A DARK ASCENSION NOVEL

The Wicked Ones

For information address
Disney Press, 1200 Grand Central Avenue,
Glendale, California 91201.
Printed in the United States of America

First Hardcover Edition, January 2023
1 3 5 7 9 10 8 6 4 2
FAC-004510-22329
Library of Congress Control Number: 2022936646
ISBN 978-1-368-07862-7

Designed by Soyoung Kim

Visit disneybooks.com

DISNEY

⚜ A DARK ASCENSION NOVEL ⚜

The Wicked Ones

New York Times best-selling author
and National Book Award–winning author

Robin Benway

DISNEY • PRESS
LOS ANGELES • NEW YORK

Prologue

MONSIEUR TREMAINE

When the man slips his wife's wedding ring off her finger, he makes sure to do so very, very gently.

After all, he would hate to wake her up.

He's waited until the house is sleeping around him, until his small children are finally settled in their beds, their tiny giggles dying down into sighs before giving over to steady, shallow breaths. His wife is sleeping on her side, facing away from him but with her hands outstretched toward the bed where he should be, reaching for a man who will never be in that space again.

The small gold band comes off so easily. He's never had

the heart to tell her it isn't real gold. He wonders if she's never had the heart to tell him that she knows and still loves him anyway.

It's an interesting thing, being loved, he thinks as he tiptoes to the other side of the bed and reaches under the duck-feathered mattress for his bag, the one that holds the few valuable possessions his family has, the ones that only he will now possess. He thought he knew love when he met his wife, or when his children were born, the two girls just pink wriggling things that reminded him in the moment of newborn puppies, eyes screwed shut, mouths open wide in a scream.

To be loved is to have a responsibility, he thinks as he checks the bag to make sure it's all there: the jewelry his wife's mother left her; a few francs he squirreled away over the past several months; an opal-backed hairbrush that belongs to one of his daughters, he isn't sure which. The people who love him have come to rely on him, and unfortunately, he is not a reliable man. He is not responsible.

He is just a man, he tells himself as he looks back at his wife. Who could ever expect him to be more than that?

His wife is still young, face only starting to show the barest cracks of age. The tiniest lines have begun to gather around her eyes, but it's easy to say that they're from smiling too much, even though her smiles have appeared less as the debts have grown. She is beautiful in her sleep, less austere, her brown hair fanned out across her pillow. He's always loved her hair; it was the thing that first drew him to her when they saw each other on the street all those years ago, back when he still imagined himself to be capable of reliability and responsibility.

He would be lying if he said he didn't think about cutting it off and selling it on some nights, of taking the shears and holding the thick strands in his palm. Four or five snips and it would be done. She would be angry, of course. She would probably even sob, but he could have said that it was for their family, for them. Didn't their daughters need to eat? Weren't they tired of avoiding the bill collectors who posted notices on their front door? It was just hair, after all. It would grow back.

But he never did it. The man is many things: a liar and a cheat. A thief, a gambler, a drunk. But, he thinks, he has never been cruel.

He tells himself this as he watches his wife now, as her hands twitch in her sleep, her legs giving a slight kick. She has never slept well; she awakes in the middle of the night and gets up to look out the window, searching for something that they both know isn't there. He knows there is unhappiness, because she never talks about it. When the man once asked about her childhood, her body went so stiff and straight that he began to suspect that the memories were not in her brain, but her bones, buried deep in the marrow. To get at them would mean breaking her open, and again, he is many things, but he is not cruel.

He watches his wife now, waits for her to move again, but she never does, not even when he kisses his palm and ghosts it over her glorious hair.

What a fortune he could have made from it.

He takes his bag and leaves the bedroom, then eases himself down the hall so that the floorboards don't creak too much. During the day they're rarely noticeable, but in the silence of the countryside night, they sound as if a cannon has been fired. Even under their daughters' small feet, the floors are rickety and splintered. The man and his wife can hear the girls coming into their room at night even when they're still ten meters away, even before they quietly complain about an ache or pain or dream and he lifts them up into their bed. He'll miss their small warm bodies pressed between them, but it's better this way. His daughters' memories will only be good. He will never have caused them pain. When they think of their father, they'll remember a man who held and loved them, who tossed them high into the sky but always made sure to catch them on their way down.

They're certainly better than the memories that his father left him.

The girls' bedroom door glides open without a single squeak even as the floorboards gently protest. They still share a bedroom despite their now very advanced ages of six and seven, even though they squawk and fight and have tearful episodes several times a week over who did this and who took those and who said that. He lets his wife handle those conflicts, lets her separate them into corners and fix their ripped dresses and wipe their eyes. From the moment they were born, he's always been in awe of his daughters, of how strong and tough they are. They remind him of everything he is not, of everything he can never be for them, and it shames and angers him in equal measure.

He would say he never resents them for it, but that would be a lie.

Now, though, tucked into their beds, he feels only fondness, a warm, syrupy emotion that all parents have when they see their sleeping children. His older daughter, Drizella, is in her bed by the window, sleeping facing the moon and stars that peek in from the dusty curtains. She is the daughter who looks up at the night sky, pointing without asking or demanding an answer, and he laughs and names the constellations over and over again, making up the ones he doesn't know by heart. He is the one who always grew tired of their game first.

They named her Drizella after his wife's mother, who arrived a week after the baby was born only to look at the child, sniff twice, and announce that any girl born with that much black hair was doomed to trouble. "She looks like she came from a coven" were her exact words, which made the news of Drizella's name that much harder to deliver. The man saw the light go out of his wife's eyes that night. It took weeks before it began to flicker back.

Drizella's hair is still black, now twisted up in rags so that she'll have perfect ringlets in the morning. His wife twists tight and fast so that tears spring to the girls' eyes, but they know better than to cry, know that crying will only make her pull tighter, tug harder. The man sometimes wishes he could intervene, but she is their mother, and he is only a man.

Girls, he thinks, always need their mother.

He leans down, setting one hand on the straw mattress for balance, and gently kisses the top of Drizella's small head. He tries to impart as much love as he can, enough devotion and adoration to carry her through the rest of her life, but there is only so much that a small body can hold. One day, Drizella will grow up and the love that her father presses into her hair tonight will only become smaller, will occupy less and less space until it becomes a tight knot behind her ribs, a quiet stabbing reminder of what has been and what is no longer there.

The man will never know this. He thinks he's done the right thing. After all, she hasn't even woken up. He would hate to disturb her sleep. She's only a child; she needs her rest.

He goes across the room to Anastasia. She still sleeps with her thumb in her mouth. Sleep is the only time she can do so safely without having it yanked out, having it soaked in vinegar so that it's sour and puckered. "If you keep doing that," his wife tells her, "your teeth will grow ugly," but that doesn't faze Anastasia. She's his redheaded stubborn one, his lucky copper coin. The day she was born, he won big at a local chicken fight and burst into their bedroom waving fistfuls of francs while the midwives fanned his exhausted, sweating wife. He didn't even hear the baby's cries at first, not until she realized she was being ignored in her cradle and decided to raise the volume by a few decibels. He cheered with her, then went out to celebrate, the money and the alcohol both gone by midnight.

He leaves her thumb in her mouth, hating to deny her a small comfort, and gently smooths the blankets over her. They're cotton when they should be wool, threadbare where they should be thick, scratchy where they should be soft. Children don't need too much, though, he tells himself. They have wonder and imagination on their side. Didn't he eat garbage scraps as a child and tell himself that it was as good as a holiday feast? A thin cotton blanket seems like nothing compared to that. He doesn't think of the upcoming autumn, how the cracks in the walls and windows will let cold air in all night long. He doesn't think of his two daughters sleeping in one bed for warmth, desperate not to be alone, aching for the kind of comfort that he won't be there to provide.

He will miss his girls so, so much.

He thinks that's the same as loving them.

He fixes their blankets one last time and slips out of the room. The old rugs that line the stairs are starting to show signs of wear, sunspots dappling the rich colors with bleached spaces, but he doesn't notice. He is a man who knows how to make decisions, who knows how to follow through, who can leave without looking back, not even once.

When he shuts the front door behind him for the very last time, no one, not even the mice nestled in the house's walls, notices that he's gone.

1

– Ten Years Later –

DRIZELLA

Every morning that Drizella wakes up, she hopes for clouds.

She wants gray skies, heavy fog, drizzle and rain, maybe even snow if it's winter. She wants the sky to look like it's padded with dark blankets and heavy goose-down duvets, the kind that she's read about in fairy tales but never owned. She wants to feel like the sky is pushing down on all of them, holding them all tight against the earth, keeping them from spinning away.

When she pulls back the worn velvet curtains this morning, she makes a wish and holds her breath.

The gorgeous late September sun glares back at her.

She lets the curtain fall shut as she tumbles back onto the bed and surveys the room. Her bed is pushed up under the window, which gives her a view of the curtains and, sometimes, the sky but also lets her feel the draft of chilly dawns and the heat of shimmering summer mornings. In the corner across the room is an old rickety armoire, which houses not only her clothes and several pairs of slippers but also what seems to be an entire colony of moths, judging by the nibbles at the hems of several of her dresses. There's also an old armchair that no one ever sits in and a dresser with a basin and a chipped pitcher perched atop it. And there's a mirror, but Drizella doesn't care to use it very often.

Sunny mornings used to be her favorite, but now they remind her of the morning after her father left. Or at least her mother said that he left. She was the one who woke Anastasia and Drizella that morning, howling and screeching so loud that Drizella at first thought there was a wounded owl in the tree outside her bedroom window. When she finally saw her mother, she was pulling at her fingers as if she was looking for something, and that was when Drizella noticed that her mother's wedding ring was no longer on her finger.

That was also when she wisely decided not to ask where her papa was.

The sky was glorious that morning, so blue and sharp

that it looked like it could shatter, raining shards down on all of them, but instead it stayed in place while the rest of their world fell apart.

Drizella puts one foot out of the bed and onto the floor, testing to see how cold the room is. Summer was miserably hot, and their drafty home held on to every last ray of heat, leaving the girls on top of their blankets, sweating through their nightgowns and waking up clammy and irritable. But Drizella wishes she had a little of that warmth now, because the floors are cold. It'll be another month before they're icy, though. She already knows that.

She puts another foot down, then heaves herself out of bed so she can see herself in the mirror.

Her papa's face looks back at her.

It's no secret that Drizella looks just like him. The way her mother's face sometimes pinches when she looks at her oldest daughter tells Drizella everything she needs to know about the slope of her nose, the curve of her jaw, the sharp point of her cheekbone. None of it quite adds up, and it didn't for Papa, either, but she remembers that her father's face seemed to fall into place like a finished jigsaw puzzle whenever he smiled. That smile appeared less and less during their last year together, no matter how hard Drizella tried to make him happy.

She smiles in the mirror now. It looks more like a grimace.

She drops her mouth back down and somehow likes herself better that way.

She's wearing Anastasia's old nightgown, the one that she outgrew last winter. It feels unfair that her younger sister is taller, but a lot of things feel unfair in their home, so it doesn't surprise Drizella. In addition, she has Anastasia's old house shoes, a jade green skirt, and several of her petticoats stashed away in her armoire. (Later this month, she will discover that a few moths were also stashed away in the armoire, ruining the skirt entirely. Also unfair.) She pulls the nightgown off now, leaving it in a laundry pile for her stepsister, Ella, to deal with, and pours water into a chipped porcelain basin so she can quickly wash herself in the icy water. She listens for the sounds of Anastasia awakening in the room next door to hers, but as usual, the rest of the second floor is silent. Anastasia has always been a late sleeper. If she ever wakes up first, Drizella sometimes thinks, it will only be because their house is on fire, and even then, she'll probably still take her time getting out of bed.

It's all routine, familiar, boring. If it weren't for the tiny calendar Drizella keeps stashed under her sagging mattress, the one that shows her every single day in a tiny, neat square, she would have trouble keeping track of the weeks as they drag by. She saw that particular calendar in a catalog at the fabric store, discreetly tore the page out, pieced together enough money to post an order for it, and then waited near the mailbox every day after, trying not to look like she was expecting anything at all.

Sometimes, when the nights are especially dark and they are out of oil to light, she brings the calendar up and tucks it under her pillow instead, her hand closing around the pages that hold the future as she drifts to sleep. She is always careful to put it back in its hiding place the next morning, lest her mother or Ella see it. She doesn't care about Ella, but her mother—she cares about her.

She still hasn't forgotten what happened to Anastasia last year. None of them have.

Drizella brushes her hair with a worn wooden hairbrush. She only remembers the barest glimpse of the one her father took, the one with the swirling blues and greens on its back, smooth and cold to the touch. It looked like the sea, or at least what Drizella imagined the sea to be like, so crystalline and pure.

She hopes she can go to the sea one day. She hopes she can leave their run-down home with its crumbling walls, its damp bedrooms, its suffocating heaviness, but on the bad days, she suspects that there's an entire world, an entire *galaxy*, that she will never see, and the longing burns inside her.

Instead, she just brushes her hair. She's supposed to do one hundred strokes, but she stops at twenty-eight, because there's no point. Drizella would fall down on a rusty rake before she'd ever tell Anastasia this, but she thinks her sister's hair is beautiful. Her own hair is inky black, but it doesn't seem to shine or hold a curl or bounce in the breeze. It's just . . . *there*. Sometimes, when her mother is angry at her for some reason or another, she'll pick up a lock of Drizella's black hair and say, "Your grandmother was right about this," and Drizella never knows quite what she means. She has no memory of even meeting her grandmother. She hopes that whatever she had to say was good, but judging from her mother's glare whenever she says that, Drizella suspects that it wasn't very good. Not at all.

Still, she knows she's her mother's favorite daughter. Even Anastasia with her crop of red hair can't take that away from her. She knows this because, whenever she kisses her mother good night—a quick, dry peck on a cold, powdered cheek— her mother whispers, "You are my one last hope," directly into her ear. It feels like both a promise and a threat. She doesn't even have to ask what her mother is hoping for. It's already obvious from everything else that has fallen down around them, leaving them in the kind of poverty that none of them would ever admit to.

Drizella is seventeen years old. She's the oldest. She needs to marry, marry well, and marry *fast*, but whenever she thinks about it, it feels like someone's hands are wrapped around her neck, squeezing tight, turning her vision into black pin-pricks as she gasps for air. In her short life, marriage has never seemed to be about love or happiness, just misery and illness and loss, a business transaction in the best of times. She's watched her mother grieve two husbands, but Drizella knows that her mother expects her to find better, do better, *be* better. And with the Prince's debut party just two months away, Drizella feels those imaginary hands grow tight around her neck once again. The tiny circled date of the party on her hidden calendar still looks so far away, but Drizella knows it's approaching like a team of runaway stallions.

She pulls back the curtain a bit and stands on her tiptoes, squinting against the light until she can see the shiny copper turrets of the castle in the distance, the purple flags waving with the royal insignia. From this far away, they look like tiny drawings, but the castle is all too real in her mind. The Prince's debut is the biggest thing to happen in their small village since, well, his father's debut many years before Drizella was even born. In theory, it is intended to celebrate his birthday, to introduce him to modern society, as nearly every man, woman, and young person in the village will be attending the celebration.

Drizella knows what it *really* is, though: a big meetup to marry off the Prince to a beautiful, young, beatific maiden, who will no doubt be beside herself to accept his hand in marriage as she beams up at him, her cheeks flushed, her eyes sparkling with the honor.

Drizella climbs back down off the bed and catches another glimpse of herself in the mirror. Her cheeks are pale, her eyes flat, and there's a pillow crease going halfway across her forehead.

Royal material, she is not.

She pushes the thought away before she can fall too far. There's time to worry about that later. There's always time. Her calendar has promised her that.

Drizella dresses quickly before she gets too cold, putting on a dress that was tighter the previous spring, back before the summer came and it was too hot to wear. It's light pink, meant to heighten the natural flush in her cheeks, but instead it just makes her look washed out and pale. She tries tying back the curtains and begrudgingly letting the morning light into the room to see if it lends her some color, but it doesn't help.

There's no point in once again wishing for gray skies, but Drizella does all the same.

She can hear her sixteen-year-old stepsister, Ella, in the kitchen downstairs, banging around with some pots and pans, making the kind of shrill noise that will no doubt annoy their mother. Drizella cannot figure out why Ella doesn't think about these kinds of things, doesn't learn from her mistakes, doesn't try like the devil to keep a good distance between herself and the lady of the house. She's always had her head in the clouds, though, and, back when her father was alive, in storybooks.

Drizella doesn't have a lot of memories of her stepfather. He was married to her mother for less than a year before he caught the wet, hacking cough that seemed to be burning through their small village. Eleven months after their wedding, he succumbed to his own lungs in a violent wheezing fit that left Anastasia and Drizella huddled together in Anastasia's room and Ella sobbing loudly at his bedside.

There are several nights that Drizella never wants to think about again. That night is one of them.

She feels a little bad for Ella now and then. Their mother has made it clear, painfully so at times, that she is just a *step*-sister, not a real flesh-and-blood sister, but Drizella still feels an ache in her chest whenever she thinks of Ella's tears in those first few weeks after her father's death, how her mother would threaten her if she didn't quiet down *now*, that her weeping was keeping the whole house awake, and didn't they all need to *finally* get some rest? Was she *really* that selfish? There was a tone in her voice that everyone in their household, even the animals, knew to obey.

Losing a father to death, Drizella thinks, must be worse than just losing him. At least she could go out and look for her own papa, could try to find his mismatched face on a crowded street or even inside a store. Ella's father is gone forever, and that may also be true for Drizella's father, but at least he's *somewhere*. Sometimes Drizella indulges herself long enough to wonder if he was actually kidnapped by pirates, banished to the seas, longing for his adored family, so that leaving was never his choice, his decision. She wonders if he looks at the moon at night, too; if he's thinking about her.

It's stupid to wonder, she knows, but for a lonely girl who can't sleep in the heat of the night, wonder is sometimes the only thing there is.

Another bang and clang from the kitchen downstairs, and Drizella sighs. She needs to wake up Anastasia anyway. It's almost time for them to leave for their morning lessons.

Anastasia's door is still closed, but Drizella barges in, letting it slam against the wall. Her sister is just a lump under her thin cotton blanket, unmoving, but Drizella knows she's awake.

"Hey," she says, then reaches out and nudges her sister's body with her foot. "Annie. Get up. Time to start another day."

The tone in her voice, as always, is anything but thrilled.

"Annie," Drizella says again. She's the only person who's allowed to call her Annie, mostly because that's what their father had sometimes called her, and the name in anyone else's mouth would feel like a betrayal. Anastasia always seems to soften a little when Drizella uses the nickname, which in turn makes Drizella feel protective, like the big sister she is.

Which is ironic, considering that Drizella is still kicking Anastasia in the thigh. "Annie," she says for a third time. "Come *on*."

"Quit kicking me," Anastasia mutters into her pillow, still unmoving. "I'm awake."

2

ANASTASIA

When Anastasia feels her sister's foot kick directly into her thigh, she doesn't move.

She's well familiar with this kind of wake-up call. Drizella seems to think that the only way to rouse her sister out of bed is to somehow commit bodily harm, and even though it never really hurts, it's still not her favorite way to wake up. A soft sunbeam would be nice, or maybe just some birds singing outside her window?

She stays in bed as a silent protest against this daily injustice.

"I don't care if you're awake, you should be *up*." Drizella moves her hand up to her ribs, digs a few fingers in through the blankets. "You're going to be late, which means I'm going to be late."

Anastasia keeps her face buried in her pillow while her mind scans through her daily schedule. The days have gotten kind of wobbly ever since they stopped going to school, having been pulled out so they could attend finishing lessons: music and singing and—for one horrible, humbling session—dance. In a few months' time, the Prince will be turning eighteen years old and having his debut party at the palace, and as soon as their mother had an official party date in hand, the girls' formal education was over. Anastasia always assumed they didn't have the money for such lessons, but with the stakes suddenly very high, their mother somehow found a way.

And when their mother finds a way, that is the way her girls will go, no questions asked.

It's not that Anastasia doesn't want to go to a debut. A party? At the palace, the most gorgeous building she's ever laid eyes on? A chance to meet an actual prince?! All of it is the stuff of Anastasia's romantic daydreams, the swoony-eyed thoughts that often carry her through her boring and dusty days. But in those dreams, she's wearing a beautiful gown, her hair is beautifully coiffed, and the Prince has eyes for only her.

The reality, Anastasia sometimes thinks, will be quite different.

The evening will probably be fine in the beginning, of

course, and here Anastasia indulges herself a little bit, imagining sipping from a glass of champagne, giggling politely at something another suitor has said to her, lowering her eyelashes just enough to appear demure but not shy, her mother smiling with warm approval from the sidelines when she sees how Anastasia has managed to charm half the room. (Where's Drizella in this scenario? Anastasia doesn't know. Let Drizella get her own daydream.)

But when she starts to think past that, that's when Anastasia gets the anxious butterflies in her stomach. All the eligible girls are encouraged to perform at this ball, a small song or a quick dance to impress the Prince, and Anastasia knows that not only is neither she nor her sister exactly performance ready, but it's a matter of talent, not time. The instructors their mother has arranged for them to meet with each week are not miracle workers, after all, and Anastasia tries not to think about everyone watching her and her sister struggle through a performance of "Sing, Sweet Nightingale," or worse, watching them make mistake after mistake, all with the undivided attention of the newly debuted Prince.

Anastasia shakes her head a little, the daydream evaporating. Ever since they left school, it sometimes feels like her imagination is the only thing she has to carry her through the weeks. Tuesdays and Thursdays and Saturdays all feel like they've been painted with the same few watery colors, their edges melting into each other so that it's hard to sort out where one begins and another ends.

But today? Today is Wednesday.

Flute lesson day.

Anastasia groans.

"Yeah, I know." Drizella sighs, then gives her sister's hair a quick pat that's far more gentle than any of her other ministrations. "Me too."

Anastasia turns her face to peek up at her sister with one eye. "I hate the flute."

"Well, based on how it sounds when you play it, the flute hates you, too." Drizella gives her one last pat. "Could be worse. You could have to sing like me."

Anastasia's heard Drizella's singing. She wouldn't wish that upon her worst enemy.

"Hurry up," Drizella says as she leaves the room. "And get all those pillow marks off your face before Mom sees. She'll have a fit and probably lose another clump of hair."

Anastasia sits up then, right as the birds start their cheery warbling just outside her window.

✣

Anastasia knows that she's technically not supposed to be in the kitchen while Ella is there. "Are you a servant?" her mother asked her sarcastically when she found Anastasia helping Ella chop vegetables one day. Anastasia was confused about how to answer, because, well, of course she wasn't a servant, but neither was Ella, right?

She never got an answer, because her mother grabbed her wrist with a sharp sigh and dragged her out into the dining room with a warning: "Don't let me catch you in there again."

But lately her mother has been sleeping late, and besides, the kitchen is the only warm place in the house on cold mornings. The fire is constantly being stoked, there are pots bubbling, and all the animals seem to congregate there, as well, making their drafty, cold house feel like a home, like Anastasia is almost part of a family, like she is loved.

As usual, the animals all scuttle around Ella this morning, sometimes so close that they inadvertently and gently nudge the back of Ella's calf with a wet nose. Anastasia watches from the doorway as she finishes tying the sash of her dress, a flare of jealousy in her chest competing with the blue flame under the teakettle. She's always loved animals, but they've always been ambivalent about her. She suspects it's because Drizella would sooner kiss a wet mop than acknowledge any of their ragtag menagerie, and her sister's bad spirits have rubbed off onto Anastasia. Even now, Drizella stays ensconced in the dining room, far away from anything that might have feathers or fur.

A kitten would be nice, Anastasia thinks. Something soft and purring to warm her at night when the cold is too harsh to keep out. Something to love her unconditionally.

Their stepfather loved Ella a lot. Anastasia can barely remember his face now, just that he had a shiny bald spot on top of his head that made her think of a gold coin, but she remembers how he sounded whenever Ella entered the room: like it was his luckiest day ever. He'd even pick her up and send her flying into the air, catching her at the last minute and making her laugh and laugh while Drizella and Anastasia stood off to the side, wondering when it would be their turn.

It was never their turn.

They all attended a party one evening when they were eight and nine years old, where the other children giggled and ran around the adults' legs like they were on an obstacle course. Anastasia and Drizella had been instructed to behave *immaculately* and not to touch *anything*, and for goodness' sake do not run like you're an *animal*, which not only made the party boring for them, but made all the other kids think the sisters were boring, as well. Instead, they sat on a divan with a pink-striped silk cover and kept their hands in their laps. They could hear the loud boom of their stepfather's voice as he held Ella in his arms, gently bouncing her as he spoke with a few friends.

It made Anastasia's throat feel empty, so she looked away.

"And how are the other two girls?" a partygoer asked Ella's father.

"The other two girls?" he repeated, then chuckled to himself. "Well, they're . . . *interesting*. Shall we leave it at that?"

When she thinks about it now, Anastasia can feel the burning shame of knowing that someone was laughing at her, but not knowing why, not knowing how to fix it. It was a shame worse than a torn skirt or a morsel of food stuck between teeth. This shame ran deeper, ran right alongside the cold of her bones. Next to her, Drizella sat ramrod straight, her eyes staring ahead at nothing. When Anastasia tried to take her hand, she shook her off, so she petted the silk divan until their mother came and said it was time to go home.

Anastasia hasn't been to a party since.

Of course, it *was* sad when their stepfather died so suddenly, and scary when their mother's eyes looked as if someone had taken a candle snuffer to them, like a window whose drapes had been pulled down for the final time. It was only a few days later, their mother dressed in traditional black, tugging the three small girls behind her while hissing at Ella, that Anastasia realized everyone in the town was watching them with wide, curious eyes. She felt embarrassed even though she wasn't sure why, and her mother jerked her hand and said, "Eyes straight ahead, Anastasia. Head high. Give them nothing."

Anastasia sometimes wonders if her mother holds her own head high just so she can keep looking down on everyone else.

In the kitchen this morning, Ella adds the hot water to the teapot so the tea can steep, its black and orange pekoe scents filling the room, along with the smell of hay and grass from the yard outside. "If that's not ready when she comes down . . ." Anastasia points to the tea, leaving the rest of her sentence unfinished.

"I know, I know," Ella says. "But I can't make water boil faster. I don't have magical powers."

Anastasia tears a hunk of bread off a loaf that's poking out of a clay canister and stuffs part of it in her mouth before her mother comes down and sees her eating a) bread, b) in the kitchen, c) like a mouse. "You're lucky she's not here to hear you talking to me like that."

Ella just looks over at her, cutting her eyes from Anastasia to the bread in her hand, then back up. Anastasia swallows fast and leaves the room in a silent agreement that neither of them will rat the other out.

Drizella isn't that nice. She always says that Anastasia is a pushover, that she'll fall for anything. "You'd starve if it meant a stray dog ate," she said once, and Anastasia couldn't even argue, because it was true, plus the mere image of a starving dog put a lump in her throat that made it hard to talk. And Anastasia would never say this out loud, not to anyone, but sometimes Drizella reminds her of their mother. To them, life is a competition, and if you're not winning, you're losing.

Anastasia isn't quite sure where she is on that scale.

The air suddenly resettles itself, and in a breath, Anastasia's moving out of the kitchen and into the back courtyard, tearing the rest of her bread into small pieces before scattering it on the ground, just like she's seen Ella do. Only this time, the animals ignore her, and a few chickens even sniff at the offering before walking away as if Anastasia has offended them. She sighs. Even with food, she can't make them like her.

Anastasia moves out of the sun, forever afraid of freckling, and then realizes that she's in the shade of the tall, looming turret that rises up from the back of their house. And instantly she's cold. Its presence is a memory that hangs as heavy as the drapes in their home, and sometimes at night Anastasia still wakes up from nightmares, remembering the dampness, the darkness, blindly reaching out for her father who will, of course, never be there to embrace her.

She will never set foot in that tower again. At night, she whispers the words out loud under her stacked blankets. They sound like both a threat and a promise.

Anastasia makes it out of the kitchen ten seconds before her mother appears in what she refers to as the breakfast room. It's really just the dining room, but neither Drizella nor Anastasia is dumb enough to argue with her about it. And technically, they *do* eat breakfast in there.

Anastasia has seen other parents greet their children on the street, meeting them in the schoolyard or looking after them at the market. She's seen the way other parents' faces light up when they spy their children, the smiles that go all the way up to their eyes, the way their cheeks get rosy with joy and love and tenderness. They sweep them up into their arms for hugs and kisses, and Anastasia can almost feel the warmth. It makes her teeth hurt sometimes, her body aching to feel that kind of heat, that level of safety.

Anastasia's mother is not that kind of parent.

She stalks into the room this morning like a woman unaware of how run-down her house is, like the drapes aren't literally hanging on by threads and there aren't mice skittering throughout its walls. After their mother married Ella's father, they all moved into his house, and while it felt grand at the time, the years of neglect and disrepair have taken their toll. Sometimes, it seems to Anastasia, the neglect and disrepair have taken their toll on all of them.

Lady Tremaine's dress is heavy and dark, not quite a widow's outfit but also not a dress worn by someone whose life experiences radiate joy. Her now-gray hair is done up in its normal bouffant-ish bun, with not a single strand of hair daring to be out of place. Anastasia remembers when her mother used to wear it looser, softer, but one day several years ago, she happened to be walking past her mother's room and realized that the door was slightly ajar. She didn't mean to spy, she really didn't, but she caught a glimpse of her mother's scalp as she tied her hair up. The stress was literally eating away at her hair. The bald spots made her look almost vulnerable, like a moth-bitten sweater that's useless in winter. Making her mother look vulnerable was a feat Anastasia had thought to be impossible, and she slunk away, trying to ignore that gnawing, cold feeling in her stomach.

"Anastasia," her mother says when she sees her now, nodding in her direction.

Anastasia cannot remember the last time her mother touched her. Well, actually, she can remember, but that memory of the tower isn't one she likes to revisit. She tries to think of her last hug, her last gentle touch, the feeling of fingertips sweeping hair off her forehead when she is fevered or a soft kiss placed to the top of her head when her mother thinks she is asleep.

She tries so hard to remember. But there's nothing there.

"Good morning, Mother," she greets her now, her words echoed by Drizella, who's seated at the table and already working on her second cup of tea. Her mother nods to both of them, and the twitch of her lips reminds Anastasia of her sister. Their movements are the same, always with heavy steps and narrowed eyes as if even walking into the breakfast room is a potential battle. Her mother has a bit of a smirk while Drizella has a pout, though. Anastasia often checks her own face in the mirror, making sure that she has neither, just a pleasant disposition. She used to smile more until her mother commented that it made her look simple, so now she just tries to hold the corner of her mouth up a bit, like she is vaguely amused by a passing memory that only she can recall.

"I assume that you've practiced for today's lesson," her mother says now.

"Yes," Anastasia says. She has, of course. Once. For nearly ten minutes. She has hated the flute ever since the metal object was put into her hands, an instrument found in the attic during one of her mother's late-night cleaning binges. It isn't uncommon for Anastasia and Drizella to awaken in the middle of the night to hear their mother rummaging through the attic, tossing out piles of old papers, rags, gardening shears, all the things that gather in an old home's crawl space over many years. Sometimes, privately, Anastasia wondered if her mother was looking for her father. She mentioned it to Drizella once, who just replied, "That's stupid. Why would Father be upstairs?" and they never talked about it again.

Their father was never found in the attic, of course, but the flute was, and when Anastasia said "What's that?" upon seeing it in her mother's hand, it became hers.

It could be worse, though. At least she doesn't have to take singing lessons like Drizella.

"And I trust that you've also practiced, Drizella," her mother says as she sits down at the table. In a fancier home, there would be someone to pull out her chair for her, someone to attend to her napkin and make sure her water goblet is filled, but theirs is not a fancy home. Drizella and Anastasia sit in their own seats at opposite ends of the table.

Neither of them ever sits within arm's reach of their mother. It just isn't done.

"Of course, Mother," Drizella says, and Lady Tremaine raises an eyebrow toward her, always ready to knock down any words that may be perceived as insolence. "I mean, yes, Mother."

"Good. I hope you girls realize how expensive these lessons are, how much it costs to make sure that both of you grow up refined, not slinking around in a scullery like"—she gestures toward the kitchen, apparently not having enough energy to even say Ella's name—"her."

"Yes, Mother," Anastasia says, placing her own napkin in her lap. There's a small burn mark in the corner, probably from a too-hot iron, but she doesn't mention it. All that will do is get Ella in trouble, and Anastasia's stomach turns over when she thinks about her mother's temper focusing in on any one of them.

"And speaking of her, where is the rest of our tea? Where is our food? Why is it so hard to get a simple task done?" Her mother sighs like someone has punched the breath out of her body. "Ella!" she calls, sharp and mean, and both Drizella and Anastasia flinch a little at the noise.

There's a rustling sound behind the door before Ella

appears, her arms laden down with several serving trays. Her cheeks are flushed from the heat of the kitchen and Anastasia clutches her cold hands together under the table, trying not to feel jealous of the warmth.

"I apologize," she starts to say, but their mother waves the words away with her hand.

"Your silly *sorry*s are useless to me," she says. "Either do the job correctly the first time or we'll find someone who can."

Ella's face pales, even though both Anastasia and Drizella know it's a bluff. If they could afford actual in-house help, Ella wouldn't be here now, they're both sure of it. And the windows and cracked walls would be repaired, and they would host parties and dinners with roasted pheasant and champagne and other things that Anastasia's read about in stories but never seen in real life.

If that ever happened, Anastasia's not sure where Ella would go, but one thing is for certain: she would no longer be here.

Their mother waits for Ella to pour the tea for her first, then sips at it as she moves on to the girls' empty cups. "And it's ice cold," she says. (Anastasia takes a tiny sip of her own tea and finds that it's lukewarm, but she says nothing.)

The only thing that seems to be ice cold at the table is their mother's eyes as she focuses her glare onto Ella. "We have been extremely charitable with you," she says, her voice low and calm, and across the table, Drizella's gaze meets her sister's, both of them silently acknowledging how stupid it would be to say anything right now. Their mother's temper has always had the potential to boil over like a teakettle. Best to just let some steam out every now and then.

"Extremely," their mother continues. She smirks a tiny bit as if amused by her own foolish generosity. "We've given you a home here."

Nobody bothers to point out that, technically, it was Ella's father who gave *them* a home. Anastasia looks up at the cracked plaster walls, the chandelier so weighed down by dust that it looks like it could fall from the ceiling at any moment. *A home.*

"Anastasia and Drizella have been quite kind to you, as well, never complaining about the time and attention that you've taken away from them." Their mother wipes at her mouth with a napkin even though she hasn't taken a single bite of food yet. "Do you feel as if our treatment is beneath you?"

"Oh, *no*—" Ella starts to say in a rush.

"Did I say you could speak?" their mother says quietly, and even the mice in the walls stop their rustling. Anastasia suspects that the grandfather clock in the corner has also paused ticking, too scared to move its hands for fear of retribution.

It's almost as if the house itself is frozen in time.

"We have given you everything, and all I ask—all *we* ask—is that you return some of the generosity that has been bestowed upon you. But you don't even know how to adequately boil water, do you." She gestures toward her cold teacup. "And now my darling Anastasia and Drizella have to hurry off to their lessons, and not only will they be late because of your inability to do anything correctly, they will also be hungry, because if you can't boil water, then how can you be trusted to cook anything?"

Their mother gestures toward the platters that Ella is still holding on her arms. Anastasia can see somewhat runny eggs sliding around on the plate, and her stomach turns. They've eaten *so* many eggs over the past several years. The chickens keep providing them, but more importantly, they're free.

"What, exactly," their mother says slowly, her icy gaze traveling all the way up from Ella's feet, shoved into hole-ridden slippers, to the top of her head, "is your use to me? To us?"

Anastasia squirms a tiny bit. She's always wanted to be an "us," but the way her mother says it makes it sound like an army, a weapon.

"Actually," her mother continues just as Ella opens her mouth to answer, "I already know the answer to that simple, simple question. You have no use. You're useless." She waves her hand at Ella, shooing her away. "Leave."

It's like watching a cat play with a ball of yarn, batting it around, unraveling it, then leaving it a pile on the ground, bored with the game before it even gets started. Ella starts to slink away, but their mother's voice immediately calls her back.

"Leave the food!" she thunders. "What, do you want us to starve?"

"No, ma'am," Ella says, moving the plates quickly from the platter to the table. When she sets Anastasia's food down in front of her, Anastasia can see her hand shaking. She wants to reach out, grab Ella's wrist, tell her that it will be all right, but she knows she'd be choosing a losing side in a game of winner takes all.

And Anastasia would never admit it, not even to herself, but deep down, she wants it all.

3

DRIZELLA

Drizella leaves the house still hungry from breakfast.

The eggs—always eggs; Drizella's surprised she doesn't have pinfeathers growing out of her skin by now, she's eaten so many of them—were slimy and, by the time Lady Tremaine got done with her tirade, cold, to boot. Drizella supposes she should just feel lucky that Ella didn't actually drop the serving platter and officially ruin breakfast.

Besides, once the whole ordeal was done, Drizella had pretty much lost her appetite.

In the beginning after Ella's father died, Drizella would secretly think that it was a little fun to watch her mother taunt

Ella, watch her make the girl squirm under her steady gaze. It felt like some sort of cosmic payback for the way her father had adored her, for the way he had never left her except in death, for the way that she always seemed so . . . *perfect*. Never misbehaving, never getting up to naughtiness. Anastasia and Drizella would sometimes invite her to play a game with them, but she always demurred, preferring her storybooks and solitude, remaining unruffled as the sisters stampeded around getting sweaty and dirty and, inevitably, in trouble. But as the years progressed, the taunting started to feel more sinister, and in any case, what Drizella and Anastasia think about it has never mattered.

Drizella trudges down their narrow path to the main street, very aware that Anastasia is walking a few steps behind her; always behind her, never in front. On these kinds of mornings, they tend to walk in separate silence, neither of them acknowledging their mother's frustrated anger or their stepsister's impotence. To acknowledge it would mean admitting that it happened, and if they admit that it happened, then that means it could happen to them.

Drizella still has nightmares about watching Anastasia disappear up into the turret, the high tower never seeming more sinister than it did that night. Seeing it all happen to her sister, Drizella often thinks, was worse than its happening to herself. Every so often, she gets a quick flash of a memory from that night, and it always makes her body go cold, her arms break out in goose bumps, even on the hottest of days. Sometimes she thinks that if she could open her brain and take out one bad memory, it would be that one, and not the one where they woke up on a sunny morning and their father was gone.

"I can hear you breathing behind me," Drizella finally says as Anastasia pants while attempting to catch up. "You sound like an old horse."

"Better to sound like one than look like one," Anastasia shoots back, which, as far as comebacks go, isn't the best, but Anastasia's never been one for wit. She's too soft, too sensitive, too easily bruised. Drizella can remember seeing her stand in the yard as a child, a moldy handful of birdseed stretched toward the sky, her small voice begging the birds to come to her, to be her friend.

Drizella hates those dumb, noisy birds. And of *course*, the next day Ella tried the same thing, and the birds flew right into her hand and acted like she was their personal savior. Traitors.

She doesn't respond to the horse comment and just keeps walking. She does slow down a tiny bit, though, waiting for her sister to finally catch up.

"So what do you think Mother does all day while we're gone?" Anastasia says when she's finally at her sister's side, and Drizella tries not to roll her eyes. They've played this game way too many times before, both as children and now as young women, their answers getting progressively darker as the years go by. "Sewing clothes for us!" little Drizella used to guess as she hopped on one leg down the road, with Anastasia trying and failing to imitate her. "Catching butterflies! Flying a kite!"

But now?

"Drinking," Drizella replies. "Heavily."

"Drizella!" Anastasia is so easily shocked that sometimes teasing her is way funner than it should be.

"Do we really have to talk about her?" Drizella asks. "Isn't living with her enough?"

"I'm just always curious. Aren't you?" Anastasia nudges her a bit, a smile spreading across her face. It's a sweet smile. Drizella knows that her own grin is a little sharper, a bit more pointed, vulpine. (She saw that word in a book the other day and loved it, loved the way it felt in her mouth when she whispered it out loud, loved how good it felt to discover something new in a house filled with old things.)

"Not really," Drizella replies now. Her bonnet makes her head feel way too warm in the sun and she wishes she could rip it off and toss it under her boots. Everything this morning feels too tight, too hot, too loud, too much too much too much.

"I don't believe you," Anastasia says. She's still huffing a little bit to keep up, but Drizella doesn't slow down. "Are you in a race or something, Drizzy?" She laughs. "You're always in such a hurry!"

Drizella *is* in a hurry. She just doesn't know why. All that's at the end of the road are her stupid singing lessons and the forever disappointed wince on her instructor Monsieur Longmont's face. He seems to look a bit more pained with every passing week, and Drizella sometimes wants to turn to him and say, "These lessons weren't even my idea!"

But she doesn't. She wouldn't. She could never. Drizella is all too aware of how high the stakes are with the Prince's debut just a few months away, and the more she thinks about it, the more anxious she feels. Other girls have been in these lessons for years, their own mothers grooming them for the finest of opportunities, and Drizella knows that her mother expects her and Anastasia to be able to compete with them. In Lady Tremaine's house, at least, you don't come home until you win, and this time, the Prince will be the prize.

The only thing that nauseates Drizella even more than the idea of the debut party is how excited Anastasia is for it. She sometimes catches her waltzing around the bedroom with an imaginary partner, smiling and gesturing demurely, and Drizella feels the heat of secondhand embarrassment flood her own face, the impending shame pooling in her stomach. In those moments, Annie's face looks so hopeful that it makes Drizella's dread double in size.

She knows this debut party will be nothing but a disaster. She and Anastasia will never stand a chance in that ballroom, not with so many other girls, each of them prettier and more talented than the last.

"You don't have to be such a Negative Nellie," Anastasia scoffed when Drizella brought it up to her one night after dinner. "Not everything has to be terrible! Look at me. I hate playing the flute. I'm awful at it, but I'm still—"

"Now who's the Negative Nellie?" Drizella grumbled.

Anastasia stopped for a few seconds, then cleared her throat. "Anyway, you could just *try*, Drizella," she says quietly. "Wanting something good to happen isn't the worst thing a person can do."

Drizella snorts to herself now, remembering her sister's annoyed tone. Good luck with that, she thinks. She'd probably clear the ballroom in fifteen seconds flat if she tried to sing any of the notes that Monsieur Longmont has attempted to teach her. For goodness' sake, they're still on the warm-up scales, and even though it has been more than a year since lessons began, Drizella still hasn't learned an actual song. "Practice is imperative, my dear," Longmont says, but Drizella can hear what he doesn't say: *There's not enough practice in the world for you.*

At home, though, in the privacy of her bathtub, with the door shut and secured, Drizella actually *likes* to sing. She can be quiet and soft as she scrubs herself down, singing into the soap bubbles until they burst. She's her own favorite audience. She's never as good as she is when she's by herself. Her voice isn't perfect, but it's all hers.

"Do you think Mother goes back to bed and takes a nap after we leave?" Anastasia says now, picking their game right back up, and oh, please someone give Drizella strength this morning.

Drizella shrugs. "Who cares? Let her do whatever she wants. Just as long as she leaves us alone."

Anastasia's shoulders sink a little, her posture drooping, and Drizella feels a quick tug of affection for her sister. At least that's one thing they have that Ella doesn't: each other.

"Or," Drizella says, smiling a little, "Lady Tremaine might have a stream of male suitors all morning long. A line so long that it leads into the yard!"

She keeps walking forward, giggling to herself as Anastasia stops in her tracks, letting out a shriek of horror. "C'mon!" she calls over her shoulder. "Gather your delicate brain and hurry up before you make us late."

Behind her, Anastasia sputters. Drizella just continues to walk forward, full steam ahead.

⁂

Once the girls get to the village, they both go their separate ways, Anastasia lugging the sad-looking flute case toward her lesson and Drizella trudging down the opposite road to her voice lesson. Anastasia's case bumps against her legs over and over again, and Drizella thinks that it must be painful, feels a little sorry for her sister as she stumbles down the road and turns the corner, disappearing from view.

It's a strange thing to have her sister so far from her, even though they go their separate ways every week. Anastasia has always been within arm's reach of Drizella since she was born, and when you're used to losing people, you learn how to keep a tight grip on everyone who's left.

Drizella takes herself in the opposite direction, doing her best to avoid muddy puddles from yesterday's quick end-of-summer rainstorm. The last thing she needs to hear from her mother is how careless she is, how she always manages to sully the beautiful things she has, why can't she be more careful and genteel like Anastasia, who would probably cut a foot off before dirtying it.

Drizella tamps down the urge to jump into the puddle like a misbehaving child, to stomp her feet and send the mud flying everywhere, to make people notice her even if it's for all the wrong reasons. Instead, she carefully navigates her way down the road, keeping her eyes down, even though she knows nobody is really looking at her.

Monsieur Longmont's studio is above the dressmaker's shop, whose windows are full of beautiful designs and some of the most gorgeous fabrics that Drizella has ever seen. When they go into town with their mother, Lady Tremaine just turns up her nose and never lets them go inside. "Why would you want such cheap materials?" she always huffs whenever Anastasia or Drizella ask and plead, but to Drizella, they don't look cheap at all. They look lush and soft, the kind of material that would make a dress that would fit forever, that would never become thin with holes, silks and brocades and lace so delicate it looks like it was woven by a spider.

A *black widow*, Drizella's brain quickly corrects itself.

There are several young women inside the store, accompanied by older women who must be their mothers, and Drizella stays a safe distance away and watches them through the window. Their cheeks are flushed with delight, not exertion like Drizella's bright red face, and their hair is perfectly curled, not like Drizella's stringy strands. (They're probably not also keeping their arms pressed tightly against their sides, desperate to hide the wet spots earned from hurrying along a a dusty road in late September. Those girls probably have carriages they ride in. Their feet probably never touch the ground.)

Drizella watches and wonders what it would be like to have a friend.

She has Anastasia, of course, but it's not the same thing. She and a few other girls in school were friendly, as well, but when Drizella mentioned spending some time with them outside of school, Lady Tremaine waved the thought away with a bony, big-knuckled hand. "Simpletons," she said, and that one word dismissed both those girls for being dim-witted and Drizella for thinking they were worthy.

Drizella watches until one of the girls looks up, then scurries past the window and up the stairs, tamping down that dark feeling that crawls through her body like poison ivy along a path.

Feelings are useless, she thinks. All they ever do is hurt you.

She waits upstairs, restlessly pacing in front of Monsieur Longmont's closed studio door. He's never late, and she wonders for a minute if maybe he's been injured, if his heart finally stopped beating, if he's fallen down in front of a carriage and perhaps been trampled by a team of the King's finest horses? Drizella is not proud of the fact that the idea gives her a bit of a carnal thrill. There's only one voice instructor in the entire region, after all. Maybe if he has indeed been dashed across the road, she won't have to sing anymore? Or at least, not for anyone else?

Drizella decides that she is, in fact, a terrible person for having such ugly thoughts. Anastasia would never think this way.

She paces a bit more, and just as she's about to go back downstairs and head home, a woman Drizella doesn't recognize comes up the stairs, a bit breathless from the climb and the heat of the late summer day. "Oh!" the woman says, startling when she sees Drizella's stormy face about to charge down the stairs. "My apologies! I didn't realize you were on your way down." She smiles, her cheeks looking like ripe autumn apples as she steps out of Drizella's way. "As you were, dear."

Drizella can't remember the last time someone smiled at her like that, their face so lit with kindness that it seems as if they are glowing from within. Certainly not her mother, that's for sure. The closest Lady Tremaine ever comes to a smile is a sneer, only half of her mouth rising, and more often than not, it ends in a cruel word or, worse, a quick pinch on the inside of Drizella's upper arm.

The woman is still standing there, and when Drizella doesn't say anything, she blinks a little, that kind flame flickering just a bit. "My dear?" she says again. "Are you all right?"

"I'm fine," Drizella says automatically. She learned a long time ago that no one ever expects an honest answer when they ask that question. "You, um, you just surprised me, that's all. I'm sorry, I'll be going now."

"Were you waiting for Monsieur Longmont?" the woman guesses, gesturing down the dusty hallway toward the empty studio. "I'm afraid that he was coughing a bit as he locked up last night. He may be under the weather today."

Drizella feels another pang of guilt about hoping for Monsieur Longmont's imminent demise. At least he wasn't crushed under the hooves of a horse, she thinks.

"Oh," Drizella replies, and is grateful that her mother isn't there to hear her stammering out one-word answers. Drizella can always hear her voice in her head, though. Her mother could be dead and she'd probably still hear her sharp words and annoyed inflections, trailing after Drizella no matter where she goes in the world; no avenue for escape.

What was the saying? No rest for the wicked.

The thought fills Drizella with such a dizzying amount of sadness that she takes a step backward.

"My dear," the woman says again, but this time it isn't a question. "Why don't you come into my office with me for a bit, get out of this morning sun?" Her smile is back. "At least rest up for a few minutes. It's so warm, and these roads are dusty. I've only just moved in a few days ago, so you'll have to forgive the mess, but you're welcome to wait. And if Monsieur Longmont makes a miraculous recovery and suddenly appears, you'll still be here!"

The thought doesn't fill Drizella with quite the same joy as it does this strange woman. She glances toward the studio, which appears to be dark through the windows, but with some interesting plants lining the sills. And the woman herself looks about as threatening as a fluffy white cloud. Drizella quickly weighs the pros and cons and decides that she'll take her chances in the dank studio.

"All right," Drizella agrees. "I guess it would be nice to wait somewhere it's a bit cooler."

"Wonderful!" the woman says. "I'm Madame Lambert. It's lovely to meet you . . ." She raises an eyebrow, waiting.

"Drizella," she fills in.

"A beautiful name!" Madame Lambert cries, and now Drizella is sure that this woman is either kindness personified or a compulsive liar, because nobody in their right mind would ever say such a thing about her name. Even the sound of it seems to annoy and frustrate her own mother, her brow knitting together as if she's remembering sour food, a bad memory. Drizella doesn't know why she gave her such a name if it bothers her so much, but she knows better than to ask.

She knows better than to question her mother about anything.

"Right this way," Madame Lambert says, holding one arm out to guide Drizella down the hallway, and once they're in front of a large tiger-oak door, she pulls a brass key out of her blue cloak and wiggles it in the lock for a few seconds, muttering some words to herself until it pops open. Drizella wonders briefly if she's made the wrong choice, if she should have just risked sunstroke waiting for Monsieur Longmont instead. Maybe all her mother's warnings about murderous strangers are about to come true! Drizella can still remember the stories their father used to tell them at night before bed, about wicked women in the woods beckoning greedy little children and then gobbling them up. She always thought they were fairy tales, but what if they were premonitions instead?

And then the door swings open and Drizella walks into the most beautiful room she's ever seen in her life. If this is her last stop before falling to her doom, it will have been worth it, she decides.

The ceiling is painted a dark navy blue, the same color as the sky on cold January nights, and Drizella can see tiny gold stars spread out across the expanse, each of them twinkling slightly from the sun that shines through the open door. There are several globes lining the wall, their perfect spheres looking almost majestic as they stand next to one another. Drizella has the urge to spin them as fast as she can, to feel the bumps of mountain ridges and the smoothness of the oceans under her fingertips as they rotate. Heavy rugs are spread over the bare wooden floors, making the room feel cozier than any of the rooms at their château, and even the dust seems to shimmer and dance in the sunlight, floating past her as if it were magic.

"Are you a witch?" Drizella says before she can stop herself. It's best just to know now so she can accept her fate and perish with dignity. Anastasia will be thrilled to have her bedroom. She's coveted the view of the castle for years, and now it can finally be hers.

Madame Lambert just laughs, though, untucking her bonnet and settling it down on a desk. There are preserved things in jars, things that Drizella can't even begin to imagine would ever need to be preserved. Their basement at home has preserved lemons and ripe tomatoes that used to grow in their now bone-dry garden, but Drizella's pretty certain that's not what Madame Lambert has in these jars. These things look spiny, with tiny suckers and pickled appendages, and Drizella's both disgusted and very, very intrigued.

"I'm fairly certain there are no witches here," Madame Lambert says with a laugh. "Just science. You're welcome to look around, of course." Her hair is the color of snow right after it falls, before it melts and becomes dirty and slushy, and Drizella resists the urge to reach out and give it a pat. With the woman's bonnet off, Drizella can see that her skin is lined but soft, like an unfolded piece of tissue, and her cheeks are pink in a way that implies happiness rather than frustration or exertion. Drizella has never thought this about anyone before, but Madame Lambert looks *kind*. She seems like the type of person who would offer a hug instead of a shove, or a gentle word rather than a sharp scolding.

Drizella's not quite sure what to do with any of this.

Madame Lambert hangs up her cloak as Drizella slowly walks around, taking everything in. Bunches of dried lavender hang from one corner of the room; plant cuttings line the windows, packed into small clay pots as they stretch toward the warm sun; half-melted candles are gathered in a circle on a large table, their wax overflowing and running together so that it all joins and seeps into the tabletop. It's all so different from anything Drizella has ever seen before that it feels like her brain is bouncing off her skull, like her heart is about to beat right through her chest, punch a hole out of her ribs and dance merrily across the floor.

It takes Drizella almost a full minute to realize that what she's feeling is *happiness*.

The back wall has several shelves full of books, their spines stacked on top of each other sideways and set upright so as to fit as many as possible on the wobbly-looking shelves. Drizella glances toward them, then back at Madame Lambert. They have a library at home, of course, but it was their stepfather's, and no one is allowed to enter it.

"Go ahead, my dear," Madame Lambert says when she sees Drizella's questioning look. "I told you, you're welcome to look around."

Drizella nods her thanks, then goes closer to examine the spines. Words like *astronomy* and *biology* are etched into the soft cloth with gilded ink, the words somewhat faded from years of sunlight. When Drizella pulls one off the shelf, she has to blow dust off the top before opening it.

There are diagrams of plants and leaves and roots, numbered charts explaining what each part is, its importance to the world. Drizella wonders how she can feel so unimportant while this tiny drawing of a plant seems to hold all the secrets of the universe, and she feels her world tilt just a little bit.

"Do you know how to read?" Madame Lambert asks, not unkindly.

Drizella nods. "Yes, we—my sister and I—went to school for several years." She turns back to the book, flipping its pages. The paper is so old that it feels like she could tear it just from breathing too hard. "My mother says only boring girls read books, though."

Drizella's gaze is still focused on the worn pages, so she misses the brief frown that crosses Madame Lambert's brow. "Well, that is a shame, indeed" is all the woman says, though. "There's so much to be found there. I find that I myself am *more* boring when I'm not reading a book."

Drizella puts the book back and reaches for another, one that has drawings of stars and lines connecting them. The word *Cassiopeia* is written underneath one of the pictures, and Drizella carefully traces the *W*-shaped pattern with her fingernail. The word is so familiar, like a ghost in the back of her brain. Someone has said this word to her before, has whispered it against her hair, but she can't remember who or why.

"What's this?" she asks, holding up the page, and Madame Lambert puts on a pair of thick reading glasses and comes over to her side. At this angle, her eyes look absolutely huge in her face, and Drizella suppresses the urge to giggle.

She finds herself never wanting anything to ever hurt Madame Lambert.

"Oh, this," the woman says with a smile. "This is a constellation. It's a Greek theory that the patterns of the stars tell a story. This one is Cassiopeia." She removes her glasses and smiles so openly at Drizella that Drizella finds herself smiling back. "The evil queen," Madame Lambert continues with a wink.

Well. Drizella definitely knows something about that.

Madame Lambert points up at the ceiling. "I've re-created it there the way I used to for some of my former students. You can see the five stars just below that cobweb. I apologize, I've only just moved into this space, and I'm still handling the housekeeping." She smiles as she brushes away some dust.

"So you work here and . . . ?" Drizella says, letting her voice trail off in a question. Her suspicious nature is getting the best of her, even as she's warming to the woman.

"I do, yes. I'm a scientist and somewhat of an amateur astronomer. Emphasis on *somewhat*." She grins.

Drizella blinks. "You're a scientist? *You?*"

Madame Lambert nods, her gaze elsewhere as she straightens a few haphazardly stacked books. *Newts, Warts, and Other Essentials*, one of their spines reads. "I am indeed," she says. "I know, people don't often think that women can be scientists, but I assure you, our brains do indeed work every now and then." She smiles up at Drizella, but the edges of her mouth are a little bit tighter than they were before. "My husband and I studied together. He was a very big supporter of my work before he . . ."

"I'm sorry," Drizella says quietly, understanding what Madame Lambert cannot voice aloud.

"Thank you, but it's all right. Everything has a beginning and an end, including all of us, and my husband's end just came a little bit sooner than I would have liked." Drizella can't say for sure, but Madame Lambert's eyes are a little glassy, and Drizella politely looks away. "Anyway, he was an astronomer and I studied biology, so now I do both."

"Do you miss him?" Drizella whispers, and thinks of her father tossing her into the air, always there to catch her, never letting her fall until, one day, he did.

"In every second of every day," Madame Lambert replies, her voice equally quiet. "But I see the stars and I know he's there." As if to underline her point, one of the gilt stars suddenly drops from the ceiling, and they both jump, startled. Madame Lambert just laughs, though, and goes to pick it up. "A falling star," she says, holding it up. "Make a wish!" Then she blows a little dust off it. "As I said, housekeeping is not one of my greater skills."

"You should see what's in *our* house," Drizella says before she can stop herself, thinking of the mice that seem to scurry in the walls at all hours of the day and night. Their tiny, high-pitched squeaks compete with all the other noise in their house and, sometimes, late into the dark night, Drizella could swear that they might actually be *singing*?

She has never told anyone, even Anastasia, this. They would all laugh her right out of the house if she ever said such a ridiculous thought out loud.

Madame Lambert just smiles, though, and turns the page to show Drizella more constellations, then points them out on the ceiling. What looked like cheap paper stars stuck haphazardly to the ceiling now seems wondrous and magical, and Drizella wonders how it's even possible that Madame Lambert has such a unique space in the same building as her dry, boring, pinched singing instructor, whose studio contains only dusty corners and a desk piled with paperwork. There's no magic there.

Speaking of.

A hacking cough comes up the stairs, followed by Monsieur Longmont, and Drizella feels her heart sink down into her toes. She's used to disappointment, but this time it feels especially harsh. "Well, look, he's alive!" Madame Lambert says cheerily, but Drizella doesn't know that that's the best word to describe him. Even on his healthiest days, Longmont always has a gray, ashen appearance that reminds Drizella of dirty January snow.

"Well, he's not dead, at least," Drizella says, and Madame Lambert laughs.

"You're a clever one," she tells her. "Now hurry along, you don't want to upset him."

Drizella drags her feet toward the door, then puts her hand on the cold brass doorknob and turns back around. "Could I . . . ?" She lets the question hang in the air, unasked.

"Of course, my dear," Madame Lambert says, and Drizella feels something warm plant itself at the base of her stomach. "You are always welcome here. Come back and visit Cassiopeia anytime you'd like."

Outside the door, Drizella can hear Longmont hack again. She's probably going to catch a late summer cold from that wretched man. Wonderful.

"Thank you" is all she says, though, and opens the door to slip out and hurry down the stairs so that Longmont doesn't see where she's been. He's too occupied coughing into a handkerchief and struggling with the lock on the door, and she tiptoes downstairs before making a ruckus running back up them, pretending to be out of breath.

"My apologies!" she cries. "I'm so sorry. My sister—"

"Mademoiselle Tremaine, did I not say that tardiness will not be tolerated?" He's standing in the doorway now, a fine sheen of sweat on his forehead. If Drizella didn't know better, she would think that he was the one waiting for her instead of the other way around.

Worth it, she thinks.

"I apologize," she says again, then skirts around him and heads straight toward the music stand where the sheet music she can never seem to read waits patiently for her.

They do scales all morning, but Drizella is too busy with her thoughts to hate even a single minute of it.

4

ANASTASIA

Anastasia always feels a little lonely when she and her sister arrive in the village and go their separate ways.

Sometimes she wishes she could follow Drizella, see what her singing lessons are like, stand up and clap or just do something to ease the effects of what she's sure is the same strained, sad look on Monsieur Longmont's face, week after week. (Anastasia has seen him buying fruit at the market. He looked strained and sad even then, and anyone who looks like that while buying summer fruits will probably never look any happier.)

But her flute lessons call her. Or screech at her. Either

way, Anastasia has somewhere to be, and so she trudges forward, trying to keep the flute case from whacking away at her legs. She has never told anyone, not even Drizella, but when she was being dragged up that horrible staircase, something had twisted in her finger, causing the bone to shift and never settle back in its right place. The pain was excruciating at first, making her breath shallow and weak, but it eventually settled into a dull ache and now acts up only when it rains.

Or when she plays the flute.

The thing is, Anastasia was actually not a terrible flute player before. She wasn't the best, but she enjoyed it, enjoyed the fact that she could manipulate an instrument to make whatever beautiful sounds she wanted. But now she can never get her finger into quite the right position and it catches on the keys, pinching her skin so that sometimes she even cries out in pain.

She never says a word, though, not even when her instructor glares at her and raps his cane against the ground and makes her play the same scales over and over again until they're perfect, until Anastasia has tears in her eyes from the way her finger is throbbing in agony. The shame of explaining how she hurt her finger is almost too much to bear, the memories too dark to revisit, and lying about it would almost make it seem like nothing ever happened, like Anastasia doesn't still have scars both inside and out from the experience. She says nothing and keeps playing.

She turns the corner, almost bumps into a white-haired woman wearing a blue cloak, and drops her flute in the process. "Oh!" Anastasia cries.

"Sorry, so sorry, m'dear," the woman says, hurrying off, muttering something under her breath, and Anastasia picks up the flute case, bending down to look at it. If there's even a single mark, her mother will notice, and God help her if the flute itself is damaged.

Anastasia inspects it carefully. There's a dent in one corner of the case.

Rats.

She sighs, already thinking hard about how to spin this. She was accosted in the street by a crazy old lady! She was startled by a pair of drunkards! She was hit by a bolt of lightning in a freak storm, and the flute case was the only thing that was damaged! Thank goodness it's only a dent!

Anastasia is so busy trying to think of a good solid excuse that she doesn't even hear said excuse charging toward her at full speed, complete with bellowing horns and the thunderous clop of horses' hooves. Someone shouts to her, but Anastasia is too busy worrying about the dumb case and the even dumber flute inside.

In fact, Anastasia only notices that something is coming toward her when she's suddenly lifted off her feet by a strong arm wrapping tight around her waist and nearly tossing her to the side of the road. Anastasia looks up from the ground just in time to see a carriage go speeding by, turning the corner so fast that it almost tips onto two wheels.

"Are you okay?" It's a man's voice, urgent and rushed, and Anastasia feels a deep flush creep up her chest toward her throat. When she gets nervous or upset, she gets all splotchy and red, making her look like she's having an allergic reaction to human emotion. Drizella used to tease her about it, but since the tower incident, she's never said another word.

"I'm fine," Anastasia says with a gasp, and then looks up at him.

He's peering down at her, moving his arm from her waist so that he can put his hands on her shoulders. There's a cowlick at the front of his hairline and his eyelashes are ridiculously long and his eyebrows are just a tad too bushy, almost like baby caterpillars, and he smells like butterscotch and fresh laundry and, oh, is he smiling now? Oh dear, he's smiling. At *her*. And his hands are so warm on her shoulders, and Anastasia feels herself start to lean in to his touch, the first touch she's had in so, so long, and—

"Are you hurt?" he asks.

"I'm fine," she says again, even though what she feels is anything but *fine*, and wrenches herself away from the man's touch before she accidentally leans in to it any more and causes the gossips in their town to go into overdrive. And with the Prince's debut party just a few short months away? No thank you, Anastasia thinks. It's not as if anyone in their village ever tries to speak to their mother, but Anastasia knows that good gossip has a way of traveling on the wind to everyone's ears.

"Well, I was fine before you knocked me down," she adds, brushing out her skirts. How dare he be so handsome, anyway? Who does this person even think he is?

"I'm sorry," the man says. "Sometimes the carriage goes way too fast for these narrow streets, and I just jumped off when I saw you on the road, and—"

"*And* you've dented my flute case!" Anastasia huffs, suddenly and deeply grateful for a good excuse (or lie, but whatever) to give to her mother. "Where am I going to find another one, hmm?"

The man crouches down to pick it up for her, and when he hands it over, Anastasia's eyes travel from his leather shoes to his velvet pants, to the royal blue sash around his waist, to the royal insignia that's pressed into his sleeve—

Oh, no.

No no *no*.

The royal insignia.

Anastasia would know that symbol anywhere. Not that she ever actually goes anywhere, but still, she would know it. Her mother drilled it into her and Drizella's heads for years and years, starting, Anastasia later realized, the day after their father abandoned them. A lion with its mouth open in a roar, a crown perched regally on its head, surrounded by a wreath of intricate, thorny vines. Their mother would describe it with an almost frenzied sort of passion, her voice rising higher and higher in volume until she caught herself and immediately cleared her throat, snapping back into her serious, stoic self. "Whenever you see that insignia out in the village," their mother said over and over again, "that means the Prince is there, too. Which means that *he* can"—here she would point, her finger as gnarled as an old branch—"see *you*."

Anastasia wasn't sure, but it always felt like her mother was looking right through her when she would say those last few words, like she—Anastasia, of all people!—was going to marry the Prince and deliver them all into the safe arms of lifelong royal status.

But Anastasia's anxiety over meeting new people is such that she can barely even acknowledge their mail carrier without feeling sweat pool under her arms. Meeting the Prince would probably cause her to pass out, hit her head, and forget her own name.

Still, her mother seems undeterred. She sometimes comes into Anastasia's room at night and stands behind her as Anastasia brushes and brushes her long red hair before affixing her nightcap. "You know," her mother says, unprompted, "Drizella is very intelligent. But you're the pretty one."

It never feels like a compliment, especially when she adds, "If only we could do something about this garish hair color of yours."

Instead, Anastasia says, "Yes, Mother," and prays that

Drizzy never overhears them. Sometimes she'll try to keep the conversation going, desperate for any tiny bit of attention her mother may mete out, but her mother just responds with "Mm-hmm" before walking out of the room, carefully closing the door behind her with a solid click. Anastasia longs for her mother to maybe pick up the brush and stroke her hair with it, smooth out the tangles with the palm of her hand, perhaps even press a kiss to the top of her head. If she thinks about it too much, Anastasia's back teeth start to ache for wanting to be touched in some loving way, even if it is for only a second or two. Just some kind of warmth to ease all the coldness in her bones, to make her feel more assured, less alone.

But her mother's hands have never been known for their kindness.

Which is why, just maybe, this man's hands felt so good when they were resting on her shoulders.

The man smiles, revealing teeth so painfully white that Anastasia has the urge to squint. "I'm Dominic," he says, bowing a little. "Official groom to the royal family. And I can probably have the royal cobbler hammer out that dent in an hour or so."

One front tooth is a tiny bit crooked. It's very charming. It's very . . . yes. Is it exceptionally warm out today? Anastasia wonders, and resists the urge to fan herself with her hand. "Groom?" she repeats.

"It's a fancy way of saying I train and take care of the

horses," he replies. "That was actually one of our newer horses' first time on the carriage, so I was riding along to make sure she did well. And seeing as how we almost ran you over, I'm thinking maybe she needs more practice." He rubs his chin and looks thoughtfully to where the carriage disappeared around the corner.

Are all chins like his? Rounded but not too round, with just enough point, maybe the tiniest hint of a dimple?

"Mm-hmm" is all Anastasia says, though. Her mother probably should have given up on the flute and sprung for diction lessons a long time ago, because Anastasia's having a hard time getting the words to go from her brain to her mouth.

"I'm very sorry about your flute case, and for the high-speed chase of sorts," he says, apparently mistaking Anastasia's shortness for anger. "I'm sure we can have someone repair it."

"No, it's fine," she says. "I'm sorry, you just startled me. That"—she gestures toward the path of the carriage, which has disappeared from view and has hopefully not taken out too many other pedestrians in its wake—"startled me, as well."

She tries to smile, but she fears she looks more like Drizella baring her teeth. (That poor girl and her incisors.) Plus her mouth feels dry and hot all of a sudden.

Dominic just smiles, though, wide and warm, tucking his hands behind his back as Anastasia does the same, one hand gripping the dented flute case. "I'm sorry we startled you," he says. "Unfortunately, the crown prince was extremely late this morning to an official appointment and the driver was instructed to drive—well, I can't say the actual phrase, but please trust that the instructions were explicit."

Anastasia smiles at that, a real one this time. "I understand," she says. "He's the Prince; his time is very important. I'm sure it was imperative that he arrive on time."

She feels like she's playing a role: the Well-Spoken Young Woman of the Village. She can't even remember the last time she used the word *imperative* in a sentence, but now here she stands, acting like she speaks this formally all the time.

Her mother, Anastasia thinks, would be proud.

"The Prince is very important to our village," she continues, now very aware that she's rambling but unable to make her words stop. "I'm sure that wherever he was off to—"

"He was on his way to christen a slaughterhouse."

Anastasia blinks. "Oh," she says. "Well, um, again, I'm sure—"

Dominic waves her words away. "Very important, yes yes yes. But how about you? Can I escort you somewhere? Unfortunately, the carriage won't be back for a bit, but if you'd like a doctor to look at you, I can wait with you for it, or I can walk with you back to the palace."

Anastasia knows what she's supposed to do. Her mother has trained her for this moment. Wait for the carriage, get Drizella into it as fast as possible, and take it back to the palace for all it's worth. This is the golden opportunity that all of them seem to have been waiting for: a chance to marry a sister off to a prince, to fix their fortune and realign their stars.

But there's something about Dominic that makes Anastasia want him all for herself. She doesn't want to reveal him to Drizella, or expose him to her mother, or show him their dilapidated, run-down château, with its leaky walls and dusty floors. He feels special, golden, chosen just for her.

"No, that won't be necessary" is what Anastasia says instead. "But I'm going to meet my sister, if you'd like to keep me company."

"That would be very nice," Dominic says, bowing a bit again, and then offers her his arm. She hesitates at first, but then realizes that it would seem strange not to take it. She may have just been nearly run over, but Anastasia still has her manners, thank you very much!

Even still, she has to bite back a tiny squeak when she loops her arm through his, not necessarily because he works for the royal family, but because he's a person. As good as his arm felt around her waist, this is softer, less urgent, and Anastasia lets her fingers curve into his elbow, feeling the barest hint of a pulse, feeling someone else standing next to her, alive and warm and *there*.

Anastasia is pretty sure that this is the loveliest thing that has ever happened to her.

"So where is your sister?" Dominic asks as they walk away from the music atelier.

"She's at her voice lesson," Anastasia replies, then holds up the case. "I'm just coming from my flute lesson."

"So you both sing or play instruments. Very talented," he says with a smile, and Anastasia has to resist the urge to tap his mouth just to make sure he's even real.

"Well, I don't know that you could say that," she hedges instead. "We, um, we take lessons. Our mother wants us to prepare for the debut party in a few months' time."

"Ah, yes, the famed debut party," Dominic says, nodding to himself. "So you'll be attending?"

"Oh, *yes!*" she says, then forces herself to take a breath and not seem too eager. "Well, yes, of course. I believe everyone in the entire village will be attending. I'm not sure they'll enjoy hearing what my sister and I have to perform, though. We're, um, we're not the most skilled musicians, is probably a generous way to put it."

"I bet you're not that bad," he says. "People are their own worst critics, after all."

"No, I'm actually pretty bad," she admits, and his smile grows wider. "My fingers, they get stuck, it screeches, and I think my instructor has used the word 'hopeless' more than a few times."

Why is she being so honest with this total stranger? Why is she even *talking* to him? Anastasia feels like someone's turned the tap on her brain; all this information is suddenly gushing out of her, and none of it is refined or ladylike.

"What about you?" she asks, eager to stop talking about herself for fear she'll completely run out of things to say. "What's it like living at the palace?"

He pauses for a moment, the same way Anastasia sometimes does when her mother asks her a question that she doesn't want to answer. *Have you practiced today, Anastasia? What are you doing sitting like that, Anastasia? Have you seen that wretched Ella, Anastasia?*

"Ah, the palace" is what he says after nearly fifteen seconds of silence, which is, Anastasia has now realized, a really long amount of time when it's just two people in conversation. "It's . . . the palace."

"Well, yes," she says with a laugh. "It is indeed a palace. Do you get to go to balls? How big are the chandeliers, really?" She leans toward him and whispers conspiratorially, "Is it actually boring there? My sister thinks it's probably boring."

"And what do *you* think?"

The question takes her aback. What does she think? No one's ever asked her that question before.

"I think," she says slowly, "that it must be very beautiful. And maybe a little chilly, what with all of the marble floors and those high ceilings. And maybe kind of intimidating, too. I know sometimes"—why is she still *talking*?—"even at our home, which isn't a palace *at all*, believe me, I feel intimidated there."

Dominic stops walking and looks at her. "What did you say your name was again?"

"Anastasia," she says. "Anastasia Tremaine. My sister calls me Annie sometimes, though."

"Anastasia," he repeats, then smiles at her. "You are very, very right about the castle, Anastasia Tremaine. More than you know."

Her heart suddenly feels like a sunrise, like the world has been lit with the most beautiful colors, waking her up to all its possibility, its perfection, its radiance.

She just smiles back as they continue to walk.

Anastasia spends the next fifteen minutes speaking to Dominic about her flute lessons, about how her instructor once looked like he had stuffed cotton in his ears minutes before her arrival. She talks about Drizella and their old dog, Bruno, and how she never wants to eat another egg for the rest of her life. And in return, he tells her about the castle, how the beautiful shiny marble floors really just make it feel like an icebox, what it's like spending so much time with the royal family but never actually speaking to any of them, how sometimes even the most beautiful place can feel like a prison when you have nowhere else to go.

"Can I ask how you ended up at the palace?" she says.

He shrugs. "I always thought that I'd go into a trade, a shop owner, a blacksmith, something like that. But then my parents died when I was twelve, and a friend of the family was one of the royal horse trainers, so he brought me in. He said that nothing is free and that it was time to work, and that's what I did. Polished shoes, fed the horses, cleaned their stalls. I had nowhere to go and nobody else wanted me, so it was as good as anything."

Anastasia tries not to picture Dominic as a young boy, missing his parents horribly, living in both physical splendor and emotional poverty. She wonders if anyone was ever there to comfort him when he awoke in the night, or when he fell ill, if he was just as lonesome in those dark moments as she was as a child, without a mother's gentle hand to soothe her forehead or shush the nightmares away.

The only difference was Dominic's mother was dead. Hers was still very much alive.

"I'm sorry," she murmurs. "That must have been a very difficult time."

They've found a small bench a good distance away from both Drizella's music studio and the slaughterhouse so that they can see the Prince's carriage. "It's all right," Dominic says. "It was a long time ago. The palace took me in and kept me fed and clothed and warm, and that family friend became a wonderful mentor, but he passed away several years ago, so here I am." He holds up his hands in a shrug. "Didn't really have a lot of other options."

Anastasia's long forgotten about being ladylike, having

yanked off her gloves to ease her sweaty hands and leaned against the bench so she won't have to keep her posture so straight. If her mother could see her now, she'd lock her in the tower forever.

A chill runs through Anastasia at the thought. Dominic notices.

"Are you all right?" he asks, and she waves away his words.

"I'm fine," she says. "Just the breeze. And the corset a bit, maybe." She shifts her posture back to being ramrod straight.

"Is that even comfortable?" Dominic asks. "Do you want to wear it?"

"Nobody wants to wear it," Anastasia says. "We women prefer breathing instead." At that, he laughs so hard that she ends up laughing, too. "I'm speaking the truth!" she protests. "You try walking around all day with this thing on. I feel like a fish out of water." She grabs at the boning of the corset as if that could help her breathe easier, but she squeezes too tight and her finger pinches, making her gasp a little.

"What is it?" Dominic frowns. "Your wrist? Your hand? Did you hurt it when you fell?"

"No, it's my finger. It was a long time ago," she says, flushing again. "I had . . . an accident. It was nothing. I'm fine. Anyway, corsets. *No.*"

Another chill goes through her, though, and she pushes the memory away.

They continue to talk, both of them keeping an eye out

for Drizella and the Prince, the two people who will eventually pull Anastasia and Dominic away from one another. Anastasia finds herself looking at his eyes a lot. They're not anything special, not hazel or green or the color of the sky right before the sunrise. They're just brown, the same as hers, but the more Dominic speaks, the more beautiful they become, and she feels something heat up right behind her heart, like a tiny coal that's been set aflame, burning her from the inside out.

"Can I tell you something that may be forward?" he asks her.

"Well, I already told you about my disdain for corsets, so I can't imagine it'll be any more bold than that."

He laughs again, but then his face grows serious. "Your hair color is really beautiful."

Anastasia's hand flies to the top of her head as if she could cover it completely with her palm. "Oh," she says, flustered. "It's just . . . yes. I'm the only one in our family, so it's sort of a . . . it's different."

"Beautiful," he repeats, correcting her. "It's the color of a sunset. Or like when the farmers burn back their fields every October and the skies get all orange and red."

Anastasia is so used to her mother's careless scorn, to Drizella's teasing about her "carrot top," to her now-dead stepfather's calling her "interesting" when he really meant "strange," to her father's never calling her anything because he isn't there. It's been so long since anyone's paid her a compliment that she feels her eyes fill with salt water, a weird rush that stings and embarrasses her.

Dominic looks panicked at first. "I'm so sorry, I didn't mean—"

"No, no, it's all right," she says, waving away his concern. "I just . . . I don't come from a family that says very many nice things." It's odd to say that out loud, even though, now that she's thinking about it, it's the truth. "Sometimes my mother says I'm the pretty one, though." She's trying to make both Dominic and herself feel better, but it sounds pathetic even to her own ears, as if beauty is a sliding scale, meant for comparing to other people and things and never just beauty for beauty's sake.

"Thank you," she says, wiping quickly at her eyes before she can make an even bigger scene. "For that."

"Well, I meant it." His face is still concerned, though, and he reaches inside his coat, pulls out a small waxed paper bag, and holds it out to her. "Butterscotch?"

Just as Anastasia's about to respond, there's a furious cacophony of trumpets from just around the corner, heralding the Prince's departure from the slaughterhouse.

"Goodness!" Anastasia cries, putting her hand to her heart. "Does that happen every time he comes and goes?"

"I'm afraid it does," Dominic replies.

"How are you not deaf by this point?"

"What did you say?" he asks, then waits a few seconds before grinning. "I kid, but I also have to go. Duty calls and all. I'll try to make sure they don't run you over this time." He gestures toward the royal assembly as he stands. "How can I see you again?"

"See who?" she says. "Me?"

Dominic pretends to look around her, then over the top of her head. "Unless someone else is standing next to you that I can't see, then yes. You. I'd like to see you again."

Anastasia tries to think fast, but her head is spinning in a completely different direction, not logical or thoughtful but instead caught up in a whirlwind of heat and smiles and brown eyes. "I have lessons every week," she says, and then, so emboldened that she'll wake up later that night and be absolutely ashamed of herself, "We live at the end of that road, way down past where the dead trees are. You'll know it's us because of the pumpkin patch. That's dead, too."

"Dead trees, dead pumpkins, got it." He smiles again, then points at her hair one more time as he starts to run off. "I'm going to think about you when the sun sets tonight, Anastasia Tremaine!" he calls, and Anastasia almost hopes that someone else heard what he said, because it seems too good to be true, too impossible to hold such a statement all by herself.

That tiny lump of coal grows hotter, glows stronger, and Anastasia has the vague realization that perhaps this is what happiness feels like.

By the time she and Drizella find each other on the path, they're both dazed. They'll each tell themselves it's from the midday heat, but of course, it's impossible to lie to oneself.

"Where's your flute?" Drizella says when she sees Anastasia, who glances down at her empty hand and then gasps.

"Oh, goodness!" she cries. "One minute, one minute!" She flies around the corner, finds the miserable thing still sitting by the bench, snatches it up, and hurries back to her sister.

Drizella is just shaking her head. "You're probably the only person who can go to a flute lesson and then forget to bring home that exact instrument." Anastasia's used to these kinds of comments from her older sister. She can barely put a shoe on without Drizella making a snide remark or a haughty tsk. But this time, her sister sounds almost . . . fond? Like she's amused instead of annoyed.

Anastasia looks at her. "Have you been in the sun for too long?"

"Hardly." But Drizella's cheeks are flushed pink, even though she's still got her bonnet on, and there's a smile pushing up the corners of her mouth. She looks completely different from the sullen sister Anastasia is used to seeing, like she's just been reborn or something, and Anastasia has the sneaking suspicion that she herself looks the exact same way.

"I just had a really good lesson," Drizella says, then starts to head up the path toward their house, going slow so that Anastasia can hustle to catch up. "I learned a lot today."

"Yes," Anastasia agrees, then falls into step with Drizella. "I believe I could say the exact same thing."

5

DRIZELLA

After her encounter with Madame Lambert, it takes Drizella six days to find a chance to break into her stepfather's old library.

It's approximately five and a half days too long.

She's never been curious about anything left behind by that man, of course, and Drizella has no memories of his being in the study or even picking up a book, for that matter. Years ago, Drizella couldn't even see a book without thinking of her own father, but time has dulled to the point where she can think about him without feeling that sharp stab of abandonment.

But after seeing all the books in Madame Lambert's studio, Drizella can't help wondering what's in that study, what sort of secrets and ideas are hidden in the pages behind those locked doors. Was he the one who whispered the names of constellations to her? Did he hold her outside at night and point out the stars? Drizella both wishes she could remember and is grateful that she doesn't.

The big, drafty estate feels stifling and small now that Drizella's been able to see what a different space can look like, and the days seem to stretch ahead of her like a road with no destination, just the same boring, quotidian things done at the same time, in the same places: waking up, dressing, breakfast, lessons, sewing, changing for dinner, dinner, bed.

Drizella's head feels floaty now, too, like she's been up to space and seen the Earth from a whole new perspective, and she hasn't quite gotten her bearings again. (*Imagine doing something like that!* she thinks, then has to hide a grin behind her clenched fist, pretending to yawn instead.) Still, she can feel her mother watching her with an especially sharp eye, and, alas, Drizella keeps giving her reasons to do so: her embroidery is jagged, and she accidentally stabs herself with the sewing needle twice during the same lesson, drawing blood from two separate fingers as well as a terse rebuke from Lady Tremaine; she misplaces her voice sheet music and can't find it anywhere, not even after shaking out her bedding and checking under the fainting couch and the dining room table; when she tries to gently crochet a lace collar for a dress, it ends up looking more like a noose, and the whole thing is so ghastly that she quickly unravels it, too frightened to have it in the house and bring even more bad luck upon them.

Lady Tremaine isn't the only one who's noticed that Drizella is acting different.

"Why are you being so *strange*?" Anastasia hisses at her one evening as they get ready to go down to dinner. Their mother insists on everyone—except Ella, of course; that would be *ridiculous*—dressing for the nightly meal, regardless of whether or not they have guests. (They never have guests. Drizella can't remember the last time a stranger's feet crossed their threshold.)

"I'm not being strange!" Drizella snaps back, then shoves her sister out of the way of the mirror so she can inspect her hair with a sigh. Forever disappointing, she thinks.

Anastasia bumps her right back and then fluffs her own red strands. Drizella stands back and burns with a little bit of jealousy over Annie's russet hair, how red and shiny it is, how it sometimes makes her look like she's on fire, ready to blaze a path to her own destiny. Again, she would rather be trampled by a horse than let Anastasia know any of this, but it still remains true.

And then Anastasia sticks her tongue out at Drizella in the

mirror, and all her generous thoughts evaporate into smoke.

"You're the one being strange!" Drizella says to her, then gives her a shove so hard that Anastasia goes sprawling onto the settee with an "oof!" "How many times do you plan on standing on my bed at night and looking out the window, anyway?"

Anastasia has the sense to look a tiny bit embarrassed, and Drizella feels a muted thrill of victory. "See?" she says. "Strange."

It's true, though. Nearly every night for the past week, Drizella's come to her room to get ready for bed and found Anastasia already in her nightclothes, standing on her tiptoes and craning her neck to look at . . . what? The castle? The moon? The stars? Their ugly pumpkin patch with all its deadened vines? Anastasia used to do the same thing when they were both young girls, but it's been years since she put her filthy feet all over Drizella's blankets. And Drizella's pretty sure that her sister has exactly zero interest in constellations, stars, or the moon, and nobody gives a shake about their garden, not even Ella or their old horse. Lady Tremaine won't let any of her girls touch the land, saying that they'll just get filthy and sunburned the minute they go out there, and anyway, who would ever marry a girl with dirt under her nails and freckles across her nose?

"Just keep your stinky feet off my bed, is all," Drizella says to Anastasia now, examining her own light freckles in the mirror. "I don't know what you're looking for, but it can't be good."

"No," Anastasia agrees as her face melts into a moony grin. "It's better than good. It's *wonderful.*"

Drizella grabs a pillow and playfully bops her in the head with it. No matter what, she's still Annie, and it's not often that Drizella gets to see her little sister smile. "Strange!" she hisses again, then drops the pillow and runs out of the room, giggling as Anastasia gives chase. She's almost caught up to her sister when suddenly Drizella comes to a dead halt and Anastasia smacks into her.

"What—?" she starts to say.

"I know I'm tired and starving," Drizella says, "so I might be hallucinating, but I'm fairly certain that I just saw a mouse—"

Anastasia laughs. "You're not used to that yet?"

"Wearing pants and a hat."

Anastasia looks up, alarmed.

They both say it at the same time.

"*Ella.*"

"Girls!" their mother calls from her bedroom down the hall. "I can't imagine those are *my* daughters running around like wild elephants instead of two well-mannered young women on their way to dinner this evening."

Drizella catches Annie's eye, then puts on a mean face and mimics her mother's annoyed tone. "Stop it!" Anastasia whispers, slapping her arm, but they're both still snickering to themselves. "You're going to get in trouble if she catches you! She'll put you in the tow—"

They both stop laughing then. A terrible silence hangs between them, laden with guilt and thoughts that have been unspoken for far too long.

"Annie," Drizella starts to say, but Anastasia just turns on her heel and starts to go downstairs.

"Coming, Mother!" she chirps, leaving Drizella alone once again, surrounded only by her darkest memories: her sister's screams, her mother's shouts, and Drizella standing at the bottom of the stairs, watching her baby sister disappear behind a dark wooden door, shaking with both terror and love.

⚜

The next day, with Anastasia taking a catnap upstairs and Lady Tremaine inelegantly passed out on a faded wingback chair in their drawing room, Drizella seizes her moment.

Her stepfather's study has been closed off since the day they moved into the château, their mother depositing a flurry of books and boxes inside and then twisting the lock tight with a *click!* that sounded more like a revolver firing than a key turning. Drizella can still remember the moment, the feeling of sudden, childish panic at the idea that she might never be let back into the room. It was so stupid that she had a hard time even admitting it to herself, but what if her father was asleep in there? What if he hadn't abandoned them? What if her mother had locked him inside the study forever? What if he had left them a secret note, a treasure map to his location, flowers pressed into a book so that they'd have something to remember him by?

Drizella tried for days to get the key away from her mother, convinced that there was a secret in there she needed to find, but all that earned her was a twisted ear and a threat of worse punishments if she tested her patience one more time. Anastasia watched the scene through the bars of the upstairs banister, her big sad eyes framed by red ringlets, and Drizella felt humiliated not only by her mother's actions, but by her own naive foolishness.

She knows better now. Her father was never in that room, of course. Everything he wanted, he took with him.

On this lazy afternoon, Drizella walks past Lady Tremaine several times, taking slightly heavier steps with each pass, but all that happens is that their dog, Bruno, glances up several times, one eyebrow raised as if to insinuate that Drizella is being rude. "Quiet, you," she hisses at him, and Bruno settles back down, unimpressed with her, as per usual. His loyalty lies with the person currently washing and drying the lunch dishes in the kitchen, humming to herself the notes on the sheet music she discovered the other day.

Once she's convinced that her mother is indeed heavily asleep, Drizella creeps down the hall toward the hall table where she knows her mother keeps important things. She knows the key is there, along with the deed to their home and her stepfather's last will and testament, in which he implored Lady Tremaine to care for his daughter as if she were one of her own.

Good luck, Drizella thought when she and Annie discovered that paperwork one day. Caring for Ella as if she were one of the Tremaines was not exactly the parting gift that her stepfather thought it would be, that's for sure.

Drizella rummages quietly for a minute, using her hands to keep the keys from clinking together while shooting a look skyward to make sure Anastasia isn't hovering at the top of the stairs, being her usual nosy self. Sometimes Annie can be so quiet that Drizella won't even know that she is there until she nearly bumps into her. "Sneaky!" Drizella tells her, shaking her head in annoyance, but the truth is that sometimes, Annie seems like a ghost, floating around with nowhere to be; just someone who used to be someone else.

And besides, if Anastasia knew what she was doing, she would ask Drizella a thousand questions about it. Can't Drizella just have something of her own for once?

She knows when she's found the right key because it has her stepfather's initials engraved at the top. She doesn't remember what they stand for, nor does she think it's a wise idea to ask Lady Tremaine for more information about him.

Instead, she pockets the key and slips down the hallway toward the darker end of the house, where all the drapes stay pulled regardless of the time of day. It's a little eerie, but almost comforting, like the feeling of waking up only to realize that it's still dark outside and you can go back to sleep, and Drizella creeps along, happy to be alone on her adventure, until she gets to the heavy door at the end of the hall.

She touches the brass doorknob, half expecting it to scorch or burn her as a warning to stay away, but it's cold to the touch, soft from years of use and wear. Drizella wonders how many people before her have touched this doorknob, have used this room for a study, a child's nursery, a playroom; so many lives have come before theirs, and—

Dear lord, who is she? Anastasia?! Drizella shakes her head, clearing the sentimentality away. She *clearly* needs to spend less time with her moony sister, that much is obvious.

Drizella shoves the key into the lock without ceremony, twists it once, and lets herself into the room.

It's dark, and she has to hide two quick sneezes in the crook of her elbow, the room is so dusty. A tiny sliver of light peeks out from below one of the curtains, and Drizella lets her eyes adjust to the dimness before she moves forward. There's a heavy mahogany desk in front of floor-to-ceiling bookshelves that are half-full of dusty tomes and a few knickknacks. A quill-tipped pen sits in a dried-up inkwell, and Drizella steps forward to run a fingertip over the soft feathers.

It's a space frozen in time, she realizes, and the thought makes her feel a little lonely inside.

She sinks down into the leather chair behind the desk and debates putting her feet up before a stack of books catches her eye. They remind her of the ones in Madame Lambert's studio, clothbound with gilt-edged words printed into their spines. They're in Latin, so she can't read them, and she silently curses Lady Tremaine for making both her and Anastasia stop their schooling. They had just been about to start algebra and Latin when the girls left, and Drizella still imagines all those mysterious letters and how they can create so much more than just words on a page.

She thumbs through the books, coughing a little bit at the dust before setting them back down and looking toward the desk. One of the drawers is halfway open and when Drizella looks closer, she realizes that a piece of parchment is jammed inside. It's a calendar, only it doesn't look like any sort of calendar she's ever seen before. Instead of numbers, there are circles: full circles, half wedges, simple slices that look like sideways smiles.

It's the moon, she realizes, and suddenly the Latin books are the last thing on her mind.

Drizella yanks the drawer all the way open, reaching inside to touch the parchment paper. There are twelve big squares on the page, each square divided into smaller sections with the months of the year written above them.

A calendar of the moon? Why would her stepfather have such a thing?

She takes the calendar out and spreads it open across the desk, lifts the page, and discovers that it's the following year, and when she goes back a few pages, it's the year before and the year before that. But the current page is from ten years ago, the year her father left them.

This isn't her stepfather's calendar, she suddenly realizes. It is her father's.

Drizella leans in close and sees that one of the squares has a full moon, that it's been circled with some long-gone quill pen just like the one in the now-dead inkwell, that it's the date of her father's disappearance, a full moon to light his way, that he had marked and planned it and had cared so little about them finding it that he hadn't even bothered to hide the evidence.

Drizella will not cry. She will. Not. Cry.

"What are you doing in here?"

She gasps and spins around, the skirt of her dress a few

seconds behind in its twirl. She thinks frantically of an excuse to give her mother, to ward off whatever nightmarish consequence she has in mind, but all Drizella sees is Ella's thin face poking through the crack in the door, her eyes wide with curiosity.

"Look at all of these books!" she says, her whisper louder this time, and Drizella waves at her to hush.

"Do you want to get us *both* thrown into the fireplace?" she hisses, snatching the calendar off the wall and tucking it under her arm. "Just shut up!"

"Are you even allowed in here?" Ella asks. "I thought this was locked—"

Drizella hurries toward her, out of the room, still flapping her hand at Ella as if she's a chicken. "Hush!" she says, then takes the key out of her pocket and turns the lock in the door, shutting everything away once again. "And if you tattle, I'll tell her"—no need to explain who *her* is; they all know—"that you're the one who keeps inviting the mice inside the house."

Drizella doesn't know this, of course, but she's had her suspicions for a few months, ever since she saw Ella smuggling a mouse caught in a trap *into* the kitchen instead of out of it, and she smiles when Ella gasps and puts a hand to her mouth. "I knew it," Drizella says. "Your secret for mine, okay? And keep those rodents away from my room while you're at it."

Then Drizella is hurrying away, going up the back staircase just in case her mother has heard their whispered exchange. Her heart is tight in her chest, like it can't beat fast enough, and once she gets upstairs, she flings herself down on her bed and feels her breath shake her from the inside out. If anyone passed by and took the time to look at her, care for her, they would think she's sobbing, her tears so fierce that they can make no noise at all.

He planned it. Her father wasn't kidnapped by pirates, wasn't swallowed by the seas, didn't fall into a mine. He was so intent on leaving them that he timed it precisely, letting that traitorous full moon light his path away from his own children. Her mother never minced words about his abandonment, of course, but still, Drizella had a childish thread of hope that maybe he would one day come back, bedraggled and exhausted but so thrilled to see them, full of apologies for not being able to write, his arms full of his daughters as they laughed and cried with him.

Drizella isn't crying now. Never again.

She waits for the storm to pass through her body, the lashing rage and loss eventually ebbing away into exhaustion. Ella hasn't followed her upstairs, and she feels grateful for that. She doesn't want anyone to see her this way, weak and embarrassed by her own curiosity. The lunar calendar is pressed between her stomach and her mattress, and Drizella rolls over a little bit, has half a mind to shred it between her hands and shower the pig troughs with it.

Instead, she carefully folds it and tucks it in between the pages of her sheet music, then smooths her hands over her hair again and again. It's something she started doing a long time ago, a self-soothing action that never quite manages to comfort her fully. When it's very late and she's very tired, she can imagine that it's her own mother stroking her hair, helping ease her into sleep.

But Lady Tremaine has never and would never do such a thing. Drizella should know better.

She lies on her bed for a long time after that, watches the sun set, and waits for the moon to appear. After a while, she hears a knock at her door, quiet and unsure.

Anastasia.

Drizella picks her head up off the pillow just long enough to say "Not hungry" before she buries her face again. A few minutes later, there's a small bump at the door, the quiet clank of a porcelain teapot lid being resettled, and once she hears soft footsteps head back down the stairs, Drizella pulls herself off the bed and goes to the door.

Anastasia has left her a tray of food: brown bread with butter, a few pickled vegetables, the last of the figs from the tree outside, and a pot of tea. Frankly, Drizella is astounded that Anastasia was able to carry the entire tray upstairs without spilling anything, and it makes something stir in Drizella's chest, the love her sister has for her to do something like this when she's upset. She nudges the tray into her room with her foot before quietly shutting the door again, needing to be alone tonight.

6

ANASTASIA

Anastasia has never been more excited to go to her flute lesson in her entire life.

She still couldn't care less about the flute, of course. She barely practiced this week and even had a hard time finding the case this morning, not remembering where she last left it. But going to her lesson means going into town, and going into town means the possibility of seeing people. Well, one person.

Dominic.

Just thinking about his name gives her a shiver. At night, she's practiced saying it out loud, the tiniest whisper conveying the most overwhelming feelings, and she imagines saying it to him, calling to him, him turning around and smiling at her.

It's just all so delicious that she can't stand it. Who would have thought that her stupid *flute lessons* would be what led her to such wonderful things?

The world works in mysterious ways, Anastasia thinks, and nods her head at how wise she is.

At breakfast, she can barely choke down a croissant even as she listens to her mother scold Ella over the fact that the pastries are cold and not fresh-out-of-the-oven warm. Across the table, Drizella is sullen, chewing away at the bread like it's somehow done her wrong.

Their mother notices.

"Drizella," she says, and both Anastasia and Drizella look up at the tone in her voice. She has a way of saying the *Z* in Drizella's name so that it sounds like lightning hitting the ground, creating a shock wave through anyone who hears it.

Anastasia sees a tiny mouse scurry back into a hole and says nothing.

"Yes, Lady—yes, Mother?" her sister says, quickly correcting herself, and their mother's eyes become a little more flinty.

"You're looking especially tired this morning," she says, picking up her teacup and sipping the tea. Anastasia waits to see if Ella's going to get scolded again for letting the tea water go cold, but it appears to be fine.

Drizella glances down at her lap and shakes her head a little before looking back up. "Yes, I was . . . I had trouble sleeping last night."

Anastasia suspected that something was amiss. She saw Ella quietly knocking on Drizella's door before turning away and coming back a few moments later with a small tray of food, which she left on the floor. It made a tiny jealous flame rise up in Anastasia when she saw that, like Ella could ever know what Drizella would need better than Anastasia herself, and she sulked at the dinner table for the rest of the night.

"And you appeared to miss dinner, as well," their mother continues, almost as if she were reading Anastasia's mind. It's eerie how she can just offer a simple statement and make it seem as if there is no right answer. Anastasia has fallen into that trap several times and has no desire to repeat the experience, so she stays quiet.

Across the table, Drizella's gaze falls to her plate. Anastasia knows her sister better than anyone else ever could, and she suddenly realizes that Drizella, who's usually as cool as the jarred vegetables stored in their root cellar, is nervous.

About what? Anastasia's attention is now officially piqued.

"My stomach was a bit upset," Drizella replies.

"Look at me when I'm speaking to you," their mother says, and both Anastasia and Drizella give her their full attention. Drizella swallows hard, but her gaze is steady, almost challenging.

"What are you going to do once you're married?" their mother asks, sipping her tea again. "Do you think you'll just have time to not run your household? To give in to that kind of weakness?"

Drizella goes a little pale but shakes her head. "No, Mother."

"Do you expect your husband to do everything while you just lie in bed?" She smirks at the idea of a man taking over the duties of his wife. And Anastasia doesn't know why, but it makes her stomach turn a little. She wonders if Drizella's stomachache is contagious.

"No, Mother," Drizella repeats. She's looking at their mother, but it's almost as if she can see right through her. "I apologize. I won't miss dinner again."

"I only ask," their mother continues as if she hasn't heard her, "because that day may be coming sooner than you think, my dears." She reaches into her dress pocket and pulls out a rolled piece of parchment, sealed with a crimson-colored circle of wax, the royal insignia pressed into it.

Anastasia feels her heart flutter when she sees it, thinking of Dominic and his purple coat. She hopes nobody notices the blush that rises to her cheeks, her own body betraying her secret.

"I believe," their mother says, sliding open the seal with a long, well-groomed fingernail, almost like a dagger going through a heart, "that this is the *official* invitation for the

Prince's debut party. And you two . . ." Her voice trails off as she smiles, but neither girl is reassured. "I have no doubt in my mind that you two will be ready for your moment."

Anastasia looks at Drizella.

Drizella looks at Anastasia.

"That's wonderful, Mother!" Anastasia says. She can tell that Drizella isn't able to speak in the moment, but her enthusiasm can carry them both. "The invitation looks beautiful, as well."

"Of *course* it looks beautiful," their mother snaps. "It's from the palace. You know that they produce nothing but the best, Anastasia. Everything from invitations to heirs." She raises her eyes, then fixes her gaze on Anastasia before sliding it to Drizella.

"And just like the palace, I expect the best."

⚜

"So," Anastasia says as they walk down the dirt road, her initial giddiness about her adventures tempered a bit by their mother's comment about being "the best." She knocks the thought away for another time, though, determined to enjoy her day.

"So," Drizella replies.

"Are you not even a little bit excited?" Anastasia pries.

"Just a tiny bit? Somewhere deep down in your cold, cold heart?"

She's only teasing, of course, but Drizella just kicks at a rock and continues walking ahead of her.

"Drizzy." Anastasia sighs. "It's a *party*, not a witch hunt. There will be dancing and music and gowns—"

"Tight shoes, loud people, crowded rooms."

"Oh, I'm sorry, I didn't realize that you were a debut party expert," Anastasia says sarcastically. "My mistake. Please, tell me everything you know about them."

"This is what I know: it's going to be terrible and we'll be the laughingstocks of the entire village."

"Oh," Anastasia says. She didn't realize that Drizella felt that way about the party, or, deeper down, that Drizella feels that way about *her*.

Drizella stops walking and turns around to face her sister. "Annie. Look at us." She gestures to her dress, to her hair and faded sunbonnet. "We're not like the rest of those girls and you know it. We don't have much money. We don't wear silk dresses or get our hair done at the salon. Our shoes are old. Neither one of us have any talent. And they call our mother the Black Widow, for goodness' sake. Do you think anyone's going to want to marry or even court us, much less the Prince?" She scoffs.

Anastasia does know it, but it's much harder to hear it

come out of her sister's mouth than to think it inside her own head. "It's not *that* bad," she says, dragging the toe of her shoe in the dirt before thinking better of it. Drizella's right; their shoes are old, and she suspects the leather sole in her right shoe is about to wear out.

Drizella raises an eyebrow. "Not *that* bad?" she repeats. "A bunch of girls all gathered there to present themselves to someone they've never even met? That sounds terrible."

"Drizzy." Anastasia sighs, rubbing her forehead with her hand. "That's called meeting people. That's how people *meet*. Everyone's a stranger at first."

"We're going to be like those fluffy white poodles that sometimes dance in the village square!" Drizella continues. "All dressed up for someone else's entertainment!"

"We're not like the toy poodles," Anastasia insists. "People throw coins at the poodles. Nobody ever throws money at us."

Drizella's brow is still knitted together, but a smile spreads across her face. "You know what I mean."

They split at the fork in the road once again as they go to their separate lessons. Anastasia's, of course, goes terribly, even more so than usual since she's barely practiced and her poorly healed finger doesn't exactly allow her to be the kind of flute savant who can float by on her God-given talent.

When her rendition of "Sing, Sweet Nightingale" is over, her instructor looks like he's just witnessed a terrible accident.

"I truly have never heard the song played quite like that" is all he says, though, and Anastasia is smart enough to know it's not a compliment.

She's just about to launch into a new song when she glances out the window and sees a familiar figure standing outside, peering down the street as if he's lost, or maybe looking for something.

Or, Anastasia realizes with a sudden rush of adrenaline, looking for *someone*.

"I have to go!" she blurts out, and her instructor whirls around, confused.

"But we still have thirty minutes left, not to mention that you missed last week's lesson *entirely*, and your mother has strictly said that you must—"

"Yes, yes, I know," Anastasia says, even though she doesn't know and she *really* doesn't want to talk about her mother at this moment in time. "But I, um, I have a stomachache. My sister had one last night. It's probably contagious." And then she coughs for good measure, even though the two things aren't related.

The instructor blanches a bit. He always has at least two handkerchiefs in his pocket at any given moment, and Anastasia has long suspected that he's afraid of every single speck of dust in the studio for fear of its giving him a cold. "Oh, well, in that case," he says, but Anastasia's already disassembling her flute and tossing it haphazardly into its case, keeping one eye on the window. It's definitely Dominic; she can tell from the royal insignia on his coat and the tiny tuft of his cowlick blowing in the breeze, and she can feel her breath coming faster, her heart moving the blood through her body like it's never done before. The urge to see him, to be in front of him again, is almost suffocating, and this damn corset isn't doing anything to help the situation.

"See you next week!" she calls over her shoulder as she rushes down the stairs, nearly falling as she grabs on to the banister for support. A sharp shock of pain runs up her finger, but she's dealt with far worse for less reward, and it doesn't slow her down at all.

Just before she gets outside, she smoothes down her hair with her palm and tries to catch her breath, tries not to look like a fish that's just been pulled out of the water, all gasping and bug-eyed. She's just a normal girl leaving her flute lesson, that's all. A cultured, refined, sophisticated—

She sees Dominic turn the corner and takes off running down the street behind him.

"Hi!" she says, sounding like, well, somewhat like a gasping, bug-eyed fish would. "Dominic! What are you"—she feels her breath hitch as a cramp appears under her rib cage—"doing here?" She smiles and tries to breathe through her teeth so it doesn't look like she's panting.

He turns around and grins at her, and, oh, Anastasia suddenly understands why you're not supposed to look directly at the sun. He's all warmth and light, golden amber hair and soft brown eyes, tan in a way that suggests he's not part of the porcelain-skinned nobility who remain forever indoors, but is still no less noble, and Anastasia feels a rush of heat run through her blood.

It's entirely possible that nobody has ever felt like this in the history of the world. If they had, why would anyone ever fight, start wars, battle with one another? Why wouldn't this feeling be everything that someone could ever need?

"Hello," Dominic says, and Anastasia looks for a pillar or signpost to clutch in case she swoons. "I thought you might be here today so I, ahem, perhaps invented a small errand or two to run." He gestures toward her flute case. "Still have that beast with you, I see."

She grins and tries to hide it behind her legs like it's a shy child. The dent is still there, but she's managed to keep it hidden from her mother, at least for now. "Not by choice," she replies. "We're sort of a package deal today. Unfortunately. But I'm glad you're here. I, um, yes. I'm just happy to see you, is all."

They stand together under the sun's hot beams, smiling at each other like two lovesick songbirds, until Dominic finally says, "Do you want to go for a walk? Maybe get out of the heat for a bit?"

Anastasia would happily walk right into the fires of hell if he asked her, but she's wise enough not to say that part out loud. "I would be delighted," she replies instead, and when he holds out the crook of his elbow, she slots her hand into the space and can't but think that they're an absolutely perfect fit.

He leads her just past the last street of the village and into a clearing near a wild lavender field. He's right: it's slightly cooler over here, and the breeze makes the ends of Anastasia's wild red hair dance in the wind.

"So, do you bring lots of girls here?" Anastasia says, tracing her hand back and forth through the soft blades so that they tickle her skin.

"Only five or six," he says, then laughs when she looks up, speechless and scandalized. "I'm joking, I promise. I've actually never brought anyone here before. This has always been my spot, but . . ." His voice trails off, and he shrugs, then picks a handful of grass and starts to tear away at it with his fingers. "Sometimes I get a little lonely, I guess."

Anastasia's ears prick up at the word. "You?" she says. "But there must be dozens—no, hundreds of people there to assist the royal family. You must be surrounded by people all the time."

"Having people around you doesn't mean that you're not lonely," he says quietly. "Sometimes that's the worst kind of loneliness. When you're lonely but never alone."

Anastasia watches as her fingers go back and forth against the green. "I suppose that's true," she says.

"And besides," he adds, "not a lot of people actually want to talk to me. *Dominic*. They only want to talk to the Prince's *head groom*." He says the last two words in a haughty tone that Anastasia's sure she's heard her mother use before. "They always want to know where the Prince is, where he's going next, what he's doing now, what he's doing later in the evening, if he's looking to marry anyone . . ."

He looks over at Anastasia as he says that, his eyes narrowing slightly, and Anastasia easily picks up the hint that he's dropping.

"You think that I'm spending time with you to get closer to the Prince," she says.

"You wouldn't be the first."

"Have I done anything to make you feel that way?" She's genuinely curious. Her mother sometimes says that she's manipulative, but Anastasia can never figure out what she's done to make her mother think so harshly about her. But it's also not like she can just ask her mother what she's done to upset her, because then that would be both ignorant and insolent. It's a tricky dance, one whose steps Anastasia can never learn.

"No, not at all, but the best ones never give away their sneaky plan," he says. He seems a little wounded, like Bruno the morning after they made him sleep out in the barn for the first time. "I guess I just want to say that I like talking to you, and if you're not—"

"Oh, I really like talking to you, too!" she says, interrupting. (Is it manipulative to interrupt someone? She's not sure. She'll have to ask Drizella.) "I'm happy to see you, *Dominic*, if that helps. Not the Prince. Just you."

Dominic smiles at that, and Anastasia feels the invisible string that ties them together pulling her a little bit closer to him. "How did you find this place?" she asks. "It feels as if it's hidden in the middle of nowhere."

He gestures out toward the field and the skies beyond it. "My mother used to bring me here for picnics in the summertime, and after she passed, I kept coming back. Not many people ever come here. It's like you have space to—"

"Think." Anastasia finishes his sentence before he can. (And there she goes, interrupting again.)

But Dominic doesn't seem bothered by the interruption at all. "Exactly. There's just space out here. No crowded streets, no cold hallways. Just . . . space," he says. He looks at her carefully. "Do you live with your parents?"

"My mother and my sister and our . . . my stepsister. My father, he . . ." Anastasia's not sure what she's supposed to say here. It's no secret in their town that their father abandoned them all those years ago, but at the same time, she's not sure if she's supposed to divulge this information to a stranger, especially one that she likes. What if that makes her less desirable to him? What if the light goes out of his eyes when he sees what Anastasia really is, a girl so homely that even her own father couldn't stand to be around her any longer?

"Anastasia?" Dominic murmurs, and she shakes her head, bringing herself back to the conversation.

"He left," she says, the words rushing out of her before she can stop them. "Ten years ago. He waited until we were all asleep and stole my mother's wedding ring right off her finger while she was sleeping and disappeared forever." She glances up toward Dominic, too intimidated by her own admission to make direct eye contact with him. "You were honest with me, so I feel like I should be honest with you."

"I'm very sorry," Dominic says, and his forehead is furrowed with concern. "What a loss."

"I know."

"I mean for him, not for you."

Anastasia rolls her eyes and scoffs, waving her hand at him and looking away so that he doesn't see the spark of tears gathering.

"No, I'm serious," Dominic says, then reaches over, takes her arm, and turns her back to face him. "I don't know what your father took with him the night he left, but I do know that what he left behind was infinitely more valuable."

"You . . ." Anastasia starts to say, then laughs and chokes back a sob at the same time. "You are a very good flirt, is what you are."

"Perhaps," he says. "But you said it first: I'm also honest."

She bites her lip and nods. "That you are," she says. "So, if we're being honest, tell me: what would you do with your life if you weren't in the palace? If you could do anything?" She's curious, but she's also a little desperate to change the subject, not used to having so much empathetic attention focused on her.

He sits back with a sigh. "I'd go to Paris," he says. "Or London. China. New York. Vienna. Everywhere, I guess. I don't know exactly what I would do when I am there, but I like working with animals. Maybe I could still be a horse trainer? A veterinarian?"

"A what?"

"An animal doctor," he clarifies. "I am not sure, and I guess that's what I'd like best about it. At the palace, I always know what to expect. There's always a schedule, never any surprises. I like the idea of just waking up one morning and not knowing what the day will bring." He looks over at her and smiles. "Kind of like today."

"A *very* good flirt," Anastasia repeats, but she smiles back.

"Is it working?"

"Unfortunately," she says, then reaches out and nudges his arm with a finger. "It's not like you have a lot of competition, though."

Dominic rolls his eyes at that, then sits up and brushes the grass from his hands. "What about you? Where would you go if you didn't live with your mother and sisters?"

It sounds strange to hear the word *sisters*, plural instead of singular. She guesses Ella is technically somewhat of a sister, but it's never felt that way. Neither her mother nor her dead stepfather ever tried to unite the three girls in bonds of sisterhood, and Anastasia deep down suspects that it's because her stepfather thought that Anastasia and Drizella were beneath Ella.

The thought still makes her burn with embarrassment, even all these years later.

"Me . . ." she says instead, thinking about the question. "Well, I guess if you're going to Paris, I may follow you." She pretends to look upset about it. "Oh, no, all of that lovely food, all of those gorgeous buildings. However will I survive the experience?"

"Can you eat while wearing that?" Dominic asks, pointing toward her corset. "How do you even sit? I've always wondered. Wait, is it rude that I'm asking?" Now it's his turn to blush, even the tips of his ears going slightly pink. "I don't talk to many girls, as you can probably imagine," he adds. "And the horses aren't great at conversation, either. I'm a little rusty here."

"You're okay," she reassures him, and resists the urge to pat his hand, even though it's a very pattable-looking hand. "Let's switch the subject. Tell me something about the palace that you'd never tell another soul."

"I am *not*—"

"I won't tell anyone, I swear," she promises, and indeed, she won't. "But there must be some gossip, some dirty secret that's burning a hole in your pocket." She's mixed the metaphor, she knows, but oh well. She wiggles her eyebrows at Dominic, still grinning maniacally, and he purses his lips together before finally bursting out laughing.

"Okay, okay," he says. "But if this ever gets out, I'll be flayed alive and thrown onto a funeral pyre to burn, so you cannot repeat it."

Anastasia makes a quick *X* with her finger over her heart. "Swear."

"So," Dominic says quietly. "We have a nickname for the Prince. But you *cannot—*"

"I've sworn I won't," she protests.

"Okay. We call him"—Dominic looks over his left then right shoulder, as if there are spies hidden in the lavender fields, just waiting for some good palace dirt—"Prince Charming."

Anastasia's posture sags. "*That's* your gossip?" she says. "My sister and I could have come up with something much better."

"No, we call him that because it's ironic. He's actually really, really boring."

Well now. This is definitely an improvement.

"Really?" she says, leaning in as if she too is now expecting spies to jump out of the fields. "Wow. Why?"

Dominic shrugs. "I think just a lifetime of being told what to do, where to go, how to act and bow and eat and think. He has no idea how to think for himself. There's just nothing there. I've had better conversations with a pile of sawdust."

All Anastasia can think is that she cannot wait to tell Drizella, but she's sworn that she won't. She wonders if Drizella will be able to read it in her eyes, if that will count as divulging a secret. "That's so disappointing," Anastasia says. "My mother is desperate for me or my sister to marry him."

"Don't," Dominic says. "You'll die of boredom within a year."

She laughs at that, full-throated and delighted by his cheekiness. "Noted," she says. "Sorry, Drizella."

"Does your mother know that we've talked?" Dominic asks.

Anastasia shakes her head and looks down at the grass. "No, I would never tell her. And besides," she quickly adds, "if she knew I was talking to someone who had access to the palace, forget it. She'd be obsessed. Ever since they announced the Prince's debut, all she's cared about is preparing us to impress him."

"Ah, yes, the debut ball," Dominic says, pulling his knees into his chest. "Those poor royal calligraphers have been working night and day to finish those invites."

"Ours arrived this morning," Anastasia admits, a little nervous to mention a ball where she's supposed to meet someone when the only someone she wants to meet is sitting right here in front of her. "The calligraphy was very beautiful, if that helps."

"I'll pass the compliment along." Dominic laughs. "You and your sisters must be excited."

"We're . . . some of us are more excited than others," Anastasia concedes. "I think Drizella is nervous. She think it's going to be a disaster."

"What do you think?"

There he goes, asking Anastasia about her opinions. The concept is so novel that it still gives her a zing of excitement. "I think I'm looking forward to seeing the palace, getting dressed up, maybe trying some champagne, and possibly seeing a very handsome boy there."

She looks up at Dominic and he's looking back at her, their gaze charged as the wind shifts and tousles their hair.

"I don't know," he finally says. "They don't let the stable hands debut. But I'll find a way to dance with you that night, Anastasia." He winks at her and makes her smile. "You can trust me on that. Not a single royal guard will be able to keep me away from asking your hand in a dance!"

Anastasia barks out an unladylike laugh. "My mother would absolutely unravel!" she cries.

"You really don't like her, do you," he says once their laughs die down.

"I don't think even my mother likes my mother," Anastasia replies. "And she certainly doesn't seem to like any of us that much, either. It's very sad, actually. I think maybe she thought she was going to have a different kind of life. Marriage, a husband who stays and doesn't steal or betray, two adoring, beautiful children, a grand home, all of that. Instead she got . . ." Anastasia's voice trails off as she raises her hands and then lets them fall into her lap. "Us."

Dominic just watches her as she talks, not saying anything. It's nice to have the space to speak out loud, Anastasia thinks, without being ridiculed or told to be quiet. "It's funny sometimes. I think that my mother has been so disappointed by all of these things in her life, and yet, those are the same things she wants for me and Drizella. It's hard to not feel a little afraid that we'll end up like her one day, no matter how hard we try to resist it."

Anastasia looks up at him, surprised by the softness of his expression. "You could never be like her," he says when her eyes meet his. "I can't imagine it."

"Well, good," she says. "I hope we know each other long enough to see if that turns out to be true."

"We will," Dominic replies with a nod of his head. "If you believe in one thing, Miss Anastasia Tremaine, believe in that."

Anastasia wonders if it's the same thing as wishing on the

first star of the night, a foolish habit that never seems to yield the results she wants. But here Dominic is, shining like he's the most golden of suns, and she thinks, what better star to wish on than him?

This time, Anastasia doesn't resist the temptation to place her hand on his. It's quite odd to see her body react instinctively, her heart dominating over her head, and she's just about to say something when she spots a tiny black-and-white fluffball dive headfirst into a lavender bush.

"Did you see that?" she asks Dominic, and then she's off and running.

By the time Dominic catches up to her, Anastasia has pulled a kitten out of the bushes and into her arms. She's shocked that it hasn't run away from her the way all other animals seem to, and while she wouldn't exactly call it docile, it's shivering in her arms, too weak to put up much of a fight.

Anastasia knows that feeling all too well.

"It's starving!" she says as soon as Dominic is close enough. "Look at it! Skin and bones! And so small!"

Dominic reaches out to scratch the kitten's head, but it mewls weakly and half-heartedly bats a paw at him. Anastasia hugs it a bit closer and wishes she had a coat to wrap it in. "It seems strong enough to me," Dominic says, pulling his hand back and looking warily at the kitten.

"You little devil," Anastasia coos, then runs a hand over its ears, which quickly pop back up again. The poor thing seems too scrawny to release back into the wild, and Anastasia thinks about all the ways a predator can descend upon and consume something too weak to defend itself.

The kitten mewls again, sealing its fate.

"I have a perfect home for you, darling," Anastasia tells the kitten. "Do you like mice? Hmm? Do you, sweetheart? Then I know *just* the place."

7

DRIZELLA

After Anastasia disappears down the road, Drizella trudges to her voice lessons. She feels the same as she does in the most humid days of summer, the air pushing down on her body and making it hard to move, and by the time she climbs the stairs to the second-floor atelier, she wishes she could just return home and take a nap in the quiet darkness of her bedroom.

When they left the house, the fancy invitation was still sitting on their breakfast table, its bold lettering searing itself into Drizella's brain. It's not like the debut is a surprise, of course, but it's been a generation since the palace has opened its doors to commoners, and Drizella knows as well as anyone that this is a very important event.

She also knows that she and Anastasia are doomed.

All her baby sister can picture are the soft lights, the beautiful music, the clink of champagne glasses, and the quiet murmur of polite conversation. She can't imagine the stares of the rest of the townspeople, frowning at their cheap, hand-sewn dresses, their lack of ladies-in-waiting, with no father beaming proudly from the wings as their names are announced to the Prince.

Drizella can handle all of that. She doesn't want to, but she will. What she doesn't think she can handle is Anastasia's inevitable disappointment, the way her face will fall, the way the harsh realization will make her eyes dim, her head bow. Anastasia so rarely gets what she wants, after all, and Drizella hates to see it all dangled in her sister's face before it's cruelly yanked away.

Just like that terrible night in the tower, Drizella would take it all on her own shoulders if it meant she could spare her sister.

And, of course, she arrives at the studio to find that Monsieur Longmont is once again late.

This news does not exactly upset Drizella. In fact, the idea of Longmont's being on time and ready for her to practice would have probably been the latest in a series of epic disappointments, and Drizella isn't exactly sure how many aches her heart is supposed to withstand, but she's not willing to find out. At least, not today.

As soon as she sees Longmont's studio is dark and empty, she immediately turns around and goes down toward Madame Lambert's . . . What to even call it? A studio? A magic shop? A *home*? Drizella's not sure what a home is supposed to feel like, and heaven knows her own house hasn't provided any answers, but she's spent the past week thinking about how warm she felt while she was in there, poring over plants and maps and stars, how safe the cozy space seemed to be. In her old storybooks from childhood, at least, all the homes felt that same way, like a place where you were happy to arrive instead of aching to leave.

Drizella pushes her shoulders back, shakes her hair out a little to try to revive the limp strands (no luck, if her reflection in the door's window is accurate), and then raises one pale fist to knock three times. Three is a lucky number, after all, and she needs all the luck she can get.

The door opens a few seconds later. "Well, hello again," Madame Lambert says, her smile widening to reveal tiny white teeth that look almost like the chicken feed Ella spreads out for their animals every morning. Her grin makes her cheeks seem even rounder, and it hits Drizella with the force of a fist that nobody ever smiles when they see her. They seem unimpressed at best, and, at least in Lady Tremaine's case, disappointed at worst.

She breaks the promise she made to herself only the day before, and promptly bursts into tears.

"My dear!" Madame Lambert says, then takes her by the hand and brings her inside. No one's touched Drizella, either, not like this. She and Anastasia will bump shoulders, or she'll give her sister a kick to get her out of bed in the morning, but there's never any warmth behind any of it. No hugs, no cuddles, no snuggles before bed. In fact, the last time Drizella remembers anyone treating her that way was when she was younger, when her father was still at home—

Her wails increase, and Madame Lambert shuts the door behind her, then guides her to a stool to sit down. "My dear," she says again, fluttering around Drizella, "whatever is the matter?"

"Nobody smiles!" Drizella cries. She knows that will make zero sense to this kind woman who already seems very perplexed, especially since Madame Lambert actually *does* smile, but it's hard to say anything else. Drizella sniffles and tries not to wipe her eyes on the back of her wrist, because that would be the height of indecency, but luckily Madame Lambert has a fresh handkerchief that she presses into Drizella's hand. It has a constellation of tiny yellow stars embroidered into it, along with a thin sliver of moon.

Drizella cries harder.

"Drizella," Madame Lambert says. "Just take a deep breath. You're fine here. All is well." Her voice is both sweet and serious, and it makes Drizella's heart race just a little bit less. "Take your time," she says, then pulls up her own chair to sit next to the girl. "I'm right here."

The reassurance goes through Drizella's body and down into her bones, spreading relief through her. She's not alone in her room. She's not combing through the study all by herself, finding hard evidence of her father's need to escape from them, from *her*. She's instead here with a kind woman whose face always seems to glow, even when she's looking at Drizella with concern, much like she is right now.

Drizella gathers herself after a few minutes, drying her eyes and surreptitiously wiping her nose while Madame Lambert pretends not to notice. This studio must have magic in it because of the way it seems to calm her instantly, like it can draw out her worst feelings and make them dissipate into thin air, leaving Drizella with a little bit more light than darkness.

"I'm very sorry," she says when she can speak, then swipes at her cheeks again. "Goodness, I don't know what came over me!" She lets out a shaky little laugh, and when she glances over at Madame Lambert, the woman's face looks nothing but kind. Drizella wonders if she always appears that way, if she's still serene after she stubs her toe in the middle of the night or cuts her finger on a knife. It's hard to imagine her looking like anything other than this.

"Please don't apologize," Madame Lambert says, then waves her hand toward the room, almost as if she's casting a spell. "It's just the old stars and me in here, after all. And a few dusty tomes, but they would never say a word about this." She smiles wider, making Drizella smile, as well. "There, that's better." She pats Drizella's shoulder, then gets up and walks toward the back of the atelier, where there's a small woodstove with a tarnished copper teapot on top of it.

"Would you like some tea?" she asks. "I was about to make myself some, and I was just thinking that it would be a little lonesome to drink it all by myself."

It's clearly a lie, but one that Drizella is grateful for nonetheless, and she nods as Madame Lambert busies herself at the stove.

"I'm afraid that poor Monsieur Longmont's cough seems to have worsened," Madame Lambert says. "That man, I swear upon this room. I told him to stay home, that he would spread germs everywhere and infect our entire village, but he just replied that germs are made-up things. I mean, *honestly*." And yes, it turns out that even when she's complaining, Madame Lambert still looks kind. Drizella wonders how she manages to do that. Even when Drizella's *smiling*, she knows she appears to be baring fangs, and it's quite a burden.

"In any case, he hasn't been in his studio for the past several days. Not that I'm spying or anything," she adds, before wiggling her eyebrows at Drizella as if to say *I have very much been spying, thank you*. "Which, of course, means that I get to enjoy the pleasure of your company once again, Drizella." The kettle starts to hum, then whistle, and Madame Lambert pours it into a teapot, then brings it and two cups and saucers over to the long table where Drizella is still sniffling a little.

"Some people say that it's bad luck to drink tea on a hot day, but I don't mind pressing my luck every now and then." She passes the empty cup to Drizella, who picks it up to study it. It's robin's-egg blue, with the faintest gold lace pattern around the rim, without a crack or chip to be found. The handle reminds Drizella of Anastasia's impatient stance, one fist on her hip as she pouts over something or other.

"Thank you," Drizella says now, hearing the drain in her own voice. "I don't have much luck either way, so I'll take my chances."

"Well, I have a hard time believing that," Madame Lambert says, "but for argument's sake, I'll let it go. Now, we can talk about why you're suddenly crying here in my atelier, or we can talk about nothing of the sort. Your choice." She reaches for the teapot and pours out a dark red tea that looks almost purple at the bottom of the cup.

Drizella shrugs a little, putting her hands around the

porcelain. It's warm outside, of course, and she can see the sun dappling through the trees that line the small street, but she still feels cold. "It's nothing," she says.

"I feel like anything that makes you cry is certainly not *nothing*," Madame Lambert says gently.

"Well, I can't fix it, so there's no point in talking about it."

"Also untrue." Madame Lambert pours her own cup and then sits down across from Drizella.

After sitting in silence for nearly a full minute, which is a very long time when you're actually sitting in silence, Drizella reaches over, pulls out her folder of sheet music, and sets it in front of Madame Lambert.

"My dear, alas, I cannot read a single note—"

"Just look inside," Drizella says, then realizes that she sounds extremely rude. "Please."

Madame Lambert does, flipping it open and seeing not sheet music (which is still missing; Drizella has turned the house upside down and can't find it anywhere) but the lunar calendar that Drizella discovered in her stepfather's office. "Well, isn't this something!" she says. "Look at this, all hand-drawn and lettered, as well." She smiles up at Drizella, but her grin fades when she sees the look on Drizella's face, tired and resigned. "I feel like this must be very important to you," she says. "Can you tell me about it?"

Drizella reaches past her teacup and gestures for Madame Lambert to hand her the calendar. It's still open to that terrible date, and she points with one long finger at the full moon illustration.

"It's circled," Madame Lambert says. "Is there a reason?"

"It's the night my father left us," Drizella mutters, then sips at her tea so she can do something with her trembling lips besides cry.

And for the first time, Madame Lambert turns sad. "Oh, my dear." She sighs. "It's dated ten years ago, I see. You must have been very young."

Drizella cannot remember ever feeling young in her entire life, but she nods anyway. "I found it in the old study. My mother, she keeps it locked up, but I snuck in yesterday. I kept thinking about being here, and seeing all of the books and stars and experiments and maps, and it made me wonder if maybe there was something like that in our house, as well." The tea is exceptionally strong and somehow seems to give Drizella a little more strength, as well.

"And what did you find?" Madame Lambert asks.

"Not much. Books, some old papers. A quill pen, ink that's all dried up. I knew my mother had stashed some of my father's old things in the study." Drizella waves her hand. "I guess I was just stupid. Before yesterday I was always look-ing out for something that maybe would show that he didn't mean to leave, after all. But then I found this."

"He needed the light of a full moon because he left in

the middle of the night," Madame Lambert says, guessing correctly.

"It's too bad," Drizella says. "Because he deserved nothing but darkness."

Madame Lambert nods as her hand stops moving. "Do you know what we call all of this?" she says, pointing to several different phases. "It's called waxing and waning. Waxing as the moon's appearance gets bigger, waning as it seems to decrease. Of course, the moon is just the moon; it never changes. It's the way the sun's light falls on it that makes it appear as if it's growing and collapsing in size."

Drizella never knew any of this. "I always thought it glowed by itself," she says.

"Not at all," Madame Lambert says with a smile. "It's a bit sad, if you think about it. No matter how brightly it shines at night, the moon will never be a star.

"And while I'm very sorry to hear of your father's disappearance, I do think that you managed to get some very good parts of him." When Drizella looks up in confusion, she continues. "Your curiosity, for one. If your father had this calendar, he must have enjoyed learning about some of the same things that I study in here." She gestures around to the plants and constellations. "Botany, astronomy, so many of science's mysteries."

"I don't want any part of him." Drizella sulks, but she

has to admit that Madame Lambert has a point. And besides, she'd rather have her father's curiosity than Lady Tremaine's cruelty.

"Well, those are things we don't always get to decide," Madame Lambert says, then pours more tea for Drizella.

"I never get to decide anything," Drizella says quietly. "Lady—my mother, she's making us go to the Prince's debut party next month."

"And you don't want to do that?" Madame Lambert asks like she already knows the answer.

"No." Drizella looks down at the tea like it has all of her missing answers. "I don't even think I want to get married. Not if it's going to turn me into my mother. She married twice, and now she's absolutely miserable." When Drizella looks up again, there are tears in her eyes. "I don't ever want to be like her."

"Dear heart." Madame Lambert reaches over and covers Drizella's hand with hers. Her skin is soft like finely ground flour and warm from her own teacup. "Women do not have a lot of options. I'm sure your mother, even with her faults, has not had an easy time of it, either. But we are more than what happens to us. We can decide how we conduct ourselves, even if we can't always choose the circumstances."

"So you think I should go and just smile and have a good time."

"I don't know enough to say whether you should or not,

nor is that something I should decide for you. You said your-self: you never get to make decisions."

"Did you go to the King's debut party?" Drizella asks her. It's not hard to imagine a Mademoiselle Lambert, her hair blond instead of white, her cheeks still rosy but less lined, her eyes still sparkling but perhaps without the glasses that are currently perched on the end of her nose.

"Oh, my dear, that came after my time," Madame Lambert says with a chuckle, as if the mere idea is ridiculous. "Besides, my own parents passed when I was very young, so there was no room for anything like that."

"But you were married," Drizella says. Anyone else would have called her impertinent by this point, but it feels differ-ent here with Madame Lambert. She never seems to mind any question at all.

"I was." She nods thoughtfully. "And I still consider myself married sometimes. Even though my husband is no longer here with me, I can still feel his love."

"But you're happy?" Drizella presses. She feels like she's fitting a lot of jagged pieces together in her brain, tying her mother's marriages and heartbreak to Madame Lambert's solo life and contentment.

"As much as one can be, I guess," Madame Lambert says thoughtfully. "There are always ups and down, of course, but that's just life, married or not."

"I don't want any part of it," Drizella says, "but I'm the

oldest. And my sister, I love her, but . . ." Her voice trails off, and she widens her eyes as if to say *She's a real piece of work.* "She'll probably only marry for love, and we'll probably all end up in the poorhouse." She knows this isn't true, that her mother would sooner shove them in front of a steam locomotive than allow them to do something as ridiculous as marry for love, but if anyone would try, it's Anastasia.

Madame Lambert chuckles at that. "Have you discussed any of this with your mother?"

Drizella bursts into laughter. It's genuine, not sarcastic, because the idea is so ridiculous that it leaves her absolutely tickled. "Of *course* not!" she says once she's able to speak again. "*Talk?* To Lady Tremaine? All she does is order and snap and berate. There's no talking in our house."

Madame Lambert's eyes go soft once more, but Drizella presses on. "We're expected to marry rich, marry well, and get money. That's it. That's what all of these dumb lessons are for, why we have to practice sewing and embroidery and I end up stabbing myself dozens of times a day. I'm forced to wear these hot, tight clothes, I can barely breathe, and my mother thinks that my sister is far prettier than I am, so what's even the point of going through the motions if I'm just going to be embarrassed and humiliated?"

There. She's said it.

"I'm sorry?" Madame Lambert says, frowning like she can't understand Drizella's last sentence. Drizella feels a stab of sympathy for this poor woman who probably thought she was just going to come into her studio for the day and get some work done, and has ended up being assaulted by Drizella and all of her *feelings*.

Drizella hates feelings. They ruin everything.

"It's nothing," Drizella replies. It's not nothing, of course, but Drizella suspects that talking about Anastasia would lead to her talking more about her father, then her stepfather, then Ella. And to talk about Ella would mean explaining how Lady Tremaine treats her, how there's a glint in her eye sometimes that seems almost inhuman, and Drizella isn't ready to do that yet.

But the fact that her mother thinks that Anastasia is prettier? She can absolutely talk about that.

"It's true, though," she says. "Annie's beautiful, I'm not. If anyone's going to marry rich and well, it'll be Anastasia. And please, whatever you do, do not tell me that beauty is in the eye of the beholder, because I will—"

Madame Lambert holds up her hand, and Drizella shrinks back a bit. Now she's interrupting just like Anastasia always does. *Wonderful.*

"I will only say that you do not get to decide what your mother or Anastasia does. You are in charge of you. That's all."

Drizella sits back a little, rocked by the force of her words. For so long, she's felt yoked to all the women in her life, all of them bending in one direction, moving just one way. The idea that Drizella could perhaps make her own choices, do her own thing? It's terrifying.

And absolutely *thrilling*.

"And for the record," Madame Lambert continues, "maybe it's my terrible eyesight, but I have a hard time seeing you as anything but lovely." She wrinkles her nose a bit like she's sharing a secret, then starts to stand up. "Stay there," she says. "I'll be back in just a shake."

When she comes back, she's holding an unlit candle and what looks like a tiny moon. "I sculpted this out of plaster many, many moons—ha, please ignore my unintentional pun!—ago for one of my beginning science classes." She hands it to Drizella, then goes over to the wall of windows and starts to pull the sashes. The heavy velvet curtains fall with soft thumps to the floor, enshrouding the room in near darkness.

But then there's a small blaze of light, and Madame Lambert's face is suddenly lit by the long tapered candle. "Ah, there you are, my dear," she says. "I always forget to light the candle first before I do the big dramatic"—she mimics the thumping noise of the curtains falling to the ground—"display.

"Now," she continues, "bring your mini moon over here. I'm going to show you how the phases work."

Madame Lambert takes the moon from Drizella and hands her the candle, then seats Drizella on a stool in the center of the room. Madame Lambert circles around her, rotating the moon both around her body and around the room, making the plaster ball light up just as it shows on the lunar calendar. It's absolutely fascinating, and Drizella sits, spellbound, as the light reflects and recedes.

As Drizella learns about the moon inside, the sun outside dips lower toward the horizon, until finally she realizes that it's time for her to go. Madame Lambert sees her to the door, and Drizella has a strange urge to . . . hug her? Drizella has never really wanted to hug anyone in her life, but Madame Lambert saves her by giving her a warm pat on the shoulder as she opens the studio door. "Take care on your way home," she says, "and give some thought to what we discussed. I look forward to another lesson soon!"

There's no need to tell Drizella that. Her brain feels crammed full with new information, like it's taken too much in and she needs to put some of it somewhere else. Madame Lambert has given her tea, knowledge, and the gentle touch that she desperately needed, and despite all of her new discoveries, Drizella feels lighter than she has in a long, long time.

Until she runs into Anastasia walking up the road and sees what her sister is holding in her arms.

"No," Drizella says as soon as she's close enough.

Anastasia just grins and holds up the tiny kitten, which looks both scrawny and furious. "Look what I found!"

"Absolutely not."

She holds the kitten a little bit higher up and moves its

paw to "wave" at Drizella. The look on the cat's face suggests that it's plotting a very painful revenge.

"Hi, Drizzy!" Anastasia says in a ridiculous, high-pitched voice. "I'm your new friend! I'm going to eat *allll* the mice just for you!"

"Please," Drizella says. "I can only handle one strange animal-talking person in our house at a time."

Anastasia ignores her. "What should we name"—she frowns, hoists the cat up higher, looks underneath it, brings it back down—"him?"

The cat looks positively scandalized and swipes at Anastasia with a tiny enraged paw.

"Lucifer," Drizella deadpans.

The kitten hisses.

"Perfect," Anastasia says. "Because you are a little devil, aren't you, just like I said?" She makes the paw wave again. "I love you, Drizzy!" she declares in that same kitten voice.

"Would you please stop it?" Drizella says, swatting at her, but there's no strength in her blows, and Anastasia just giggles at her as she tucks the kitten under her chin and follows her older sister home.

✦

That night as they're getting ready for bed (Ella pours warm water into basins and carries them upstairs; Lady Tremaine immediately deems the water too cold), Anastasia comes into Drizella's room and once again stands on her bed. The kitten is there sleeping, curled up in a ball and resolutely facing away from both of them. Upon arriving home that evening, Drizella had a sudden stab of terror that her mother would make her sister get rid of the kitten, or worse, drown it in a bucket of water, but to everyone's great surprise, the two of them seemed to have a fondness for one another. Lucifer even scampered out of Anastasia's arms to go wind around Lady Tremaine's ankles, purring his little heart out, and neither Drizella nor Anastasia could be certain, but they could have almost sworn that they saw the corners of Lady Tremaine's mouth lift up just a fraction more than normal.

"Get off my bed," Drizella says to both her sister and the cat without any real malice. "And stay away from my pillow."

Anastasia just murmurs a response, not paying any attention at all as she cranes her neck to see whatever it is that she needs to see.

"What are you looking at, anyway?" Drizella asks, patting her skin dry and looking at herself in the mirror. Under the dim lighting, she looks not quite like herself, like she's warmer and softer now. It reminds her of Madame Lambert in a way.

"Nothing," Anastasia says, then loses her balance and barely keeps from tumbling to the ground. Drizella just watches as she flails, then shakes her head.

"You're like a baby animal," Drizella says. "All limbs and nothing else."

Anastasia reaffixes her sleeping cap, then leans back on her hands in a casual way that Drizella has never seen before. It's bound to be terrible for her posture, that's for sure. "What do you think love feels like?" Anastasia asks.

Now Drizella is the one who almost falls over. *What?* she asks. "What kind of a question is that?"

Lucifer sighs and curls deeper into himself, as if exhausted by their boring girl talk.

"A good one," Anastasia says, defending herself. "I'm just curious, that's all."

They're both interrupted by the sound of yelling, Lady Tremaine's voice carrying down the hall with the kind of strength and volume held by a thunderstorm. They can hear Ella's thin reply, but it's immediately shouted down once again, this time with a simmering rage that almost threatens to make the candles blow out, make the windows rattle.

With her eyes on the door, Drizella slinks over and sits down next to Anastasia. Her sister is pale now, the glow and glassiness gone from her eyes as they listen to the rage pour down. Ella's crying now; there's the sound of a sharp slap, followed by more shouting, and the two girls sit side by side, not moving.

Drizella doesn't know what's worse: the guilt that it's

happening to Ella . . . or the gratitude that it's not happening to her.

When it's finally quiet once again, neither of them feels soothed by the silence.

"I don't know what love feels like," Drizella whispers after a minute in answer to Anastasia's question. "But I know one thing: it's not this."

8

ANASTASIA

The walls are so high, so cold, and Anastasia can't find purchase anywhere on them, her broken hand scrabbling up over the stones.

Anastasia. Annie, wake up. Breathe, Anastasia.

She tries, but her body won't work, she can't move, she's so cold and wet, and the walls seem to only get higher, pushing her back down toward the damp stone floor. She's crying, the salt burning her eyes, the darkness so thick that it feels as if it could wrap itself around her neck, strangle her.

Anastasia.

She was only trying to help Ella in the kitchen, that's all! She didn't know that her mother's fury would become all-consuming, that she would wrench Anastasia's wrist on her way to the back staircase and—

Annie. Annie, shh.

Drizella can't be here! It's not safe; she'll suffocate, too! Anastasia reaches up, tries to find her, grasping at the air, until she feels her sister's hand clutch hers, yanking her out of the tower and back into the real world.

Anastasia sits up with a stifled gasp, letting the air rush in to her now-empty lungs. Drizella's sitting on the bed next to her, her face illuminated by a gap in the curtains where the moonlight shines through.

"I couldn't breathe," Anastasia manages to say.

"I know," Drizella replies. She looks sleepy and rumpled, half-annoyed from being awoken. "You've had this nightmare a million times."

Anastasia doesn't really need to be scolded right now. What she needs is a hug, but she's not foolish enough to go looking for one, not in this house.

"Can I—can I have some water?" Anastasia asks, sitting up and wiping at her face with the sleeves of her nightgown. "Please?"

Drizella gets up to pour it and Anastasia moves the curtain back a little, letting in more moonlight as she catches her breath. "That," Drizella says as she passes the glass to Anastasia and comes back to sit on the edge of the bed, "is a waxing gibbous moon."

"A what now?" Anastasia says. She doesn't even care about anything Drizella is saying. She's just grateful to hear her sister's voice rooting her back into the real world and far away from her terrible dreamscape.

"Waxing gibbous," Drizella repeats, looking almost proud of herself. "That means it's close to being a full moon. And then after it's full, it'll go back to a gibbous again, only that time, it will be called a waning gibbous instead."

"Gibbous is a funny word," Anastasia says, then regrets it when Drizella rolls her eyes and seems to sag back down. She tries again since she suspects that this is Drizella's odd way of comforting her. "How do you know all of this?"

Drizella traces a pattern in the old bedspread with her fingertip, shrugging a little, and Anastasia lets it go.

They're both silent for a minute, the nighttime world finally settling back into its normal haze of cricket chirps and house creaks, the distant call of the cattle in their neighbor's pasture, a quiet cluck from the henhouse.

"When you have those nightmares," Drizella asks so suddenly that Anastasia startles a bit, "do you see him?"

Anastasia frowns. "Who?"

"Father." Drizella looks at her, and her eyes are as flinty as the sharp edge of a knife.

"No," Anastasia replies. "Never. It's just me and the tower and the walls. No one ever comes to save me." She pauses before adding, "I don't know if I even remember his face."

Drizella nods at that, still tracing the pattern. "I do," she says softly. "Only because I hate it so much."

That seems fair, Anastasia thinks. After all, Drizella had almost two more years with their father than she did. Almost two more years of habit and memories and love that were all yanked away with the click of a closing door.

"Can I go back to bed now?" Drizella asks. "If I look puffy in the morning, Mother will disembowel me."

Anastasia doesn't know what that word means, but she's pretty sure it's both painful and fatal. "Yes. Thank you, Drizzy. I'm sorry I woke you up. Again."

Drizella waves her words away with a tsk of her tongue, but just as she's about to leave, she rests her warm palm against the top of Anastasia's head. "Go to sleep," she says, as kindly as Drizella can manage, and the warmth eases Anastasia back down to sleep, where she dreams of nothing for the rest of the night.

⚜

Neither sister mentions it, but only because they don't have to.

It's no mystery why Anastasia's nightmare has returned.

They go to the debut party in one week.

The past two weeks have been arduous for them both, the anxiety and importance of the event looming over them. Food has been restricted, as well, leaving them both with grumbling stomachs and aching heads. "Do you *really* think you'll fit into your corset if you eat that?" her mother asks when she sees Anastasia putting butter on a slice of bread, and it's enough to shame her into throwing the whole thing toward the chickens.

Their mother has also cancelled their weekly lessons, preferring incessant rehearsals at home until Anastasia's fingers swell up so much she can't play and Drizella goes hoarse. "Why am I sending you into town week after week when all it gets me is results like this?" she says at one point after Drizella fails to hit a high note and Anastasia's flute just screeches.

It shames Anastasia not because she's wrong, but because she's right. She skipped her last two lessons, after all, focusing on Dominic instead of her flute. Each time she sees him, she feels like a lantern has been lit inside her, and the more she burns, the more she wants.

They return to the lavender fields each time, Dominic bringing a clean horse blanket from the stables and Anastasia sneaking some bread, butter, sour pickles, and dried meats from their kitchen at home. Even their meager food feels like a feast, and Anastasia lies with her head on his stomach as they look up at the trees and dare to imagine what life could be like under a Paris sky.

She'd work in a shop, of course, and he'd attend school with the money she makes. They'd take in strays (but not before a quick attitude check—Anastasia has learned her lesson with that blasted Lucifer) and nurse them into good health. At night, they'd reach for each other by candlelight, or oil lamp if they're lucky enough to afford it.

Anastasia knows how ridiculous it all sounds, but she loves the way Dominic looks at her when she imagines these things out loud. Her mother would scoff at her grandiosity, but Dominic just beams and asks questions: What kind of animals? What kind of books? What kind of shop? Every single one of his questions makes her feel as if the fantasy could be a reality.

The problem, Anastasia thinks as her mother continues to scold them about their subpar talents, is that Dominic has given her a glimmer of hope, and she's starting to feel the desperation that a glimmer of hope can bring. She feels itchy and anxious every day, like she has somewhere to be, someone to see. She fidgets so much during their sewing practice that Drizella finally throws a knitting needle at her, which manages to unravel all of the stitches that she's made, and then they get scolded again.

Anastasia can't help it, though. She doesn't know how to describe how Dominic makes her feel, but she knows she wants more of it, needs to get it somehow.

"Anastasia!" Her mother's bark cuts through the room and startles her so much that she drops her flute, which clunks to the ground. "Honestly, you are the clumsiest girl!"

Anastasia cannot argue with that.

The more they mess up, the more tense their mother becomes, until the entire house feels like it's been filled to the rooftops with nervous, electric energy. It reminds Anastasia of the game she and Drizella used to play as children, rubbing their socked feet back and forth across the wool carpets, then attempting to zap each other with their index fingers, giggling and shrieking at the shock.

The only member of their household who seems to be completely unfazed by all the tension is Lucifer. He couldn't care less about Anastasia, Drizella, or even Ella, which marks probably the first time an animal hasn't fallen head over heels for the girl.

No, the sole object of his affection is Lady Tremaine, and what's more, she seems positively delighted by him, too. He trills next to her as she dictates the girls' posture lessons, swishing his tail like someone shaking a finger at them. Anastasia thought she'd finally have a little thing to love and to love her back, to snuggle with under the covers at night, to cuddle and listen to its soft purrs, but Lucifer has different ideas. He tortures the dog, sleeps in her mother's bed, and yowls until Ella deposits food and cream into his bowls. He growls instead of purrs at them. And his claws, both Anastasia and Drizella have come to discover, are very sharp.

The day before the debut party, their nerves rubbed raw, their stomachs empty, their temples pounding, Drizella, fed up and scratched up, finally complains.

"Lady—Mother, can we just have a bit of a rest this afternoon?" Drizella looks drawn and pale, that normal fiery glare now extinguished from her face. "We're both exhausted."

Anastasia once got caught in a thunderstorm outside, and she remembers the seconds between the bolt of lightning and the clap of thunder. The silence was terrifying, even more so than the two events themselves.

That was nothing compared to the silence from their mother now. Even Ella, who has slipped into the room to announce that dinner is almost ready, slips right back out without saying a word.

"Exhausted?" their mother says quietly without turning around. "Did I hear you correctly?"

Anastasia and Drizella exchange quick glances. No way Anastasia's taking the heat for this one, not that Drizella would ever expect her to.

"Yes, Mother," Drizella mutters.

"Speak up!"

Drizella looks toward the heavens, then clears her throat. "Yes, Mother!"

Their mother turns around now, a thin curl of a sneer spread across her mouth. That same flinty look that Anastasia saw in Drizella's eyes the other night is now in their mother's.

"Do you think you have any idea what exhaustion is?" She's still speaking in that soft, scary voice that's always worse than yelling. "You two spoiled, selfish children?"

"I just . . ." Drizella starts to speak again, and Anastasia widens her eyes at her sister. *Abort, abort, abort!*

"I can't sing, Anastasia can't play the flute at all—sorry, Annie, but it's true—and we can barely walk up the stairs *without* a book on our heads, much less with one. We're going to be the complete laughingstocks of this entire debut, Mother! Those other girls, they have dresses and money and—and *fathers*! We're not like them, we never were, and I'm tired of pretending like we are!"

It's as if someone has fired a cannon directly through the room. Their mother is shocked into silence, Anastasia's jaw is on the ground, and Lucifer bolts up the stairs in less than three seconds, not willing to stick around to see what happens next.

Deep down in her stomach, Anastasia knows that Drizella is right. Back when they were still attending school in their giant hair bows and stiff, starched pinafores and dresses, the two girls had always stood to the side during recess, knowing that they were different. In a bad way. They knew that some of the other children had lost their fathers, of course, but none of them had just up and left the way Anastasia and Drizella's had. They saw the way the other girls' papas would scoop them up in the street, nuzzling their rosy cheeks and kissing their hair, pressing coins into their sticky palms and slipping candied sweets into their pockets. It made Anastasia feel so, so lonesome, her throat aching from trying not to cry, and Drizella would just say "Ignore them, Annie" as she turned around to make up a game for them in the dirt.

Anastasia plans to ignore them again, of course. Nothing is going to take away from her determination to have a good time at the debut party. But knowing that Drizella feels that way dampens her spirits, and she finds herself wishing that she could protect her sister from every perceived danger, every imagined hurt and faceless enemy. Drizella has been fighting for a long time, Anastasia thinks. No wonder she's always poised for battle.

"Of course you're nothing like them," their mother says now, her voice rising in volume. "Do you think I raised you to be as simpleminded as they are? Do you believe that I reared you up to act like those blushing, giggling, empty-headed girls?"

Anastasia doesn't know what to say, so she says nothing.

"No—" Drizella starts to say, but her mother cuts her off.

"You have no idea the sacrifices I have made for you!" Now their mother is yelling, which is both reassuring and terrifying. *Steam out of the kettle,* Anastasia thinks.

"What do you think these lessons cost, Drizella, hmm? Who do you think pays for those, may I ask?" It's clear she doesn't want a response. "Who do you think buys your fine clothes and your hair bows and the purse that you swing around as you waltz out the door every week?"

As far as Anastasia knows, their mother has never had a job in her entire life. She has often suspected that their money is from Ella's father's will, and that it will probably run out sooner rather than later.

She says nothing of the sort, of course.

"I have slaved and cut costs and worked myself to the bone to make sure that you two have everything that I did not. Do you think that my childhood involved music lessons? Do you think I was sent off to voice lessons? I was not! I was too busy trying to survive, trying to make something of myself, and your father took it all from me!"

Danger, Anastasia thinks. Their mother has rarely mentioned their father since the morning after he left, telling her two young girls to never ask about him again, that he was as good as dead, and good riddance. Anastasia broke that rule only once, when she was being shoved into the tower, calling for him over and over again like a terrified child, her brain nearly exploding as she realized what her mother planned to do.

But now it's Drizella who's broken that rule.

"He took it all!" She's shrieking now, and Anastasia can

feel her knees starting to knock together. She's so frightened, in fact, that she has completely forgotten that she still has a book on top of her head. "Your father, the sniveling thief, sold me a lie and left me with you, and now it's your turn to make good on the promises that he made!

"You will debut, you will find husbands, you will not marry for love or companionship or any of that stupid nonsense! Your job—your *only* job, you lazy things—is to marry rich, marry for money, and get us out of this crumbling house for good! Do I make myself *perfectly* clear?"

It seems as if even the house is trembling under the weight of her rage.

"Answer me!"

"Yes, Mother," they both intone at the same time.

"If I ever hear either one of you complain again about being exhausted, I swear I will move you permanently into the tower, do you understand me?"

Anastasia nods and feels the press of tears in the corners of her eyes. She knows that crying right now is the worst thing she could possibly do. Her mother hates laziness, but she loathes weakness even more.

"Yes, Mother," Drizella whispers again, looking at her shoes.

"Excellent." Their mother claps her hands together once more, and it's as if not only has the storm passed, but it never even happened. Sometimes it makes Anastasia feel like she's hallucinated the whole thing, that it was just a trick of her mind and not how her actual mother would ever act.

"Now," her mother says, smiling at them, her incisors gleaming. "Another thirty minutes up and down the stairs should do it."

�֍

Anastasia, no surprise here, has a hard time sleeping that night.

She tosses and turns for a long time, flipping her pillow over again and again, searching for the cool side that becomes more elusive with every flip. The sheets tangle around her ankles, making her feel itchy and trapped, and then she manages to somehow rest her hand on her own hair so that it pulls when she tries to flip over yet again. She yelps in pain before realizing that she's the one causing the problem, and that's when she finally gets up, smooths down her nightdress, and goes in search of something to drink, the water by her bed now too warm for her tastes.

She slips down the stairs in her bare feet, ignoring the chill of the floor, and keeps an eye out for mice wearing hoop skirts or something equally ridiculous. (She does sort of think that Drizella was imagining things—how could anyone ever find a hat tiny enough for a mouse?)

Once she's in the kitchen, she lets her eyes adjust to the darkness of the room before making a move. She's so rarely in this space that she doesn't know it as well as she does the rest of the house, its corners and countertops all unfamiliar to her body. Anastasia could wind her way through the rest of the château while blindfolded (and probably with a book on her head, to boot) and never once bump into a piece of furniture, but the kitchen is a different story. It helps that the moon looks almost full, its light gliding into the room like cool water. What did Drizella call it? Ribbons? Globules? Anastasia has always known that her sister is smart, smarter than her, for sure, and she often wonders what it would be like to be in Drizella's brain for a day, calculating figures and schemes with equal alacrity.

As soon as her eyes adjust to the moonlit darkness, though, Anastasia sees a figure huddled down by the butcher-block countertop, its dark wood stained by the blood and intestines of meals past. It's Ella, crouched down, her eyes so wide that at first, they're all Anastasia can see of her.

"Ella?" she whispers. "What are you doing here?"

"Please don't tell," Ella whispers back. She's huddled in on herself, knees pulled up to her chest almost defensively, and Anastasia feels a quiet pang of guilt. She would never hurt Ella. She's not like her mother.

Anastasia takes a step closer, peering down to see the hunk of brown bread in Ella's hands. "Are you eating?" she asks.

Ella stands up quickly, shaking her head. "No, I was, I was just—"

"Ella," Anastasia says. She's no fan of Ella, but she doesn't like seeing her scared like this. She seems more like a frightened animal than an actual person, and Anastasia's stomach twists uncomfortably. "It's okay."

"She wouldn't let me eat dinner tonight because it was late. I was just outside because—because you were all talking about the party, and she—I didn't want to interrupt." Her words are like a waterfall tumbling over sharp rocks, falling hot and fast from her mouth, as uncontrollable as nature.

"Shh, it's okay," Anastasia whispers again. "I don't care. I'm not going to tell her."

Ella's shoulders sag. The bread looks small in her hands. "Thank you," she whispers. "I was so hungry I couldn't sleep."

Anastasia moves toward the icebox where they keep the cow's milk and reaches for a glass from the high shelf near the window. "I couldn't sleep, either," she says.

"I know your debut will be perfect," Ella says, and okay, now she's just overdoing it.

"I already said I'd keep your secret. You don't have to lie," Anastasia says with a roll of her eyes. The glass is up high and she has to stand on her tiptoes to reach it.

And that's when she sees a figure sneaking past the window and into the garden.

"Oh, my goodness!" she hisses, then instinctively falls to the ground next to Ella. The bread falls from Ella's hands and rolls under the stove, which is a shame for her, but not for the mice.

"What? What?" Ella says. She's looking toward the kitchen door, no doubt convinced that their mother is about to walk in and behead both of them, but Anastasia shakes her head and nods to their garden.

"There's someone out there!" she whispers, trying to keep it from becoming a full-throated scream. "I think it was a man!"

Ella's eyes go even wider. "Do you think he wants to rob us?"

"Why?" Anastasia says before she can stop herself. "He'd be the dumbest robber in town."

Ella peeks around Anastasia's shoulder and opens the kitchen door just a crack.

"What are you doing?" Anastasia says, slapping at her hand. "Are you trying to get us all killed?" Oh, my goodness, she thinks. *Is* Ella trying to get them killed? Is this her revenge plan? Has Anastasia been living in the same house with a cold-blooded, calculating murderer this entire time?

"I just want to see," Ella replies, and okay, maybe Anastasia's getting a little too hysterical. "It looks like a boy."

Anastasia looks through the crack in the door. Now that she has a chance to focus, she realizes that Ella's right: it's more of a boy than a full-grown man. He's fairly tall, though, with a head of dark hair that sweeps across his forehead and a little strand that curls up and—

"*Oh, my goodness.*"

Anastasia scrambles up off the floor, shoving past Ella to get a better look at their so-called intruder. "Who is that?" Ella whispers.

"None of your business," Anastasia replies, even as her heart is humming the "Hallelujah Chorus," the one the church choir sings every year on Christmas Eve. It always makes Anastasia feel hopeful, like the possibilities are endless, like love is real, and she turns quickly now toward her stepsister.

"My secret for yours," she says, holding up a finger. "If you tell her about this, I'll tell her about the bread." She tries to look threatening, even baring an incisor like Drizella, but from Ella's point of view, Anastasia just looks confused.

"I won't tell her," Ella says. "I would never. I don't even know *what* to tell her, you haven't even said a single—"

"Good. Now go upstairs. You didn't see anything."

"But I sleep downst—" Ella starts to say, but Anastasia's already hurrying out the door in her bare feet, her heart in the driver's seat and her brain barely hanging on for the ride.

In their yard, Dominic turns at the sound of her footsteps, his sudden smile lit by the moonlight. Anastasia thinks he's maybe the most beautiful living thing she's ever seen. "What are you doing here?" she whispers. In the stables, one of their horses neighs softly, and Anastasia shoots a threatening look toward the barn even though none of the animals can see her.

She'll be damned if her secret is ruined by a *horse*.

"I was worried about you," he says. They're standing just centimeters apart from each other now. She's tempted to run straight into his arms but stops herself just in time, suddenly very aware of the fact that she's barefoot in her nightdress.

"You haven't shown up at the village for the past two weeks," he continues. "I thought maybe you were sick or injured or . . ." His voice trails off. "I haven't seen you in so long. You look beautiful."

Anastasia stares at him. "Did you hit your head on the way over here?" she asks. "I'm in my dressing gown and my hair looks like a bird's nest and I probably have a pillow crease right here"—she points to her cheek—"and how dare you show up without any warning? This is completely inappropriate."

Dominic grins. "But are you happy I'm here?"

Just like that, Anastasia melts like butter in a hot pan. "Yes," she says, and she doesn't know why, but her eyes fill with tears. "Yes, I'm very happy."

She takes him over to the pumpkin patch, which is very much past the point of saving, but it's away from the house enough that they can talk without being overheard. His hand is cold in hers and she looks back at him and frowns, wrapping her other hand around it to cradle it in her palms. "You're freezing," she says. He's wearing a dark coat over a white shirt and what look like jodhpurs, and, in the most charming way imaginable, he has a little bit of hay in his hair. He's disheveled and handsome, and Anastasia has to bite back a squeal of glee.

"I'm fine," he replies. They settle themselves on a giant pumpkin that's a few days away from rotting, but it's still firm enough to hold their weight. (If Dominic had shown up three days later, it would have been a very different—and messy—story.) "My hands are cold, but that's all."

"You're not wearing your palace clothes," she says.

"No, I thought it'd be a bad idea to wear those tonight, just in case," he says. "I did lose a button somewhere along the way, though," he adds, holding up one side of his jacket to show her the empty space. "No matter, though. I can just attach a new one tomorrow. But are you okay?"

"I'm fine," she says, even though the events of the previous day have left her feeling anything but that. "My mother, she pulled us out of the lessons to get ready for the debut tomorrow."

Dominic's eyes light up just as hers dim. "Will you be dressed up?"

"No, I'm going to wear a flour sack to the palace," Anastasia says sarcastically. "My mother will be thrilled. Yes, I'm going to get dressed up!" she continues as he starts to laugh. "What do you think?"

"I'm sorry, it was a stupid question," he says, but Anastasia's smiling now for the first time in weeks. "You must be excited, though. It seems like half the village is going to be there tomorrow night. The housekeepers have been working in twenty-four-hour shifts, the bakers have used up every egg and stick of butter in France and—what's wrong?"

Anastasia can't keep her face from falling as he talks, the monumental importance of the evening becoming more obvious the more he says. "I don't want to go anymore," she whispers.

Dominic frowns. "Why not?"

Anastasia waits for him to keep talking, to say what anyone else would say to her: *Don't you realize how lucky you are? Do you know how many girls aren't able to debut in such a fine fashion? Only the laziest and most ungrateful of girls wouldn't want to go to the palace. Is that what you are, Anastasia? Lazy? Ungrateful? Or perhaps both?*

It's her mother's voice she's waiting to hear, she realizes, and the thought makes her feel sick.

"It's just going to be a lot" is all she replies, though. "I don't like people looking at me."

"Well, I'm looking at you right now," he says, then moves his head down to make exaggerated eye contact with her. "Good, I made you smile. And yes, it will be a lot of people looking at you. But if it helps, I'll be one of them."

"Will you still try to attend?" Anastasia asks.

He nods. "I'll be there to assist some of the guards and the Prince and King, of course. I probably won't be able to talk or chat—"

"Oh, me either," she says. "If my mother saw me talking to you . . ." She drags an index finger across her neck. "And you probably have an actual guillotine at the castle, too, so it'd be very easy for her to do."

"Well, it's a little rusty, but . . . I'm kidding!" he says when her eyes widen. "We only have swords and a cannon that is, I have to say, fairly formidable."

"So she'll have to get creative," Anastasia says with a nod, but then she carefully, oh so carefully, like she's touching the most delicate spiderweb, leans her shoulder against his. His hands may be cold, but the rest of him is warm. "I'm glad you'll be there. That makes me feel better."

He leans right back into her, and Anastasia knows without any doubt that what she's doing is wrong. She's talking to a boy in her garden at night, wearing just a nightgown, no shoes or socks, her hair a mess, with no bonnet. She's actually touching him, too, without a single chaperone in sight. (Unless you count the chickens and the tattletale horse, which she most certainly does *not*.)

"I'm really happy to see you" is all she says to Dominic, though.

"I'm really happy to see you, too," he replies. "And I'm very glad you haven't been ill or sick or anything. I was worried."

The warmth spreads through Anastasia like a fever, the idea of someone worrying about her filling so many holes in her heart that she hadn't even known existed. "Well, the next time you see me, I'm going to be *very* dressed up, so I hope I'm not too intimidating."

He smiles, playing along. "How will I even recognize you without your nightgown and bird's-nest hair? Will you still have the pillow crease on your cheek? That will be a good hint."

"Oh, no," she says, sitting up from his shoulder. "I'm going to have the most grand dress, made out of diamonds and jewels." She grins at him, wrinkling her nose a little in happiness. "My carriage? Built with solid gold."

"Really?" he says, laughing along with her. "That must be tough on the horses."

"Horses?" she scoffs. "Oh, please. We have *unicorns.*"

Dominic laughs out loud at that, and both his hands and Anastasia's hands fall over his mouth, both of them giggling and shushing at the same time. "Stop, stop!" she whispers, burying her face in his shoulder to stifle his laughter. "My mother will fire us out of that cannon if she finds us out here!"

"To be fair, I don't even know if it still works."

"Trust me, she'll find a way to get it up and running again."

They sit close together for a moment until it's clear that everyone in the house is still fast asleep, but Anastasia doesn't move from his shoulder. "I know you're going to be at the party tomorrow," she says quietly, "but I miss you already."

His hands come up to tighten around her arms. "I know the feeling," he replies. "I'm excited to see you again, but that means I have to leave you first." He turns his head, and oh, my goodness, Anastasia has never been this close to anyone's mouth before, and certainly not a handsome boy's.

"I have to tell you," he whispers, and she feels her breath halt in her chest, "that I am *very* excited to see . . . a unicorn."

She giggles at that, pulling away slightly. "Go," she says. "We've already taken a big enough risk."

"See you tomorrow, Anastasia Tremaine," he replies, then gets to his feet and pulls her up with him.

"Why do you always say that?"

"Say what?"

"My full name."

Dominic looks surprised, then confused. "Because that's who you are. And that's important."

She looks down at her bare and now very dirty feet, blinking fast to keep the emotion at bay. She's important.

"I'll see you tomorrow" is what she says when she looks up. "Be nice or otherwise you won't see any unicorn at all."

He makes a quick *X* over his heart with his fingertip, and when he walks away, Anastasia has to force her feet to stay in place, to not run after him and follow him wherever he goes, to hold his hand and tumble right off the face of the earth if that's what she has to do to stay with him forever.

"Goodbye," she whispers instead, and watches him leave until she can no longer see the shape of his body, until the moonlight is the only thing left in his path, until she feels like she can breathe again.

And standing there in the dark, alone but not lonely, Anastasia realizes that maybe this is what love feels like. All of her lying and sneaking around, these so-called bad behaviors, seem to keep adding up to something *good*, and after a lifetime of following the rules, aiming to please everyone and everything, all Anastasia has ever gotten in return are abandonments and scoldings, fits of rage and locked rooms, disgusted looks and undried tears. She's tried to earn love again and again, only to be disappointed every time, and she's just now discovering that maybe love isn't something you earn, it's something you can just give to someone else without expecting anything back.

Maybe love is something that she *deserves*.

9

DRIZELLA

The morning of their debut, Drizella wakes up, remembers what day it is, then heads downstairs, walks out the back door to their pumpkin patch, and throws up behind a large tangle of dead vines.

When she's done, she dabs the back of her wrist against her mouth, trying to regain some semblance of decency. The morning is cool and dew has settled everywhere, leaving her bare feet wet. What kind of girl goes outside in just a nightgown, barefoot? Drizella is horrified by her own behavior. At this rate, she'll probably end up teaching those clothed mice how to waltz—

Her thoughts are interrupted as she leans over and vomits again.

It's nerves, of course. Drizella never entertains the idea that it is anything else. Her stomach is flipping back and forth like a boat caught in a storm at sea, with no bearings or safe harbor anywhere, and she stands up and wonders if she can just flee back to Madame Lambert's studio, hide there beneath the stars and moon, bury herself in the leaves of the overgrown plants that line one wall. Would Madame Lambert even shelter her, hide her?

Drizella managed to get a few more days in Madame Lambert's atelier before her mother cancelled their lessons in town entirely. It was devastating for Drizella to realize that her visits to the village square would be curtailed, but the time she spent in that mysterious, magical atelier was wonderful enough to almost cancel out her disappointment.

They mixed sodium bicarbonate with vinegar and watched as the gas it produced inflated a small balloon. Madame Lambert schooled Drizella on the constellations until she knew as many as her brain could hold: their names, origins, Greek and Roman myths combining with astronomy to create the kinds of stories that Drizella could never have imagined on her own. Madame Lambert showed her how to put tiny slices of plants and leaves on a small glass square and then look at it under something called a microscope, which magnified the sample hundreds of times; Madame Lambert pointed out the green-filled cells, how they all nestled together to create something that was alive.

They also drank tea and read in pleasant silence together, the soft sound of turning pages the only kind of music that Drizella would ever need. Sometimes Madame Lambert talked to her about her experience as a scientist, too—the cruel things that people would say to her, the way her husband had supported her independence, how much she enjoyed working with her students at university. Drizella always felt warm inside when she was at the atelier, as if Madame Lambert's presence was enough to settle her, comfort her. Drizella hadn't even realized how tense she was until she felt that tension leave.

She can hear Lady Tremaine calling her now, loud and urgent in a way that suggests anger will be quick to follow, and suddenly that tension is back. She wipes her mouth on the back of her hand and hurries inside to find Ella in the kitchen, already firing up the stove and putting pots and plates out. They exchange glances but say nothing.

Drizella never really knows what to say to Ella, anyway. Their history is too checkered to be friends at this point. She supposes they're both silent survivors, in a way, but even that sounds too corny to repeat out loud.

"Drizella!" Lady Tremaine's voice has that warning edge to it, the one that always makes them hustle, and Drizella leaves the kitchen in a hurry, the door swinging shut behind her.

"Coming, Mother!"

"Were you outside in your nightgown?" Lady Tremaine sounds shocked and horrified at the same time.

"Just for a moment!" she says, running up the stairs. "I just thought I saw something."

Anastasia comes out of her room, half asleep but still wide-eyed. "What did you think you saw outside?" she asks, and there's a strange tone to her words that piques Drizella's interest.

"None of your beeswax," she says, then hurries down the hall to Lady Tremaine's room before her voice falls off that edge entirely.

It ends up being a beautiful autumn day.

Not that any of them notice it.

Ella runs all around the house, fetching last-minute mending, steaming and ironing the girls' dresses and underthings until her cheeks are flushed from the heat, finding slippers and shoes and polishing jewelry and unearthing petticoats and bustles from storage and sewing up the moth holes so no one will know just how old and tattered everything is.

Anastasia and Drizella, on the other hand, are practicing their musical recital like their lives depend on it. Which, based on the look on Lady Tremaine's face, is entirely possible.

Drizella didn't know that Anastasia could get worse at playing the flute, but the evidence is clear to her ears, and she can tell that it's frustrating her sister, too, that she wishes she could be good at just one thing, just this once. Drizella hopes that Lady Tremaine will give Annie a break already, that she can see that nerves aren't going to help the situation at all, that the more she pressures her sister, the worse she becomes. Drizella wonders what the rest of the debutantes are doing today, if they're taking restful and restorative naps on fainting couches, being plied with water and light snacks, their mothers fawning over them and talking about how they remember when they were just teeny tiny babies and now look at them, all grown up!

"Drizella!" Lady Tremaine's voice snaps her out of her reverie. "'Sing, Sweet Nightingale,' now."

No one has ever expected Drizella to hit that high note, of course, but this is the first time that she's missed it so spectacularly. It feels as if the house itself winces at the squealing sound of Drizella's voice, the draperies and rugs shuddering in disgust.

Drizella is too hungry, too exhausted, and too overwhelmed to do anything but look at the ground. Lady Tremaine doesn't even have to say anything this time: her disgust rises around them like smoke, suffocating all the possibility that the night could hold, choking them in her contempt of their failure.

She turns on her heel and walks out of the room, and Drizella and Anastasia don't say a word to each other.

When it's finally time to dress that afternoon, Drizella

goes down the hall to her room, where Ella has laid out her green dress, along with her shoes and jewelry and hair band. Her underthings are there, as well, and Drizella wonders how, exactly, she's supposed to squeeze herself into all of *that*. The bustle looks particularly cumbersome, and despite the situation at hand, Drizella makes herself giggle wondering what she'd look like if it accidentally slipped and fell down while she was wearing it.

It'd be a memorable moment, to say the least.

"Drizella."

The door clicks open and then shut as Drizella freezes, her hands still holding the weird contraption. "Mother," she says.

"I've come to help you get dressed," she says, sounding almost formal, and Drizella takes a big, deep breath and says a quick prayer to a god who's never once answered any of them.

"Of course," she says out loud. "Thank you."

It's awkward and uncomfortable, her mother tugging Drizella into her corset and underthings with swift, sure hands. Drizella keeps waiting for a too-tight grip, a quick slap back into place, and she finds herself instinctually cringing away from Lady Tremaine as her body is squeezed and laced and reshaped into something acceptable, something entirely different from what she actually looks like.

"Honestly, Drizella," Lady Tremaine finally says when Drizella moves her arm away from her mother's cold hand. "Stand. Still."

"I'm sorry," she says, and when she sees herself in the mirror, she doesn't see her own face anymore. It's someone else pretending to be her, a girl trying to look like a woman, and she doesn't like it at all.

"You know," Lady Tremaine says, "your sister Anastasia looks absolutely beautiful in her dress. Not every redhead can wear pink, of course, but she's *stunning*. I suspect she'll be the talk of the debut this evening."

Drizella knows what this is, the verbal whip to a horse, but she still nods. "Yes, Mother."

"She also has such a pleasant way about her, don't you think." It's not a question, so Drizella doesn't answer. She knows very well that her opinion doesn't and will never matter around here. "So cheerful, so bright-eyed, so . . . *hopeful*. Even with all of our bad luck, she still manages to keep a kind attitude about her."

Lady Tremaine locks eyes with Drizella in the mirror, then yanks hard on the corset ribbons, knocking the breath out of Drizella's ribs and pushing it out of her mouth. It feels almost like a punch.

"Your sister is very sweet, but very dumb. She'll be the one who will marry the first man who says a single kind thing, mark my words. Which means that you *must* come through tonight, Drizella, do you understand me." Again, not a question, and Drizella couldn't have said a word in reply even if she wanted to. She's still trying to catch her breath. "You are my only hope. So take that sour face, put a smile on it, and go out there and finally start doing something useful for your family, Drizella. Do *not* fail me."

She raises an eyebrow in the mirror, and Drizella nods.

They finish dressing in silence, the green velvet dress shoved onto Drizella's now-unrecognizable body and the slippers made to fit on her feet, even though they're a half size too small. "There," Lady Tremaine says when they're done. "I'll see you downstairs. Don't forget what we discussed."

"Yes, Mother," Drizella says.

Once the door clicks shut, she resists the urge to tear it all off, to scrub her hands over her face and smear the makeup everywhere, to rip at her hair until the curls and bows fall out, to throw the shoes and tear the corset into tiny pieces of fabric until they can't ever pinch another girl ever again.

Instead, she just stands and looks at herself in the mirror. Even though she's so dressed up, she feels so young. She's never spent a single night away from her own house, never more than half a day away from the piercing gaze of Lady Tremaine's watchful, critical eye, but there's a refrain running through Drizella's mind that she can't stop.

I want to go home. I want my mother. I want to go home. I want my mother.

She stares at herself for minutes, daring herself not to blink, to hold her breath and pass out and wilt down to the floor. But that would mean leaving Anastasia to face the evening by herself, and as bruised and tired as Drizella is, she can't let Anastasia fight alone.

She takes as deep a breath as she can, lets it out slowly. Maybe things will indeed be all right. Maybe she should work on thinking positively, like Anastasia always seems to do. Maybe she'll hit that high note; maybe Anastasia's flute playing will be pristine. The world will not end tonight, she thinks. The sun will still come up tomorrow, no matter what happens this evening. She knows that for a fact now, knows that the Earth rotates every single day, bathing them all in darkness and light, over and over again.

It's not much comfort, but in the moment, it's all she has.

⚜

Anastasia is waiting for her downstairs, dressed in her pink gown, her hair atop her head in a way that makes her look almost elderly instead of sophisticated. Her cheeks are flushed, and Drizella wonders if Lady Tremaine gave her a version of the "don't fail me" speech. She wishes she and Annie could steal a few moments together, that they had planned this better, that they had formed an alliance before the evening began.

But it's too late now.

Both girls regard each other silently as Drizella descends the stairs, Lady Tremaine waiting near the first step. "Lovely," she says, her face full of . . . not pride, definitely not love. Triumph? Superiority? Whatever it is, it doesn't make Drizella feel any better.

"Ella!" Lady Tremaine yells, causing both girls to jump. She's loud anywhere in the house, but the front hall has a particularly strong echo to it, and Anastasia's hairdo seems to almost quiver from the noise. "Come on, girl!"

Ella tiptoes around the corner. She's wearing a dress that Drizella vaguely recognizes as one of Anastasia's old ones, and a pair of shoes that she knows were hers once upon a time. Her hair is brushed and looks clean and shiny, but her face is nervous, her hands clasped together in front of her.

"Excellent," Lady Tremaine says. "We're all here, and the carriage and footmen are waiting."

Drizella feels all her newfound positivity drain away. The truth is that, for the first time, Drizella can see how pretty Ella is. Worse, though, it's the kind of pretty that their mother always wanted for them, her raven- and red-haired daughters, and realizing it now, minutes before heading into one of the most nerve-racking nights of her life, makes Drizella feel like she's starting to unravel at the seams.

And judging from her reaction, Anastasia feels the same way.

"Ella's going to the party?" Anastasia cries, a real look of panic crossing her face. Drizella suspects that the same look is crossing her own.

"She had hay in her hair this morning!" Drizella says. "Literal, actual hay!"

"She talks to the horse like she's expecting him to answer her!" Anastasia says, and Drizella can hear the threat of tears in her voice.

"She's the reason that all of the mice in this dump are wearing hats and shirts," Drizella says.

"That *cannot* be normal!" Anastasia adds.

"We're already going to be the laughingstock of the entire ball, and—"

"Silence!" their mother cries, and once again, the echo nearly deafens all of them. Even Ella, who still hasn't said a word, shrinks back with a wince.

"Ella," Lady Tremaine says, as if she has one nerve left and her two spoiled, miserable, whiny daughters are trampling all over it, "will be attending the debut this evening as your lady-in-waiting." At this, she shoots a look at Ella, who nods meekly and fixes her eyes on the ground. "She will be making sure that you appear to have every single advantage, just as the other girls will. I'm sure I don't have to explain to either of you how crucial appearances can be, am I correct?"

Drizella and Anastasia both nod, their complaints tamped down for the moment. Nobody's thrilled by this decision, of course (least of all Ella, judging from the way she looks like she might be sick at any moment), and Drizella hates to admit it to herself, but Lady Tremaine is right. The finest girls will have attendants, several ladies-in-waiting, footmen and drivers and the grandest carriages.

Drizella has a stepsister, a bustle that feels loose, and a terrible, impending sense of doom.

"Yes, Mother," she says.

"Yes, Mother," Anastasia repeats, even though she still looks sullen.

"Wonderful," Lady Tremaine replies in a way that doesn't sound wonderful at all. "The carriage is here. Shall we go?"

As always, it's not a question, but an order.

The carriage has definitely seen better days: The wheels are covered in a cheap gold paint that makes Drizella think of Madame Lambert's painted constellations with a pang of longing; the velvet seats inside are only half stuffed, and the velvet is worn and bald in some places, including where Drizella ends up sitting; and the driver and footmen all smell faintly of ale and could use a hot shave and comb.

"This does not inspire confidence," Drizella whispers to Anastasia while their mother is outside the carriage, speaking sharply to the driver, telling him the best way to go, and the tension in her chest eases a little when Anastasia smiles. "We'll probably end up walking home at this rate."

Anastasia giggles a little bit, quickly slapping at her sister's arm. "Just try to have a good time tonight, okay, Drizzy?" she says. "For me?"

Drizella would, after all, do anything for her sister.

On the bench across from them, Ella shifts uncomfortably and clears her throat. "I just . . ." she starts to say, then clears her throat again. "I didn't ask to attend," she finally manages. "I begged her to let me stay home, I *begged*—"

"It's fine," Drizella says, even though it's not, but what can Ella do? Drizella can barely attempt to stand up to her own mother, so what power does Ella have?

Ella nods, looking relieved at the sparse peace treaty between them, and then the conversation dies as Lady Tremaine climbs into the carriage with a half-hearted assist from the footman. "Lazy fools," she mutters, then settles herself and runs a bony hand over her graying hair. For just a second, she looks frazzled, and Drizella wonders for the first time that evening if Lady Tremaine is nervous, too. She so rarely leaves the house other than to run a quick errand in the village. She has no friends, never receives any correspondence or house calls. It's been years since Drizella heard the whispers of "black widow" as she and Anastasia trailed behind their mother, but she suspects that Lady Tremaine remembers that moment, especially now.

"What are you waiting for?" their mother calls, rapping hard against the carriage door. "We'd like to arrive there before midnight!"

The carriage lurches out, jolting all of them, and Drizella puts her hand on the velvet seat and holds on for the ride.

As the palace comes into view, their silence takes on a heavy tone. Ella is staring wide-eyed, her mouth open in a way that makes her look like her jaw is unhinged, but Drizella is too busy staring herself to say anything to her. She's seen pictures and drawings of the palace, of course, and has even seen it at night from far away, looking more like a tiny pink hat than what it actually is: the grandest, most glorious building that Drizella has ever encountered.

Next to her, Anastasia whispers softly, "It's as beautiful as he said it would be," and Drizella pricks up her ears at that a bit. As *who* said? But then their carriage is falling into line with all the others, each one more ornate and gilded than the last, and Drizella shrinks back into her seat and hopes no one can see the flaking paint on the carriage door, and that their driver doesn't end up passing out before they get there.

When they finally arrive, the three girls carefully climb out of the carriage and follow Lady Tremaine up the massive, imposing stairs and into the palace, which is warmly lit with chandeliers and candles and the twinkle and shine of so many gems and tiaras and jewelry.

Drizella has a ring on, of course. She hopes no one can tell that the stone is fake.

Whatever small flicker of weakness Lady Tremaine seemed to have in the carriage is gone now. "This way, girls," she says, leading them forward with her head held high, and Ella follows them in, still agape.

"Stop it!" Drizella hisses at her, then opens her own mouth to mimic her. "You look like a fish."

"Have you ever *seen* a home like this before?" Ella asks, her gaze going everywhere like she's following a fly with her eyes.

She is truly the most hopeless lady-in-waiting Drizella has ever seen. They would have been better off with one of the costumed mice instead.

"No," she says, then hurries to catch up with Anastasia, who's starting to look giddy and excited now that they're finally within reach of the immense palace doors. She, too, is looking everywhere, her eyes scanning over the crowds of people, and Drizella feels her heart sink a little bit more when she sees Anastasia's face, shining with hopeful glee under the lights. It's one thing to manage her own anxiety and concern, but watching the lead-up to Anastasia's inevitable disappointment is another thing entirely.

If they can make it through the night with Anastasia's heart still intact, Drizella will consider it a success.

Their mother is ahead of them, smiling and nodding at everyone, and the murmurs that rise up around them seem, at first, to be conciliatory and welcoming. The women are dressed in pastel and jewel-toned gowns, the silks shimmering under the soft lighting, and the men are wearing crisp suits. The young women, of course, are dressed in their absolute finest, looking as excited as their parents do proud. There's a buzz in the air, all of them excited to see the Prince make his official debut as a royal, and, far more important, his debut as an eligible bachelor, and everyone seems to have a smile on their face.

Drizella and Anastasia even manage a few smiles in return, nodding humbly, until Drizella realizes that nobody is actually smiling at either one of them. Instead, all the gazes and murmured appreciations are for Ella, whose head is down and who seems to be completely unaware of the attention she's gathering.

"Such a beautiful girl."

"I remember when she was just a wee thing, before her father passed, the poor dear."

"What gorgeous golden hair."

Drizella feels her cheeks burn as she lowers her head.

Anyway, let them admire Ella! Sure, she's pretty, but she's spacey and collects and dresses *actual vermin* for a hobby. Golden hair is great and all, but just wait until you've got a houseful of mice that look like they're starring in a theater production. The thought makes Drizella laugh quietly, and Anastasia turns around and smiles at her. *What?* she mouths. From the look of relief on her face, it seems she thinks that Drizella has finally decided to enjoy herself.

Drizella just waves it away. She can tell her sister later when all of this is done and they're back home, with this whole experience far behind them.

Anastasia and Drizella are led toward a staircase along with several other girls. "Go on, my dears," an official-looking woman says, smiling at them as she waves them forward. "The dressing room is just that way." Her smile grows when she sees Ella trailing along behind them. "Feel free to go upstairs to prepare for the talent showcase."

Drizella sends a quick look back at Lady Tremaine, but her gaze is elsewhere, appearing both smug and alone in the crowd, and Drizella thinks that she could sneak out so easily, just grab Anastasia's hand and run down the massive staircase and along the path back to their home. The idea is so tempting that she feels her heart seize with adrenaline, but of course, there is no escape. If she attempts to make a run for it, there's no safe harbor for her, no situation in which her mother could understand why she felt so panicked, so trapped.

"Come on, lazy," Anastasia chides her, reaching back to take Drizella's hand, and as they go upstairs, Drizella watches the large palace doors close, sealing them in to their fate.

Upstairs, the dressing room feels both way too big and way too small, a flurry of young women and their entourages helping them primp and pluck and tuck every single part of them into place. A few are practicing what seem to be complicated dance steps, another girl is tuning a violin, and Drizella is fairly certain that she sees a ventriloquist-in-training in the corner.

Ella leans toward the sisters and whispers, "I'm not sure what an actual lady-in-waiting is supposed to do."

"Me either," Drizella whispers back. Next to her, Anastasia has drawn closer, and Drizella has to resist the urge to put her arm around her sister's shoulders. "Just get us some water. Look busy."

Ella nods and straightens her shoulders, and for a minute, Drizella feels a bit of warmth toward her. It's not her fault, after all, that she's been shoved into this situation, but she's making the best of it. Drizella realizes she could try to do the same.

"Here," she says to Anastasia, and leads her sister toward a large mirror that's set up behind a scrim. It'll be quiet and hidden there, giving them a chance to catch their breath and maybe figure out a plan to stick together. Drizella is the old-est. It's her responsibility to make sure that they get through this. It's only a few hours, after all: the Prince's debut followed by an hour of presentation and mingling, another hour of the talent showcase, then an hour of dancing. What's three hours in the course of an entire lifetime? Surely the two of them can make it through 180 measly minutes.

But when they stand side by side in the mirror, they just look wilted and exhausted. Drizella's hand drifts up toward her hair, where her once-bouncy curls now look windblown and limp, no thanks in part to their drunk driver's erratic pace. "You're fidgeting," Anastasia says, frowning at her own towering hairstyle. "And slouching. Stand up straight."

Drizella resists the urge to pinch the soft part of Anastasia's upper arm. "Is that meringue that's holding your hair up?" she shoots back.

Anastasia's eyes narrow. "I like your hairstyle," she says. "What's it called, the wet noodle?"

Drizella does not resist the urge this time, making Anastasia yelp as she gives her a hard pinch with a twist. She huffs and slaps at Drizella, and pretty soon they're like two small children fighting over a toy, smacking and elbowing one another while the rest of the girls preen and smile just beyond the privacy of the scrim.

"Okay, fine, fine, stop!" Drizella finally says, taking a step back. "Look, we need to be on each other's side tonight, all right? Otherwise Mother will make us sleep out in the barn with the horses."

"There are worse places to sleep," Anastasia says darkly, frowning at Drizella in the mirror, and Drizella watches as her own shoulders slump forward, as the tower looms far away. This is not the memory she wants to think of tonight.

"I know," she says instead. "I just meant that she'll probably put our heads on pikes if this debut doesn't go well, okay?"

"Oh, that sounds *far* better—"

"Annie!" Drizella whispers harshly. "Stop pouting and listen to me! I'm trying to—"

But she's cut off as a conversation reaches their ears. "Did you see that girl Ella?" says someone. "What a beauty. And so charming, too!"

"Where have they been keeping her, do you think?"

"Locked away in a room upstairs, perhaps?" a third girl teases, and everyone laughs.

"Did you see the *other* two?" There's another titter, this time of disapproval, and Drizella closes her eyes and waits for the blows to fall down on their ears.

"*Velvet* instead of silk? They look like colorful dustrags."

"Well, their father *left*, you know."

"I heard he robbed his own family blind before he snuck out."

"Well, that explains why those bustles look to be at least twenty years old."

"I wonder how many moth holes are underneath those gowns."

"And you know what they say about *their mother*."

"Are those two *truly* Ella's sisters?"

"I think you mean they're her ugly *stepsisters*," a fourth girl adds, and this time the laughter, as sharp as shattered glass, seems to float over the scrim and land directly on top of Anastasia and Drizella, the softness of the giggles doing nothing to lessen the blow of the words.

The two sisters look at each other in the mirror, cheeks burning with shared shame, indignity, and the quiet, climbing fear that the reason these ladies are laughing is because everything they're saying is true.

Anastasia's chin wobbles. Drizella has to force her own to not do the same.

The conversation continues, but Drizella's head is buzzing too loud to hear anything else that they say. She feels like she's been filled up with bees, all of them humming and stinging every part of her insides, making her hurt from the inside out. Next to her, Anastasia is shaking slightly, and Drizella reaches down and takes her sister's hand in hers, squeezing it so, so tight.

"Don't listen to them," she murmurs. "They don't know anything about us. They're just bullies."

"I don't know *what* you're talking about," Anastasia says, raising her chin high even as it continues to quiver a little. "Everyone knows that real ladies don't gossip. It's *vulgar*. And besides, I think you look very nice, Drizzy. I like that green color on you very much."

Drizella regards her own reflection. Her eyes are dark and flashing, reminding her of something, of *someone*, but before she can think too hard about it, Anastasia's squeezing her hand back, nodding at her as if to say *It's all right*.

Drizella blinks again, and now she just looks like she did

before, worn and tattered. "I think you look lovely, too," she manages to say. "Not all redheads can wear pink, you know."

"They most certainly cannot," Anastasia agrees, then pats her hair a few times. "If we have to do this, then let's just do it, all right? You and me. Like always."

It's as if she's suddenly become the big sister in their relationship, and Drizella feels a cool breeze of comfort, like she doesn't have to be the only one propping both of them up. Before she can say anything, though, Ella comes back behind the scrim, holding two china teacups full of water and appearing flushed.

"Goodness, I've been looking for you everywhere!" she says. "You two hide so well!"

"We do indeed," Drizella says airily. "Come, Anastasia. We'll get something to drink downstairs."

And she takes her sister's hand once again, feeling flushed with a newfound confidence that maybe, just perhaps, things could go well for once.

10

ANASTASIA

When the same woman who ushered them upstairs comes into the room to tell them it's time for the debut to begin, the rest of the girls head downstairs, squealing quietly to each other, clasping their hands tightly. Anastasia and Drizella are the last ones to leave, Ella tagging along behind them, and once Anastasia sees their mother, she realizes that she can't look her in the eye. She's too embarrassed, the humiliation washing over her like icy water, making her feel both numb and extremely pained.

Is that what people really think of her? Anastasia wonders.

Is it *really*? She thinks back to all the people she would say hello to as they walked through the village, smiling politely and getting generous nods in return from people who never bothered to say anything further. Did they wince behind her back, make faces to tease, call her names and giggle once she was around the corner? Anastasia thinks about all the times she was in a good mood, was *happy*, even, and the shame washes over her again.

She's never felt like the smartest person in any room, but now she just feels so, so stupid and small. She's half tempted to grab Drizella by the arm and run out of there, but where would they go? Back home to a mother who would no doubt be incandescent with rage if they dared to flee their own debut? The lavender field where Dominic took her —

Dominic.

Anastasia wonders if he's been teasing her, too. Maybe someone put him up to his flirtations, maybe made a bet that he could get the ugliest girl in the village to fall in love with him. He's the one who found her, after all, not the other way around. Her cheeks flush such a deep red that the color goes all the way to the tips of her ears, and she can feel the nervous pink splotches beginning to spread across her neck and chest.

Next to her, Drizella just looks resolute and cold, her profile sharp as she glares ahead toward the room where the debut will commence. They're surrounded by other girls with their parents, ladies-in-waiting, and friends all huddled around them, beaming with pride and good cheer at their beautiful daughters.

Anastasia wonders if her father thought she was ugly, too. If that's why he left.

"I can't," she starts to say, and her mother turns to look at her with an arched eyebrow that speaks volumes more than any words could. "I can't feel my feet," she finishes, the words awkward on her tongue. "These shoes are too tight, Mother."

"Find something of actual value to say or don't speak at all," her mother replies, turning back toward the crowd. She was standing off to the side of the room when the girls came back downstairs, surveying the people crowded into the ballroom with narrowed eyes like she was at an auction, trying to decide which priceless treasures she might purchase. "Beauty involves pain. That's the price we pay for being women." But then she suddenly turns around again, her eyes narrowed. "Why are you so flushed?"

"It's, um, warm in here," Anastasia replies, and it is. Too much body heat and excitement and the smell of silks and fabrics and perfumes make the room seem to almost shimmer with electricity.

"Don't faint" is all Drizella says, without even bothering to turn around. Anastasia can hear the unspoken threat in her sister's voice: *Don't you* dare *pass out and leave me to do this all alone.*

Next to her, Ella whispers, "I can go fetch more water if you'd like."

"I'm fine," she snaps back, and Ella withdraws, wide-eyed and wounded. At any other time, Anastasia would feel bad for snapping. It's not Ella's fault that she's beautiful even when she has hay in her hair, when she's covered with slop from the pigs' trough, when she's been out getting eggs from their ornery chickens and returns covered in scratches and pin-feathers. But Anastasia just *hurts*, and it's too much for her to hold by herself. She has no idea how to carry this much pain alone.

"You've done enough, don't you think?" she adds, throwing a look over her shoulder, and Ella looks up, confused.

Anastasia will apologize tomorrow, she thinks as she moves forward toward her mother and sister. Tomorrow things won't hurt as much. Tomorrow will be better. *She'll* be better.

Once they get into the grand hall where the Prince's debut will take place, Anastasia feels her heat rash ease a little. The ceilings are so high that it makes her neck ache to look up, all of them lined with huge crystal chandeliers that would no doubt kill everyone in the room if even one came crashing down. At the far, far end of the ballroom are two thrones, magnificent and resplendent in their golden glories, and Anastasia feels a twinge as she thinks about what Dominic said about "Prince Charming."

She wonders if Dominic is here, the way he said he would be. She looked all over for him when they first entered the palace, but hasn't been able to spot him. She wonders if he's been sent away on an errand or if he's hiding in the stables somewhere, watching her, laughing to himself at this dumb girl who actually thought she was good enough for him.

Next to her, Drizella reaches down and squeezes her hand so tight that Anastasia feels her finger throb, but she tightens her jaw and says nothing. "Forget about it," Drizella whispers through clenched teeth. "I mean it. Forget them. They're nothing."

But it must be *something* if Drizella is telling her to forget it. If she could just forget it, there'd be no need to remind her to do so. Drizella must be shaken up, too, and the idea of Drizella, the human equivalent of an icicle, feeling the same shame that Anastasia does is enough to make Anastasia's eyes begin to tear.

She has no idea how to comfort her sister, though. That's not what they know how to do in their family. Theirs is a house full of sharp words, swallowed sobs, composed expressions that never give away any emotion at all. She tries to squeeze Drizella's hand in return, but by the time she manages to tighten her fingers, Drizella has already let go.

An entire brigade of trumpets begins to wail, signaling the royal family's arrival, and over the heads of what must be every single person who's ever set foot in their village, Anastasia can see the Prince walking with his father down a broad staircase and toward the set of thrones. There's a flutter in the room when he appears, murmurs about how handsome, how regal, how royal. His hair is perfectly combed, every single strand in place, his purple suit and sash starched and pressed so that every pleat is sharp and exact.

Anastasia finds herself missing a dark cowlick, a callused hand, a wide and warm smile.

The actual debut is, Anastasia thinks, slightly underwhelming. The King presses a sword to each of his son's shoulders, a giant crown is placed on his head that makes him almost resemble one of the mushrooms that blooms in their backyard after the rains, and then the trumpets flare up again and everyone applauds politely. Drizella, still clapping, turns around to catch Anastasia's eye before rolling her own eyes for just the briefest of seconds.

It makes Anastasia laugh, anyway.

Afterward, the girls are lined up in a room just off the main ballroom and introduced to the Prince in alphabetical order, which puts the Tremaine sisters toward the bottom of the list. It's a parade of young women who have been preparing their whole lives for this night, and it shows: their fine silk dresses glow under the chandelier lights, their cheeks look as soft and pink as rose petals, they beam toward their proud parents as they gracefully take a turn around the room on the arms of the royal guards who are standing in as escorts for the evening.

Anastasia has only held the arm of one boy in her entire life. She chews on the inside of her cheek and tastes blood.

When it's her turn, her knees tremble, and she has no idea how she's supposed to walk when she can barely stand. She's never had this many people looking at her before, and somewhere in this room are people who called her ugly, who made fun of her and her sister like it was nothing. Like *they* were nothing. Every single person watching Anastasia is a potential traitor, and she wishes she could yell at all of them, scream until the chandeliers sway and fall.

Instead, she walks toward her escort, who looks bored and indifferent. Anastasia saw him escort two of the previous girls, and he smiled at them. (She didn't think he was as handsome as Dominic, though.) When he offers her his arm, Anastasia knows she's supposed to let her fingertips rest ever so gently on him, but instead she grips so tight that he winces a little. "Loosen up," he whispers through his teeth.

She says nothing, just keeps a frozen smile on her face. Across the room, she attempts to share a grin with her mother, but she's only watching her with the ever-present critical eye. There are no silent, loving exchanges between them, no bashful smiles or hastily wiped tears of pride.

"Ow!" her escort cries.

"Sorry," she whispers back, but still doesn't let go.

The whole experience is like a fever dream, a little too warm and hazy to be real. Anastasia can see everyone watching her but can't recognize their faces, her vision blurring enough to block out the sharper details. Her shoes feel so tight that she's worried her feet might pop out of them entirely, but she manages to keep everything where it belongs.

They circle the room once, Anastasia nodding to random people that she most likely will never acknowledge again, and then she's at the front of the room, the Prince standing at attention and the King smiling politely from his throne. He reminds Anastasia of the kind of doll she used to see in toy catalogs in their general store, unblinking and unthinking.

"Mademoiselle Anastasia Tremaine!" a voice booms. Her own name has never sounded so scary before.

The Prince bows and she curtsies, but he never bothers to make eye contact with her.

Prince Charming, she thinks. *Indeed.*

When it's Drizella's turn, the room is equally quiet, with very few murmurs of admiration or approval. Her hand is a light touch, though, and she moves like a shark coming up on prey, each step emotionless and calculated.

And instead of looking down or toward Anastasia or her mother, she instead makes eye contact with every other woman in the room, as if she's daring them to step forward and admit what they said in the dressing room. By the time she arrives back where she began, Drizella has a smirk on her face, one eyebrow arched as she falls back in line with the other young women.

It's intimidating. *Drizella* is intimidating. But more important, it's familiar, and Anastasia looks across the room toward their mother, whose face mirrors Drizella's own.

A shiver runs through Anastasia when she sees their similarity.

When the introductions are done, each girl has a chance to perform her talent, mostly singing or playing a musical instrument. A small riser is brought out to the ballroom so the attendees can gather around as the girls perform. Anastasia knows it's supposed to feel informal and fun, but instead it just looks like a circus ring. Maybe Drizella wasn't too far off when she compared them to the dancing poodles.

One girl is a very fine puppeteer, and the audience murmurs and applauds enthusiastically for her and her marionette. Anastasia suspects the ringing applause is as much for her talent as it is the relief of not having to listen to yet another violin or vocal solo.

And once again, Anastasia and Drizella are toward the end of the evening, and by the time it's their turn, the audience is weary from standing. A few fathers are mopping at their foreheads with their handkerchiefs, and Anastasia wonders if her own father ever does that, if he would have been here grinning at his children the way the rest of the fathers here are.

"And now we have Mademoiselles Anastasia and Drizzle—*Drizella*, excuse me—Tremaine performing a flute and vocal duet of 'Sing, Sweet Nightingale.'" Anastasia's glad she's not on the receiving end of the glare that Drizella shoots at the attendant for mispronouncing her name as she walks resolutely toward the center of the room, Anastasia clutching her flute and tagging along behind her.

Anastasia's not sure, but it feels like her throat is closing up, and the pink splotches are overtaking her body like a patchwork quilt, and it's suddenly so, so warm in the room that she wishes she could dab at her own forehead. She's clammy and hot, and she can already tell that there are damp spots under her arms, staining the velvet dress. She's supposed to play the flute in this condition? She can barely *breathe* in this condition!

The flute slips a little in her sweaty palms, her gloves abandoned so that she can play for the recital, and next to her, Drizella stands straight and tall, her own hands clasped in front of her as she glances at Anastasia out of the corner of her eye.

Anastasia can't read her sister at all. It scares her. It's like Drizella has shut out everyone, closed the door to her mind and escaped to a place where no one can follow her. And even though Anastasia is standing in a crowded room, surrounded by people, her own family, even, she suddenly feels so alone that she wobbles a little from the force of the emotion.

Someone clears their throat. Another person coughs. Their impatience is palpable.

Anastasia takes a deep breath, puts the flute up to her mouth, and begins.

The first notes are okay, not perfect but still entirely respectable, and Anastasia feels her heart perk up a little bit. But toward the end of her introduction, her finger catches, the note she hits sounds like the screeching of a baby bird falling out of a nest, and the entire room winces. Even Drizella's eyelid twitches, and Anastasia quickly pulls away, shaking her head a little as if there's a piece in her brain that she just needs to put back into place.

With trembling hands, she brings the flute back to her mouth, takes another breath, and starts over.

This time is better, but then Drizella misses her cue and that trips up Anastasia, who fumbles the next notes until it sounds like she and Drizella are performing two entirely different songs. An audience member giggles just a bit, followed by a sharp "Shh!" No doubt it's a parent scolding a child, but even the whispered hush sounds a little amused.

Then Drizella's voice cracks, not even on a high note, and Anastasia startles enough that her finger once again gets stuck in the flute. She panics and attempts to unstick it, and the force of her tugging causes the flute to go flying toward Drizella, who manages to duck in the nick of time.

Anastasia doesn't see this, though. All she sees is the darkened storm cloud passing across her mother's face, her eyes closing as if she's witnessing a terrible accident, her jaw set so tight that it appears to be wired shut. Anastasia can see one of her hands tightening into a fist, her knuckles almost looking like weapons, they're so round and skeletal.

There's another giggle, then a full-out guffaw, and pretty soon the whole room is laughing. Laughing at them, the two girls who couldn't even perform for two minutes without some calamity. And, horrors, the Prince's composed exterior has cracked, and he's *smiling*. He's politely hidden it behind a hand, but it's there nonetheless. Even the Prince is laughing at the two girls with no talent, no prospects, no beauty, no father.

Because after all, Anastasia and Drizella are just the two ugly stepsisters, nothing more.

Anastasia turns to go somewhere, to flee the room or escape into a crowd of strangers, but then there's a kind set of brown eyes looking at her from the back of the crowd, a lip caught between a pair of slightly crooked teeth, and Dominic's gaze is suddenly the only thing she can see in the room.

Was he laughing at her, too?

Anastasia can't bite back the sob that manages to escape from her chest, so she runs.

She steps over the flute and hitches up her dress and bolts from the room, the crowd parting for her as if they're afraid that they might touch her, become infected with whatever ugliness and failure seems to be on her skin. She can hear the faint sound of someone calling her, probably Drizella, but she doesn't want to stay another minute just so she can see Drizella's cold eyes.

She knows it's not her mother calling after her, that's for sure; no words of comfort are waiting for her, no gentle hand to dry her tears.

Anastasia runs away from it all.

✣

She finds herself outside after only a moment or two of frantically searching for an exit, her legs still pumping fast as she dashes down a set of turret stairs, the night air cold on her wet face. The stairs wind gracefully down until she's outside on the palace grounds, the silence of the evening stark after the loud and noisy ballroom. She's alone now, the crowds far behind her, and she lets out a small cry that soon turns into a fresh set of sobs.

The bustle that she's wearing—that she was forced to wear—is coming undone at her waist, and Anastasia stops just long enough to reach up under her skirt and yank it off, tossing it toward some nearby rosebushes, where, the following day, it will take two gardeners six hours to untangle the delicate, worn fabric from the thorny bushes. She'd try to get the corset off, as well, but it's impossible to undo by herself. She can dismantle her hair, though, and that's exactly what she does, pulling at the pins and clips until it's falling out in a tangle.

Unburdened by the impossible bustle and towering hairstyle, she takes another deep breath and keeps running. She has no idea which direction she's heading, but what else is there for her to do? Where else is there for her to go?

She runs until she comes to a graceful bridge over a quiet river. *Imagine being so rich that you have your own river*, she thinks through her tears, and the thought finally makes her legs stop. All her limbs are on fire, burning with the effort of running after not doing any sort of strenuous exercise for her entire life, and if Anastasia could unzip her legs from her body and throw them into the river, she would.

If she could throw her entire *body* into the river, she would, but instead she just stands there, leaning down to catch her breath even though the sobs are ripping their way through her lungs and throat, making it difficult to see. Anastasia hasn't cried like this since . . .

The tower.

Her mother is going to put her back in the tower, where it's cold and there are rats—not fat little mice wearing tiny shoes made by Ella, but actual *rats*—and the window doesn't shut and the walls are so, so close together, and Anastasia feels the fingers of panic begin to close around her throat and squeeze harder than they ever have before.

Someone's still calling her name, the voice getting closer. It's not Drizella; it's certainly not her mother. Maybe one of the brow-mopping fathers took pity on her?

But when she wipes her eyes and looks up, she sees Dominic sprinting across the grounds toward her, and even from far away, Anastasia can see the concern and fear that's etched across his face.

As soon as he's close enough, he's reaching out to her, slightly out of breath with his dark hair falling across his fore-head. "Anastasia," he gasps. "Where are you—?"

"Don't take another step toward me!" she yells, holding out one shaking hand. Dominic freezes in his tracks, his frown deepening just as a beautiful, lilting voice floats down from one of the palace's open windows. The beginning a cappella notes of "Sing, Sweet Nightingale" seem to make the river water almost ripple with joy, and Anastasia looks up toward the music and listens as a golden, honeyed voice fills the ballroom.

It's beautiful. Because of course it is.

Anastasia starts to cry again, the initial humiliation now doubled not only by the singer's obvious talent but also by the fact that Dominic is there to bear witness to it.

"You need to leave," she says through her tears. "Just go."

"I'm not leaving," Dominic says. "Not when you're like this."

"You saw what happened," she hisses, wiping at her cheeks with the back of her hand. "Didn't you?" she adds when he hesitates, even though his hesitation tells her everything she needs to know.

"I did," he murmurs, and her eyes overflow yet again. "I'm sorry, Anastasia, I truly am. That must have been terrible. The whole night looks pretty terrible, if I'm being honest. It's so warm in there, and all that *perfume*—"

"Am I a joke?" she asks him, hating the way her voice cracks on the last word. "Tell me the truth. Did your fancy palace friends dare you to talk to me, see if you could get the ugly girl to—?"

"Whoa, whoa, wait a minute." Dominic's voice has lost all its kindness now, replaced by a sternness that she's never heard before. "The who? What did you just say?"

"Tell me the truth," she says. She wants the question to sound unyielding and firm, but she just sounds weak and tired. Which, to be fair, she is. And hungry, to boot. "Is all of this just a game? Is it funny to you? Am *I* funny to you?"

Dominic takes a tentative step forward, one eyebrow raised in a way that's the complete opposite of her mother's habit, a question instead of a demand. When Anastasia finally gives the barest of nods, he reaches over and gently guides her toward the small set of steps at the end of the bridge, sitting her down before settling next to her.

"Did you just call yourself the ugly girl?" he asks.

"Everyone else is saying it!" She sniffles, wiping her eyes on the back of her old-fashioned velvet sleeve, and then Dominic's pressing a handkerchief into her hand. It reminds her of all the fathers from the room, dabbing at their foreheads, and she begins to cry again.

"Anastasia Tremaine," Dominic says, "you're not ugly. You're anything but ugly."

"Oh, really?" she says, waving her hand toward the palace, toward all the traitors who are now clapping wildly for that gorgeous rendition of their song. "Then you should probably let everyone in there know about that!"

Dominic just shakes his head, then puts his hands on her arms and turns her to face him. "What happened?" he says.

"You saw what happened! I ruined the performance and Drizella choked and now my mother's going to murder us and she's going . . . she's going . . ." The fingers squeeze again, cutting off her words.

"I'm not talking about the performance," Dominic says, his own voice as calm as hers is panicked. "What happened, Anastasia? Who said you were ugly?"

"They did." She sobs.

"Who's they?" His hands are tight, but not in a bad way, almost like he's keeping her above water, keeping her from going into the river below.

"The women," she admits, folding the handkerchief over and over until it's a tiny square, then letting it unravel.

"Drizella and I, we were getting ready upstairs, and nobody knew we were there, and then they said . . ."

Dominic is patient, waits.

"They said our father left us, that we looked like we were wearing rags. They said we had moth holes in our clothes." Just saying the words makes her feel like someone's stabbing a knife into all of Anastasia's most tender places, and she drops her head so that she doesn't have to see Dominic's face when he realizes what she really is. "They said that Ella was beautiful and that we were her ugly stepsisters."

Dominic sits back, the shock obvious on his face, but before he can say anything, Anastasia cuts him off.

"If I'm just a joke, if this whole thing is some big prank, I won't be angry." She will be very, very angry, but nothing would be as strong as the grief and loss she would feel, as if losing Dominic would kill all the goodness inside of her. "But I just want you to be honest with me. Are you in on this, too? Are you in on this with all of them?"

Dominic looks as if she's accused him of murdering a puppy. "Am I what?" he asks, and if she couldn't already see the disbelief on his face, she hears it in his voice. "Anastasia, look at me." He bends down to look at her face, and she reluctantly meets his eyes.

"You are *not* a joke. I don't think any of this is a joke. You make me laugh. You make me happy every single time I see you. That day when we first went to the lavender fields—I think about it all the time, how warm and honest you were, how you made me feel like I could tell you *anything*. I told you about my parents, Anastasia. I've never talked to anyone about them before. And I don't think a single part of you is ugly, not at all. The only ugly ones are the people who made you feel that way."

Anastasia shudders a little bit, then looks up at him. "Do you really mean that?"

"I always mean what I say," he replies. "But especially when I'm talking to you."

She's crying again, her spine sagging down like a reed bent by the rains. "It was so awful," she weeps. "They were just giggling and laughing at us, and Drizella, her face, I couldn't . . ." She sobs again, covering her face with her hands, lined with Dominic's handkerchief. It smells like him, soap and butterscotch, along with a hint of the rich, powdery lilac scent that seems to permeate the castle, and then his scent is everywhere, drowning out everything else.

Dominic leans forward and gathers her in his arms, resting his cheek against the top of her head. "Anastasia," he whispers, and just the way he says her name is a balm. "I'm so sorry."

He lets her cry for a long, long time, rocking her back and forth as a cool breeze blows softly around them. His arms are so warm that it makes Anastasia think of the fluffiest, softest bed, and she presses her face into his collarbone and lets him hug her. She can't remember the last time anyone did this, held her tight when she was sad, and now that she finally, finally has some comfort, she can't imagine letting go of it.

"My mother, if she sees you . . ." She manages to say, trying to sit up, but Dominic pulls her closer and Anastasia sinks down against him once again.

"I locked the door behind me," he says. "It's the only main way out to the garden. Don't worry." His hand is on top of her hair like a little cap, warming her down to her bones. "The rest of the paths here are blocked due to the debut. She won't find us, I promise."

"She's going to put me in the tower again," Anastasia mumbles, breath hitching a little in her chest. "She's going to lock me up and throw away the key."

"Lock you up?" Dominic repeats. "Your mother locks you up in a tower?"

Anastasia is quiet after that, though. She doesn't want to remember that night, how it felt to be so cold and alone, not when she's warm and the only person she wants is right here with her.

Even after she's finally calmed down and her tears have devolved into quiet shudders, Dominic still holds her. "For what it's worth," he says, and Anastasia can hear the rumble of his voice in his chest, "I thought you looked absolutely beautiful."

She rolls her eyes, but a tiny flame lights up inside her. "I did not. My hair is ridiculous and my bustle looked stupid."

"All bustles look stupid," he says, which makes her smile a bit. "But it had nothing to do with what you were wearing. I just think you always look beautiful. I wish I could have kicked all those people out of the room so I could have asked you to dance with me."

The dance. They're missing the dance. Forget the tower; their mother is going to dangle their bodies off a flagpole after tonight.

"I wish you could have, too," she says.

"We still could, you know," he replies, then helps her sit up a little. Anastasia doesn't need a mirror to know that she's a mess, and she quickly dabs at her eyes and cheeks with the handkerchief again.

"You're really suggesting—"

"Not in there." Dominic jerks a thumb back toward the palace. "Not with all of that stuffiness and rudeness and all those pompous people." He pauses before saying, "But we could dance right here."

Anastasia's eyes widen, but he's right. They can hear the music, it's a beautiful night, and, well, she's never danced with anyone before, much less at a palace.

"If you want to dance, you should ask properly," she chides him, and he immediately snaps to attention, his heels clicking together as he stands and falls into full royal mode.

"Mademoiselle Tremaine, will you do me the honor of having this dance?"

It's so ridiculous that it makes her smile, even if it's still a little wobbly and watery, but she likes that someone is willing to be ridiculous for her. "It'd be an honor," she replies, taking his hand and curtsying as deep as she can go in her too-tight shoes. Dominic bows low at the waist, then grins as he pulls her toward him.

It's not like the dances she's been made to practice at home over the past several weeks. Those are structured and separate, the distance between the two performers acting as its own chaperone. When Anastasia and Dominic dance, they fit together perfectly, his gentle swaying in perfect rhythm with her own heartbeat. It's loving but chaste, intimate without being inappropriate, even though Anastasia can't picture a single chaperone actually approving of their quiet, private waltz.

She doesn't care who approves of her, though. Let those old women and their pinched daughters laugh at her and her sister. Let them make fun. Let her father wander off the face of the earth, for all she cares. Because all she needs is right here, holding on to her with a gentle yet firm grasp, his arms warm on her back, his pulse steady under her cheek. Above them, the moon is shining so bright that it looks like the sun, bathing them in the cool spotlight of its glow.

"I think this is even better than dancing at the ball," Dominic murmurs, bringing one hand up to gently caress Anastasia's cheek.

"Too many nosy people," Anastasia agrees. It feels like his face is getting closer to hers, centimeter by centimeter, and then she's standing up on her tiptoes to bring herself up to him, and their lips touch in a kiss that's both gentle and intense, Anastasia's breath nearly leaving her body as she feels Dominic sigh against her.

When they pull apart, Anastasia feels like she's out of orbit, spinning away from everything that she knows, everything that she wants to leave behind. "Dominic," she whispers.

"I'm sorry," he says. "That was so forward of me. I didn't mean—"

Anastasia just pushes herself up higher and kisses him again.

It feels holy, Anastasia thinks. This is the kind of moment that makes people believe in things they can't see, put their faith into emotions instead of hard, cold facts. Around them, the air is so quiet that not even a leaf is stirring, as if nature itself is afraid of disrupting their delicate moment.

It's almost as if the two of them are actually alone.

If only they were.

11

DRIZELLA

After Anastasia leaves—no, *abandons*—her in the ballroom, Drizella stands alone while the rest of the guests roar with laughter. But their hearty chuckles are nothing compared to the buzzing sound in her own head, almost as if a beehive has been unleashed in her brain, drowning out the rest of the cruel sounds around her.

She doesn't look toward her mother. She already knows what she'll see in her eyes, and it won't be good.

There's a gentle hand on her arm, and Drizella glances over to see Ella coming to stand next to her. She gives Drizella a nod, and Drizella can only stare back at her in confusion before Ella opens her mouth and begins to sing "Sing, Sweet Nightingale."

She wants to duet, Drizella realizes. Ella thinks that she might actually help.

Her stepsister is even dumber than she had imagined.

And the worst part? Ella can actually sing. Not like Drizella, who can still barely hit all the notes on the scale even after months of practice. No, Ella has a beautiful voice and has decided now is the best moment to use it. The whole room seems entranced by this sudden performance, and the shocked and sneering expressions surrounding Drizella seem to fade into something softer, more generous as they turn their gazes toward Ella. Even the Prince seems enraptured by Ella's voice, and judging from the way her mother's posture goes stiff, Drizella realizes that Lady Tremaine has seen his face change, as well.

Ella nods at Drizella again, completely oblivious to the effect she's having on everyone, encouraging her to join her. And Drizella tries. She really, truly does. But her throat is so tight and all she can see is Anastasia's face as the flute went flying, Anastasia's face when the laughter began, Anastasia's face as she ran away, leaving Drizella alone under the sneering gazes of so many cruel strangers.

Ella is still singing, her voice now becoming more confident and powerful, and when she reaches for Drizella's hand,

Drizella steps away from the spotlight. Nobody wants to hear her sing. They want Ella.

Drizella ducks through the crowd with her head low, her eyes straight ahead, looking at nothing, having no idea where she's going. It's almost as if the palace and its inhabitants are crumbling around Drizella, burying everyone in her mental rubble as she stalks forward, and she's happy to leave them all behind.

She never wants to come to this place again.

She walks until she reaches the massive staircase, then heads down it, past the immense line of knights, all still standing at attention, and then stalks right out the enormous doors. Drizella had no idea you could just walk out of a palace like this—she thought it'd involve escorts, or at least a draw-bridge or moat—but instead she just heads outside, and when her lungs finally manage to get a taste of the cool, damp night air, Drizella takes a breath like she's spent the last two hours suffocating.

Which, in a way, she has.

Ella's voice is floating down the stairs behind her, ethereal and angelic but still somber, singing "Sing, Sweet Nightingale" as if the song was meant to be sung only by her.

What was it that Madame Lambert said? No matter how brightly the moon shines, it will always be because of the sun's light.

It will never be a star.

Drizella doesn't even realize she's heading toward the village until she's halfway there, nearly thirty minutes of walking that has her aching and bruised feet carrying her in the opposite direction of her home. Not that she'd ever go home for any sort of comfort, especially not after a night like this one. That's probably where Annie ran off to, and right now, Drizella doesn't want to see her sister at all. Not after being left alone like that.

She walks.

The night gets even colder, and of course Drizella has no coat, but still she heads forward, going over the dirt roads and down several small hills, the path as familiar to her in the nighttime as it is during the day. She can feel her hair becoming damp with dew, a fine layer of mist pressing down on her skin, and her velvet dress starts to feel weighted down and too heavy for her frame to hold up. She has half a mind to just wrench it off her body, but luckily she has enough awareness to realize that showing up in the village half naked will not do anything to improve her circumstances that evening.

She trudges on until she comes to the worn fork in the road, the one where she and Anastasia have split off so many times before, each going into their own worlds. The buzzing in her head has decreased now that she's outside in fresh air, but unfortunately it's been replaced by the sounds of the audience laughing. It wasn't gentle, either. It wasn't as if people were both amused by and encouraging of the sisters, like when parents clap and cheer for a child who's just learning to walk, then giggle when they tumble down in surprise on the ground. This laughter was cruel and harsh and vindictive, and Drizella has no idea why.

Is she really so ugly that there's no other redeeming quality about her? Is this why her mother is so mean to her? Is this why her father left? Is this why she has no friends aside from her own sister? Surely that's not the only thing that anyone can see when they look at her, right?

The echoing laughter, however, tells her otherwise.

She goes right at the fork and only realizes where she's headed when she arrives there, the staircase to Madame Lambert's studio beckoning her up like a crooked finger, easing her toward the warmth of the room. Drizella holds on to the rail to balance herself, her dress is so heavy with the night's dampness, and climbs up and puts her hand on the doorknob and thinks, with an eeriness that will give her goose bumps when she remembers it later, *I will break down this door if it's locked.*

Instead, the knob turns easily in her hand.

As soon as she steps into the warm, candlelit room and sees all the stars and constellations glowing, sees the green plants reaching out their leaves as if to say hello, sees a china teacup half filled with rooibos tea, she begins to shiver.

"Hello?" someone calls, and there's a rustle and clatter in the back before Madame Lambert suddenly emerges. She looks a little more rumpled than she usually does, soft in the way people look when they first wake up in the morning, but it's clear she's been working, not napping. She's wearing a smock, and there's a brush of something blue across one cheekbone that shimmers under the lights. Her glasses are hanging on a chain around her neck and she immediately tugs them up to her eyes, blinking twice and then squinting.

It's been two weeks since Drizella has last seen her, but it feels like a lifetime.

"Drizella?"

Drizella says nothing. It's obviously her, no need to confirm it, and besides, she's not sure she's able to speak right now anyway. Even in the warmth of the room, her teeth are chattering, and Madame Lambert stands and looks at her for a few seconds before immediately hurrying to her side.

"Drizella, good heavens!" she says, her hands fluttering all around Drizella as if she's not sure what to tend to first. "Your dress, child! What happened? You're almost soaked to the bone! Did you walk here?"

Drizella just watches her, feeling out of her body. She had the same experience as a child, struck down by scarlet fever and delirious from the heat of her own skin. She felt herself rise up to the ceiling and looked down at her own self, sweating furiously in her bed, before she drifted back down again.

She tried to tell her mother about it, but she said it was just a dream, that only lunatics spoke that way, and did Drizella want to end up in the madhouse?

Maybe that's where she's going after all, Drizella thinks now, because what she's feeling now is anything but sane.

"Drizella," Madame Lambert says again, her hand coming up to Drizella's forehead. "Are you ill, my dear? Are you all right?"

Drizella barks out a laugh at that question and doesn't bother to answer.

"My girl, you need to tell me what's going on."

"I walked here," Drizella says. Her voice is so low and feral that at first she doesn't even recognize that it's her who's speaking.

"From where?" Madame Lambert asks.

"The palace."

"You walked all that way? Like this?" Madame Lambert sounds horrified, her hands starting to wave around again. "My child, that's at least five kilometers."

"May I take these shoes off, please?" Drizella asks, still in a monotone state. "They hurt."

"Oh, of course, of course. Here, let me help!" And then sweet Madame Lambert is stooping down, gently taking Drizella's ankles in her hands one at a time as she helps her step out of the ghastly slippers. "You're bleeding, oh, no. I'm sure I can fix it, though, dear, don't be alarmed."

Drizella doesn't feel alarmed. She doesn't feel anything at all.

Madame Lambert runs around the studio for a moment, gathering supplies before coming back to the door where Drizella is still standing, unmoving, unblinking. "Come, my dear," she says, guiding Drizella to sit on a wooden stool. She sits with a plop, unladylike, of course, completely at odds with the weeks wasted on walking around with a stupid book on her head.

What was the point? she thinks. *What on earth was the point of all that?*

"Hmm?" Madame Lambert asks, and Drizella realizes that she's spoken her question aloud.

"What did you say, child?" she asks again.

"What was the point?" Drizella mumbles. "She knew we were going to fail."

Madame Lambert squints a little, bending down to look at Drizella's face. She's a small woman, but she seems to tower over Drizella now that the girl is sitting down. Drizella feels a bit like she's under an elm tree during a spring rainstorm, sheltered instead of entrapped.

"Why don't we do this?" Madame Lambert says gently. "Let me help you get out of these wet clothes and into something dry, and you can tell me what happened while we work? I have a few experiments whose processes I need to examine in the late evening."

It takes Drizella a minute to nod, still not making eye contact with the kind woman who probably won't ever want to talk to her again once she hears how Drizella has failed her entire family, embarrassed them all to the core, and shattered her relationship with her mother. Not that they ever had much of a relationship in the beginning, but at least there had been potential. That's gone now, and all Drizella can feel is her mother's withering gaze piercing right through as soon as she sang that first wrong note.

"All right" is all she says, though, and Madame Lambert stands up to her full, short height and claps her hands together.

"Wonderful," she says. "Before you catch your death of cold."

Drizella lets the woman stand her up and start to unbutton the back of her dress. Her fingers are deft, moving almost at lightning speed with the difficult velvet buttons. Not silk, only velvet. She's shivering now, even as the wet dress leaves her body, and she brings her arms up to hug herself.

"I know, my dear, we're almost done," Madame Lambert says. "My goodness, who laced this corset? I'm impressed that you're still breathing at this rate."

"Please take it off," Drizella whispers. "I don't care about it. Rip it if you have to."

It feels as if Madame Lambert somehow manages to undo all the lacing at once, and Drizella gasps in a good, solid breath for the first time since their terrible evening began.

The garment's ribbing has left terrible red marks along her sides and back, and Madame Lambert hisses a little. "These blasted things," she mutters under her breath. "It's like they're trying to keep us from even *breathing!*"

Drizella is still gasping, though, and her heart is racing as Madame Lambert carefully pulls her arms from her chest so she can ease them out of the dress sleeves. "Almost done, my dear," she says, and her voice is softer than any voice Drizella has ever heard before. It sounds like a lullaby, and she knows that it's gentler than anything she deserves right now.

"We failed," she whispers, and Madame Lambert doesn't stop moving, but does lean in closer to listen.

"We failed at everything," she says. "Our dresses were all wrong, our hair was wrong. We should have worn silk instead of velvet. They laughed at us."

"*Who* laughed at you?" Madame Lambert asks.

"Everyone." Drizella wonders if this is what it would be like to have a different kind of mother, someone kind instead of cruel, with gentle hands instead of harsh words. "They said we were ugly, me and Anastasia. My sister and I are ugly, that's what everyone said."

"I can assure you, dear girl," Madame Lambert says as she untangles Drizella's left wrist from the sleeve, her voice sharper than Drizella has ever heard it, "that neither you nor your sister could ever be ugly. Ugliness only comes from the inside."

Drizella shakes her head. "I feel like everything inside me is black," she says. "Like their laughter burned me."

Madame Lambert tuts at this, then gives her wrist a final, gentle tug. "Well, anyone who calls two young women ugly during a ball celebrating youth and beauty must have their own ugliness inside of them," she says. "And sometimes, in groups, that ugliness can be catching."

She pats Drizella's shoulder. "Up, my dear. Let me attack this bustle. You must have waddled like a duck the entire way here, you're so bogged down in all of these accoutrements."

Drizella stands up on shaky legs, like a newborn foal still adjusting to its brand-new world, and she puts one hand on Madame Lambert's worktable to steady herself. Across from her, the globes are still. Drizella's the one who's spinning this time.

Madame Lambert is deft and quick, her hands tossing the bustle to the side before helping Drizella out of the dress entirely. She's just in her slip and stockings now, still cold and trembling, but then a soft cloak is draped over her body, wrapping around her almost as if it were made for her. It smells like the studio, the scent of peat moss and rooibos and oil paints now more comforting than anything in her own house, and Drizella brings the collar of the cloak up to her face and breathes in deep as Madame Lambert runs an affectionate hand over her wet hair.

She sinks down onto the stool just as Madame Lambert

murmurs, "Oh, my dear girl, please don't cry," but it's too late. The tears are blurring her vision, so much so that she doesn't see Madame Lambert come up to her, doesn't realize that she's wrapping Drizella up in her arms until it's already happening. Drizella's instinct is to shove, to push, to get away from any sort of kindness so that the seared, charred feeling deep in her stomach doesn't consume anything good, but then Madame Lambert starts to pat her back, and Drizella feels herself sag into the woman's embrace, the sobs rising up like the tides of the ocean, and Drizella is drowning.

"She wanted this so much!" she sobs, clutching at the woman's dress. "Her face when they . . . I tried!"

"Who, dear?" Madame Lambert asks, stroking her hair just as Drizella has always wished her mother would.

I want to go home. I want my mother.

"Anastasia," she says, gulping down tears as she tries to speak. Anastasia's face as the crowd roared with laughter, Anastasia's face as she was dragged up into the tower by their mother, the terror so sharp and real that sometimes Drizella feels as if it's been branded onto her brain. "She was so excited, and I couldn't protect her! I keep trying, but I never can, and—"

"Shh," Madame Lambert says. "Let's just worry about you for now, all right?"

Drizella nods, finally able to be vulnerable for once under

the cover of night, in the deep hush of a world on its way to sleep, and she closes her eyes and lets Madame Lambert hold her as she cries.

Once she's emptied herself of every terrible tear, Madame Lambert helps her sit up, hands her a soft cloth to dry her face, and then turns the stool so that Drizella is sitting at the table. The collar and shoulder of Madame Lambert's cloak are soaked through, and Drizella blushes at the physical reminder of her own weakness.

"Never you mind about that," Madame Lambert says gently. "These things will dry in a flash." She smooths Drizella's hair back from her face like a mother checking for a fever, her touch soft and dry, and Drizella shudders a little.

"I'm sorry," she manages to say, her voice sounding raw and watery. "I don't know what came over me."

"There are no apologies allowed in this work space," Madame Lambert says. "And either way, you have nothing to apologize for. I know it's late, but would you like some tea? Peppermint, I think."

Drizella nods even though she knows a cup of tea will soon be handed to her no matter what she says, and presses her palms against the cool table. The ballroom had been so, so warm, with both the heat of too many bodies and the flush of her own embarrassment, and she resists the urge to lower her head and press her cheek against the metal surface.

"I can't stay in this village anymore," she says, surprised by the words that are coming out of her mouth. "I can't, even though Anastasia is still . . . I just can't do this anymore."

Drizella barely knows what "this" is, couldn't even put it into words. It's a feeling more than a statement, the pressure bearing down upon her so that she feels like she's in a vise with no way out.

Madame Lambert just brings her the tea, then sits down next to her and puts a comforting hand over Drizella's. "Don't let one terrible night dictate your entire life," she says. "I know that when I was a girl—"

"It's not just one night, though!" Drizella cries, her cup falling back into its saucer with a shrill *clank*. "It's every day, it's every night! Our house, it's not even a home, it's this oppressive space where it feels like the walls are closing in on you, like the longer you're there, the harder it will be to escape! Our mother, she never leaves, she never . . ." Drizella's voice trails off, her chin trembling again. "She's not a mother. She's a keeper." It's a word that she's only ever thought, never said aloud, and it's both horrifying and relieving to finally have it out of her brain and into the world.

Madame Lambert's eyes are both sad and sympathetic. "Oh, my dear" is all she says, though, and Drizella drops her head into her hands. She's too cried out, too tired, too embarrassed. Everything is just too much right now.

Madame Lambert places a hand on her back and lets

Drizella settle. "This may not be the best time to announce this," she says quietly once Drizella's breathing has steadied itself once more, "but I'm leaving for Paris next week—"

Drizella crumples, her hands fisting over her eyes. It feels like her spine has been crushed into powder; she can barely hold herself up. What else is there if not this room? Is she doomed to spend the rest of her life in their crumbling, decrepit manor? Who will want her now? Who will think she's smart, or even interesting? Who will smile when they see her? And who on earth will ever love her?

"And I will need someone to assist me," Madame Lambert continues.

And just like that, Drizella is back in one piece, her head up, her eyes dry. "Assist you?"

Madame Lambert nods, her lower lip caught between her teeth. "I didn't want to say anything at first, but I'll be attending a few classes at the Sorbonne and will need someone to attend to my laboratory once I'm there, plus assist me with experiments and such."

It's as if Madame Lambert has put her heart back together only to shatter it once again. "Oh," Drizella murmurs. "Of course, yes. You would need someone."

"I was going to advertise for an assistant once I arrived, but after seeing you here . . ." Madame Lambert's voice trails off, her hand waving around at the studio. "You have a great mind, Drizella. You're curious, which is a very rare gift in a person. You ask a lot of questions. You're not afraid to be wrong or to try again. I don't know the full extent of what happened tonight, but I want you to know that I think you have wonderful potential. Not solely as a possible wife or mother, but as a person, and I would love to have you accompany me as an assistant."

Drizella's eyes fill up with tears so fast that it even surprises her.

"Not that you can't or won't be either a wife or mother one day," Madame Lambert continues. "But I want you to know that you can do other things, too. If you'd like. Your worth is not based on anyone else."

Drizella nods, looking down at her half-empty teacup so that Madame Lambert can't see the emotions spreading across her face. After ten years of being told to ignore her feelings, Drizella now struggles to reveal them to anyone else.

"I would like that very much," she says, once she can keep her voice under control. "To go with you to Paris. To the Sorbonne." Just saying the words *Paris* and *Sorbonne* gives Drizella goose bumps. "I don't think I can pay my way, though."

"Never you mind about that," Madame Lambert says, patting her hand reassuringly. "Money can sometimes have a way of just appearing out of thin air, and besides, I can cover your basic expenses. I just need you to do the work."

"I can do *all* the work!" Drizella cries happily. "All of it, any of it, whatever you need!"

"Paris is quite a large city," Madame Lambert warns. "It's not like this village. There are so many people, carriages, commotion. You might be overwhelmed."

"The idea of being surrounded by commotion sounds absolutely heavenly," Drizella admits. "Our house, it's so . . . Nobody ever . . . It's just very quiet. The mice are probably the loudest out of all of us."

Madame Lambert smiles at that. "Well, there are mice in Paris, too," she teases. "But also museums and opera and the theater. We could attend a few performances."

Drizella is almost light-headed at this point. "That would be wonderful," she says. Already, the terrible, suffocating night at the palace is nearly forgotten, her vision now clouded with the idea of being so close to so many of the arts, to an actual *laboratory*. In *Paris*. "I'll take the mice. I'll take all of it."

In the back of her mind, though, Anastasia keeps appearing, her red hair flaming around her like an evil halo, her face confused and embarrassed, just as it was during their recital that evening. How could she ever leave her sister? How could she just abandon her to their mother's whims, to their dreary home, to their hopeless life?

Drizella pushes that aside. She's a smart girl; she'll figure it out. Plus, Anastasia wasn't exactly thinking about *her* when she rushed from the ballroom, leaving Drizella to face the jeers and taunts alone.

"But there is one thing," Madame Lambert warns, interrupting her train of thought. "I will need your mother's explicit permission." Her face softens a bit as she adds, "I'm not looking to add 'kidnapper' to my list of accomplishments."

"Of course," she replies. "And you'll have it." Drizella will be forging that note immediately.

Madame Lambert gives her a warning glance, like she already knows what Drizella is planning, but then her eyes soften and she smiles at her. "It would be a delight to have you join me, Drizella," she says. "Truly. I think your world would open up so much in Paris. You would have so many opportunities, meet so many new people."

Drizella is nodding frantically, agreeing with every syllable that falls from Madame Lambert's mouth. She must look like Bruno when the dog is eyeballing a bite of dropped food, and her eagerness embarrasses her a little. "I would like that very much," she says, reining herself in, hoping that she looks a bit more refined than before even as she sits at the table wearing a cloak that is easily three sizes too big for her, with wet hair still sticking to her face. "I—I'm very grateful to you, Madame Lambert. For everything."

Madame Lambert just smiles wider and pats her hand again. "No need to thank me, my dear," she says. "I'm just glad to see a smile on your face. I don't think I've ever seen that before." She gently pats Drizella's cheek, then goes to stand up. "You should do it more often."

If Drizella can get to Paris, she thinks, she will smile every single day.

✣

12

ANASTASIA

With every step that she takes away from Dominic, Anastasia can feel the dread start to bloom in her stomach, spreading out through her limbs until it feels like every nerve is on edge.

They danced to three songs before Anastasia realized that she had better get moving before her mother came looking for her. "Don't go," Dominic whispered, still holding her close, and it took all of Anastasia's physical and mental strength to separate herself from him.

"You know where to find me," she says.

"I will come tomorrow night," he says, but Anastasia rests a finger on his lips, and the act seems as intimate as their first kiss was.

"No, no, I need a few days," she says. "My mother—she'll be on a rampage. It's best just to let her settle."

"At least let me walk you—"

"No," she says again. "I mean it, Dominic. She'll be out for blood. I don't want her to see you at all."

Dominic looks unsure at that, but Anastasia just kisses him again, then once more, before walking away.

She has to go home, of course. Where else could she go? She has the fleeting thought that she should have asked Dominic to stash her in the horses' stables for the night, and the image brings a small smile to her face. He hung on to her hand until the very last second, until just the tips of their fingers were touching, and all of his warmth left her once they finally separated.

She can't wait to see him again. Even in the few minutes they've been apart, Anastasia misses him with a longing that she has never felt before. Dominic is hope and potential, the future and all of its possibilities, and for the first time, Anastasia feels as if maybe she is going to be okay.

And then she turns the corner, the castle falls from view, and she remembers where she is going, and just like that, the future feels icy and cold, but not uncertain.

No, Anastasia is absolutely certain of one thing: that her mother is going to lose it.

She keeps walking, her tight slippers getting muddy in the damp and rocky road, and as she gets closer to the village, she sees a dark-haired figure walking toward her. It's hard to see her in the dim night, the moon's light not equal to the sun's, but Anastasia would know her anywhere, would know those clumsy, downtrodden steps if there were a thousand different people walking toward her. Drizella's stride has a way of making her look like she's in a constant pouty state, but at this moment, Anastasia has never been more relieved to see her sister clomping up the dirt path.

"Drizzy," she says.

"Shut up."

Anastasia startles. "What? Why?"

Drizella closes the distance between them until Anastasia can see her sister's withering glare. Up close, Drizella looks terrible. She's carrying her shoes in one hand, with the other one clutching a satin and velvet cloak around her body. Her eyes are red and puffy, too, which shocks Anastasia. "Drizzy, where's your dress? Have you been *crying*?"

Drizella just stares at her, her jaw clenched. If Anastasia didn't know better, she would almost think her sister was smiling at her, and it's not hard for her to guess why Drizella might be upset.

Anastasia's shoulders sag, a little more of Dominic's magic dissipating into the night. "I'm sorry," she says. "I'm so sorry, Drizzy, I am. I just panicked and ran. I didn't know what to do, and she was standing there watching, and . . ."

Drizella continues to glare.

"Will you please just say something?" Anastasia finally cries, stamping her foot into the wet ground and regretting it almost immediately when the muddy water splashes up her leg.

"You and me," Drizella says, her voice dripping with mockery. "Like always."

"What?"

"That's what you said to me upstairs in that dressing room. You said that we were in it together, and I thought you meant it."

Anastasia's face, which is already flushed from the evening's events, grows even redder. "I did mean it!" she says. "I'm sorry that I'm not like you, that I can't be all stoic, that I actually have feelings once in a while!"

Drizella throws her shoes angrily at the ground. "You want to talk about feelings?" she yells. "How about what it feels like to stand in a room with every single person staring at you, laughing at you?"

"I do know what that feels like—" Anastasia starts to say, but Drizella cuts her off.

"No, you don't!" she yells. "Because you weren't alone! I was right there next to you, Annie, and you just ran away and left me standing there with *her*."

Anastasia frowns, not understanding at first. "With Mother?"

"With Ella!" Angry tears fill Drizella's eyes again, and Anastasia realizes with a jolt that she can't remember the last time she saw her big sister cry. "She just waltzed up to the center of the room, and thirty seconds later, every single person in that room loved her." Drizella swipes at her eyes, her lip trembling. "Everyone *loved* her," she says again, "and not even our own mother loved me. You left me alone."

This is the moment where Anastasia should apologize, throw her arms around her sister and beg her for forgiveness, offer her the kind of comfort that Dominic so easily extended to her. But Anastasia has spent her entire life in a cruel household, under cruel guidance, kept under a literal lock and key with very little softness to ease away the harshest edges, and there are some lessons that are very difficult to unlearn.

"Well!" she yells. "You left me, too, you know! I ran away, and you didn't even come looking for me! I'm your little sister, Drizella. I'm not your enemy! You went into this whole debut party looking for every single little thing that could go wrong, and you know what? Congratulations, you found them!"

"I did not!" Drizella protests. "I just wanted to protect—"

"You didn't even *try*!" Anastasia cuts her off. "Not one smile, not one nice word to a single person. I thought your glare alone would behead the Prince right in front of everyone."

"Why would I waste a single nice word on those simpletons?" Drizella shouts. "They didn't bother to have any for me."

"For *us*," Anastasia corrects her. "I was in that dressing room, too, you know. I heard everything, just as you did. And yes, you're mad at me for leaving, but you couldn't even bother to come find me, Drizella!"

"I had my own places to be," Drizella huffs, looking both sorrowful and defiant at the same time.

"What?" Anastasia shakes her head, trying to sort out what Drizella has just said. "I thought you stayed at the ball with Ella and Mother."

"Where were *you*?" Drizella counters, and in that moment, both sisters become very aware of the fact that, for the first time in their lives, they are each keeping a big secret from the other.

Neither of them says anything for a long time, both their chests heaving as they breathe hard with the force of their anger. It's as if all the evening's terrible events have been distilled down into this place, this moment, and Anastasia and Drizella finally have a place to store their fury, no matter how misguided it is.

"You seem different," Drizella finally says, then leans in closer. "Something happened."

"Yes, something did happen!" Anastasia says. "We were humiliated in front of the entire village at the palace, if you recall."

"No, this is different. You seem—" Drizella's about to start gesturing with an accusing finger at her sister's face, but suddenly there's a great stampeding sound, and both girls instinctively leap out of the way of their mother's carriage barreling up the road, the horses' hooves kicking up clumps of mud and dirt and soiling their outfits even more. Even at the fast pace, though, they can both see the driver swaying drunkenly in his seat.

"Well, at least someone had a good time tonight," Drizella mutters. "Come on, we better go."

"Do you think she recognized us?" Anastasia asks.

Drizella leans down to pick up her shoes. "She wouldn't have stopped even if she did."

❧

When they finally make it up the path and driveway to their front door, Drizella puts a hand on the knob, then turns back to Anastasia. She seems as if she's about to say something, but then hurt fills her eyes once more before she blinks it away, leaving a stoic, stubborn girl in its wake. Anastasia didn't know that she had the power to hurt Drizella like this, her sister who always seemed completely impenetrable. It feels like a weapon she doesn't know how to wield.

When they open the door, the house is dim and quiet, but it seems to almost be trembling with anger. Or maybe it's fear, Anastasia thinks as she creeps in behind Drizella, selfishly grateful that her sister is in front of her. Maybe the house can sense what's about to happen. Maybe it's seen enough terrible things in its lifetime to know how much worse things can get, and Anastasia feels even more of Dominic's light slip away as it disappears into the void of their home.

"Well, good evening," someone says, and both Anastasia and Drizella freeze in place, looking over to see their mother standing by the large hearth. There's a black cat tail poking out from underneath her skirt, and then Lucifer is slinking out to look at both of them. He seems almost pleased by the tension in the room. "No, please, don't stop moving now," their mother says. "The two of you seem to have no problem at all running away. Surely you can manage to come a few steps closer."

A very long time ago, when she was even littler than a little girl, there was a rare cyclone out on the horizon. Anastasia can still remember how the daytime went dark, almost black, and how it felt like all the air in the world had been sucked up into the sky. Her father grabbed both her and Drizella and tossed them into the root cellar, explaining to them that a huge storm was coming, but what Anastasia remembers most is the eerie quiet, and how it was shattered by the most ear-piercing whistle, just like a teakettle, nature raging over their heads and taking whatever it wanted, field by field, farm by farm, until everything around them was in tatters.

The silence in the house is that same way, deafening in its stillness, and Anastasia cringes, because if memory serves, the rage is about to begin.

"I wouldn't expect either of you to know this," their mother says, walking closer to them after Anastasia and Drizella stay rooted to the floor, "but the rest of the ball was absolutely beautiful. All of the parents looking at their ador-ing children, all of the young women so happy to be there."

Anastasia's knees are trembling under her dress. She can tell that Drizella's are doing the same next to her, and as her eyes adjust to the dim nighttime light, she can see Ella stand-ing back by the curtains, hiding in the shadows. Her eyes are wide and round, her hands clenched tight in the draperies.

"There was dancing, of course," Lady Tremaine contin-ues. "And the orchestra was so grand, so royal. The Prince even waltzed with a few of the girls. You can imagine how thrilled they were." She smiles a little bit, only it's not a smile at all. It's a grimace, a sneer, a warning.

"And as I watched these girls with His Royal Highness, all I could think about was how proud their mothers must be. And then I wondered to myself, and for most the evening, when it was that my two daughter became the most! Disgraceful! *Ingrates!*" Her voice rises with every word until it seems like the windows rattle on the word *ingrates*, and Anastasia shudders. The last time her mother screamed like this, Anastasia ended up in the tower.

"You have absolutely *humiliated* this family tonight!" Their mother continues to scream, punching a fist through the air to emphasize the word. "But more importantly, you have humiliated *me*! How am I ever supposed to show my face in this town again, knowing that my own daughters—my own flesh and blood—dared to pull the kind of stunt that both of you pulled this evening!"

Drizella opens her mouth, and Anastasia reaches back and grabs her arm, a silent plea with her sister to *please please please* not talk. Their mother has always been irritated and angry, but this is the kind of rage that sears itself into their skin, implanting memories on them forever. It's untouchable, unreachable, unstoppable. When a teakettle finally explodes, after all, boiling water flies everywhere.

Across from them, their mother's violent motions have made her hair start to tumble down, the gray streaks falling from her severe bun and revealing two small bald spots near the front of her hairline.

She looks so old, Anastasia realizes, and at the same time, she's acting like a child. It's a strange juxtaposition that makes Anastasia even more frightened, realizing that her mother's rage is going from anger to hysteria, that her veneer of icy calm has melted into an uncontained, white-hot fury that could quite possibly consume all of them.

"We're sorry," Drizella says when their mother pauses to take a breath. "Truly, Mother, we're very sorry." Behind her, Anastasia nods in agreement. "We didn't mean to disappoint you."

Their mother frowns, then begins to laugh. Ella is still behind her, frozen in her spot. "You didn't mean to disappoint me?" she mocks Drizella. "*Disappoint?* Is that what you think you did? No, no, darling, that's not it at all. You have completely and utterly *failed* me. That's what you did this evening." She walks toward them, and Anastasia and Drizella take a step back for every step she advances. "I keep you in this home, with food and shelter and blankets and heat and clothes and lessons, although I assume that those were a complete waste of money, after your little stunt tonight." She jabs a bony finger in their direction. "And yet all you ever do is fail me, again and again.

"You are both disappointments, that's always been a given, but this? Tonight? This was failure, the kind you cannot fix or repair. The village will see to that, I'm sure," she barks. "What prince—or what *man*, even—would want to court or marry you now? The two cowards who couldn't even keep their chins up at a simple party, who ran out of the room crying like children?"

It's as if she's reaching into a quiver and firing arrow after arrow right into Anastasia's body, their poison tips making the sting go deeper and further than she would have thought possible. Drizella is now fully trembling, but her head and chin are still high.

"You are all failures!" their mother continues, more hair spilling down over her shoulders. "All of you! *Your* father," she adds, pointing at Ella, "so weak that he went and died, and you two and *your* father!" She whirls on Drizzy and Annie. "You could have been like me, but instead you turned out just like him. You know he couldn't even stand the sight of you." She levels her gaze at them, and Anastasia feels the bow tighten, her aim narrow until the target is right over Anastasia's heart. "Why do you think he left?"

Anastasia's mouth opens, then closes as the poison of her mother's words spreads through her bloodstream, its coldness going everywhere, freezing her in place. The warmth of Dominic's embrace is long gone now, and she hates that her eyes start to well up with tears.

"Because of you!" Drizella suddenly shouts, and everyone in the room startles, even Lady Tremaine. Lucifer, who seemed to be enjoying the fight, suddenly dives back under their mother's skirts at the sound of Drizella's voice.

Drizella's not trembling with fear, Anastasia realizes with a jolt. She's trembling with *rage*.

"Because of you, you miserable, miserable woman!"

Drizella continues, her hands clenched into fists. "Because you're cruel and terrible and mean and you don't have a single drop of love in your entire body. All you do is bully and push and threaten, and you know what's worse? Nobody loves you, not even your own daughters! We never have! And we will *never* be like you, not *ever*!"

There's silence for a few terrible seconds, and then their mother starts to chuckle, then laugh. She's so close to them that Anastasia can see the backs of her teeth. "You stupid girl," she says, and her sharp incisors gleam in the moonlight that falls through the drawing room windows. She takes a step toward the girls, and Anastasia reaches for her sister to pull her back, but Drizella doesn't move.

"You may not want to be like me," their mother says quietly, her murmur louder than a howl, "but let's remember one thing, my darlings. You *are* me. You were born from me; you have my blood in your veins. It's a pity for me, of course, but you will never be able to outrun yourselves. It will catch up to you one way or another. When this youth"—she trails a fingernail down Drizella's cheek, and Anastasia gasps despite herself—"fades, when no one loves you, when you're left alone with no opportunities or options, we'll just see who you really are, Drizella. Named after my mother, did you know that? I hated my mother, too, as I'm sure she hated hers, and so on and so on . . ." She pats Drizella's cheek just a little too hard, enough to make Anastasia ready to spring into action.

"Well, blood is blood, after all. And one way or another, we all bleed."

She suddenly takes her hand off Drizella's face and turns back to the draperies, and toward the cowering girl hiding inside of them.

"But at least there's one person in this house who has none of my blood. Isn't that right, Ella?" Their mother turns and beckons her forward, acknowledging her for the first time, still smiling even though it looks like it hurts. "Come over here, my dear. That's it, right this way."

Stop, Anastasia thinks, trying with all her might to send Ella a message with her mind. *Stop. Run. Leave. Go.*

"Now," their mother says once Ella is closer to her, the girl still wise enough to stay out of arm's reach. "We know that Ella is not like any of us for many, many reasons, but a brand-new one appeared this evening."

Anastasia thinks of the golden, honeyed voice floating down toward the river, drifting over her and Dominic, and feels her hands go cold.

"It appears that our lovely little Ella has some semblance of talent. She can *sing*." Their mother says this as if she's announcing that Ella has a contagious, incurable disease. "Did either of you know about this?"

Anastasia shakes her head once. Drizella stays perfectly still.

Ella just trembles.

"How kind it was of her to showcase this hidden talent in front of everyone," their mother continues, taking a step toward Ella as Ella takes one step back, a slow and terrifying waltz. "And at such a moment, with you two running off and whining like little children, suddenly every single eye at the palace was on her." She gives Ella a wink, and Ella blinks furiously in response, almost as if she's twitching.

"Drizella," Anastasia whispers. She's not even sure what she needs, what she's asking for, but she's scared, and summoning her big sister is the only thing she knows how to do.

But Drizella doesn't respond.

Instead, it's Ella who speaks.

"I was only trying to distract from—"

It's as if her cautious sentence is the thing that finally summons the furious storm that's been brewing in their house, and suddenly their mother is moving, and so is Drizella, and Ella, and Anastasia, all of them coming together in the worst of ways.

Their mother is shouting, grabbing Ella's wrist in her wrought iron grip, and Ella is crying out, her face pained. "Mother, no!" Anastasia shouts. She doesn't like Ella, never has, and is certainly no fan of the stunt she pulled that evening.

But she doesn't want to see anyone actually hurt.

"Mother!" Drizella is shouting, and she tries to pull at her mother's dress, but her hands slip off the cheap material before she can pull her back. Ella is yelping almost like a wounded dog, the sound high-pitched, just like the storm's whistle had been, and Anastasia resists the urge to cover her ears and take shelter.

"Who said you had any right to open your mouth and utter a single word, much less a note?" Filled with rage, their mother seems to tower over Ella, who's crouching down as much as the woman's grasp will let her. She's twisting her wrist now, pulling hard to bring her back up to her full height, and Ella cries out again. "Nobody will remember you by the time I'm done with you, that's for sure," their mother mutters.

"Stop, Mother! Let her go!" Drizella cries, this time trying to grab Ella, but she's yanked away as their mother begins to half march, half drag her through the room and toward the back staircase, where—

Oh, no.

"Mother!" Anastasia screams. "No, don't do that to her! She doesn't—It was just a song, that's all!"

Mother, please! I won't go in the kitchen again, I promise! Please, Mother!

Drizella, sobbing alongside Anastasia, trying to hang on to her sister even as their mother furiously tugs her up the rickety stairs.

Their mother whirls on them, sending Ella into a half spiral that has her crying out in pain, using her free hand to clutch at the woman's tight fingers. "Do you feel sorry for her?" their mother says. "Do you, Anastasia? Would you like to take her punishment for her, in that case?"

Anastasia's vision goes blurry for a moment.

I'll never bring up Father again! I'll never do it again. . . .

Yes, I'll make sure of that. You'll remember this, Anastasia, if it's the last thing I ever do to you.

Anastasia still wakes up thinking of that tower, even though it's been more than a year since she was locked up in it. She wants to be strong enough to say yes, to shove Ella aside and march up the stairs herself.

"That's what I thought," her mother says with a sneer when Anastasia doesn't answer. "What about you, Drizella? Would *you* like to take her place?"

Drizella is blank, almost stone-faced, and she's not looking at her mother or Anastasia or even Ella. Her eyes are fixed somewhere else, almost as if her mind has left the room entirely.

"Please," Ella is sobbing, now dangling from their mother's tight fist. "Please, please . . ."

"Like I said," their mother says to them, yanking Ella back up and making her cry out. "We'll just see who you *really* are."

And then she's hurrying away, dragging Ella behind her as she stumbles to keep up, half running and half pulling as they begin to ascend the rickety wooden staircase.

The splinters in Anastasia's ankles and feet from being dragged up the stairs, the way they scraped up her knees and toes and made tiny bloodstains in the wood grain. The sound of the lock clicking shut, the way the panic crawled up through Anastasia's body until it felt like she was made of spiders, everything crawling all over her, around her, in that terrible unknown darkness.

Anastasia's heart was pounding against her ribs so hard that she thought it might just burst right out of her body, the same way it's doing now, her panic for Ella all too real, because she knows what she's about to endure, and she wouldn't wish it on her worst enemy.

The screaming eventually starts to dissipate as they ascend the stairs, and Anastasia bends over at the waist and clutches the settee with a shaking hand. "Drizella," she whispers, gasping for air, and that seems to be the thing that shakes Drizella from her spell. She looks down at her sister, then pries her hand off the furniture and leads her through the house and out the back door, taking her toward their old, decrepit pumpkin patch.

The cold and damp bricks pressing into her freezing skin. The rats' bodies brushing against her in the night, no matter how tightly she curled herself into a ball. The bone-crushing loneliness of thinking that no one was ever going to save her, that no hero was going to ride up and rescue her the way her childhood storybooks had promised.

"Breathe," Drizella keeps saying, and it's not like Anastasia isn't trying, but she just can't seem to make her lungs work. She collapses onto the same pumpkin that she had shared with Dominic as Drizella takes a seat next to her, eyeing Anastasia warily.

"Breathe, Annie," she says again.

"I'm trying!" Anastasia says, wheezing, putting one hand to her chest. She wishes Dominic was here with her now, holding her again, whisking her away from the horrific chaos and violence of the evening. Was it really just a few hours ago that she was dancing with him? Can two things wonderful and terrible both happen in the space of a single evening? The faint memory of his all-encompassing warmth tells her that they can, and she shivers and tries to breathe.

"What are we going to do?" Anastasia whispers once she can speak again.

"About Ella? Nothing." Drizella gestures up toward the tower, where Ella's sobs are beginning to grow in strength now that she realizes the full extent of her torment.

"There's nothing we can do," Drizella continues, unaware of Anastasia's flashbacks. "Even if we took her place, she'd find another way to punish her. Probably worse, too."

Anastasia nods, hating that her sister is right, just like she always is.

"Drizzy, I'm sorry," she says quietly. "I'm sorry I left you behind."

Drizella sits for a moment, then reaches out a hand to Anastasia without even looking up at her. Anastasia grasps it immediately, squeezing her cold fingers around Drizella's trembling ones.

"I know," Drizella says. "I'm sorry, too." She's grinding

her jaw back and forth as she glances up at the full moon. "It'll never be a star," she whispers, then drops her gaze to the ground before tightening her grip on Anastasia's hand. "Annie," she says. "I have something I need to tell you."

Anastasia pictures Dominic, feels his warm arms around her, hears his soft laugh like the peal of church bells on a wedding day, joyous and free with the promise of so many good things ahead. "I have something I need to tell you, too," she replies.

And as they talk, Ella's voice once again floats down around them, but this time it's the sound of tortured, terrified sobs. Gone is the beauty and light.

Even under the glow of the full moon, tonight only darkness remains.

13

DRIZELLA

Drizella spends the next twenty-four hours reeling from the events of their debut night.

And then she starts making a plan.

Lady Tremaine hasn't come out of her room in two days, which means Ella hasn't eaten or had anything to drink in two days, either. Drizella suspects that Anastasia is sneaking food to her under the door, but she can't be sure, and either way, she wants no part of it. If Lady Tremaine finds out that the girls have been helping Ella, she'll lock them all away, and Drizella has no time for that.

Because she needs to get out, get to Madame Lambert's studio, and get to Paris.

And despite all the terribleness of the past several days, it still makes Drizella smile to remember her sister's face as she told her about Madame Lambert and her upcoming trip to the Sorbonne, and how she invited Drizella to come along as her assistant. "I don't know what the Sorbonne even is," Anastasia said breathlessly, her eyes round as the moon, "but it sounds *amazing*."

"It is," Drizella assured her. Not that she's ever been past their village's boundaries, but it must be amazing if it's in Paris. Why else would Madame Lambert be going there?

Still, nothing could have prepared Drizella for the fact that Anastasia has a suitor who works at the palace. Truly, *nothing*.

"What?!" she cried. They were still in the pumpkin patch on that terrible night, their voices low, their heads together as if they could hide outside with each other, far away from their mother's fury. Anastasia flapped her arms before slapping her hands over her sister's mouth. "What?" Drizella said again, this time muffled by Anastasia's palms. "How did you even meet?"

Once she heard the whole story, she was flabbergasted. But, if she was being very honest with herself, she was glad that Anastasia had someone to run to after that terrible recital. She had found comfort in Madame Lambert, the woman's being the maternal presence that Drizella had desperately needed, and it warmed her to think that Anastasia had someone to take care of her, as well.

Ella had not had anyone, of course, but Drizella couldn't think about that right now. They didn't have time.

"Dominic said that we should run away to Paris," Anastasia said. "I wonder if he really would."

"You should ask him," Drizella pressed her, leaning forward to make her point once her sister had uncovered her mouth. "Really, Anastasia. We could go together, be there together without *her*."

"But what about Ella?" Anastasia bit at her lower lip. The desperate sobs coming from the tower had softened into steady, quiet weeping, which was agonizing in a different way. Defeat always sounds worse than fury.

"We can always come back for her," Drizella says after a thoughtful few seconds. "Think about it. We'll work, make money, or Dominic can find a job and we'll figure it out. We could even just send her money and tell her to come to us. Lady Tremaine can't stop us, Annie. We're almost grown. We can make our own lives."

It sounded so simple, so straightforward. Madame Lambert had once said that the shortest distance between two points was a straight line, meaning that the solution to a problem tended to be the easiest one, and this was exactly that. Leave, make money, get Ella out, and the world would be wide open to them.

It was supposed to be just that easy.

�֍

On Monday morning, Drizella stays in bed until the sun is too bright to ignore, then dresses and goes downstairs to forage for her own breakfast. Both girls know all too well that the kitchen is off-limits, but with Ella still in the tower, they have to get their own food. Drizella finds the heel from a loaf of bread and some strawberry jam left over from the summer. The simple nature of her breakfast appeals to her, and as she pours hot water over tea, she thinks that this is what her life will be like in Paris: making food, preparing for her day, using her mind to come up with plans and solutions to some of nature's most complex problems, with Madame Lambert smiling benevolently at her.

The sun diffuses through the window into the kitchen, and Drizella takes that as a good sign.

Her mother is still in her room, she and Lucifer hidden behind her closed doors without even a sliver of light peeking out from the cracks. Drizella doesn't know what she is doing in there, and she doesn't care. She just knows she has to act fast, before her mother emerges and they have to resume tip-toeing around her, waiting for the house to settle once again like feathers after a pillow fight.

There is no time to waste.

This morning, Drizella slipped her stepfather's office key out from underneath her mattress and tucked it into her dress pocket. She never put it back that day after Ella caught her in there, not wanting her stepsister to know where it was kept. She pats it now as she walks toward the office, reassured by its heavy weight. Her heart is pounding fast from knowing that she is breaking into her stepfather's office even as her mother is just one floor away, but Drizella has no choice. She has to take the initiative. She has to make things happen for herself.

It kind of sounds, she realizes with a bit of a sinking feeling, like the sort of thing her mother would do.

The house is silent as Drizella turns the key and lets herself into the room once more, shutting the door behind her just in case anyone comes snooping along. She feels far more emboldened than she did the last time. Her stepfather's office now seems merely dusty and shabby instead of wondrous. It still looks as if no one has been in here for years, which is perfect.

Drizella moves fast, opening up the top desk drawer and looking for paper and fresh ink. The ink, miraculously, is sealed and still usable, and she grabs the quill off the desk and smooths out a piece of paper on the blotter. Her hand is shaking, she realizes; it's been so long since she's written any-thing. School was just recitation and repetition, writing lines over and over again until the words looked like squiggles. Her penmanship is good, of course, but her thoughts are now far more difficult to organize.

Drizella takes a deep breath and sits down in the chair. "What would Lady Tremaine say?" she whispers to herself.

Then she writes the opposite of that.

My dear Madame Lambert,

It is with great pleasure and respect that I hear about your offer to my daughter Drizella. As you know, she is quite bright and would so benefit from this opportunity, and I cannot express my gratitude enough to you. Paris will be a wonderful experience for her, and my only regret is that I cannot, due to time and money, provide it for her. But she has my permission to go, with my only request being that she send home weekly letters so that her sister Anastasia and I can still keep in touch with her.

It will be hard to say goodbye to my eldest daughter, even if it is only temporary. She is named after my mother, after all, and the affection I feel for Drizella is what I'm sure my own mother felt for me, God rest her sweet soul. It is so hard to see your children grow and thrive as they leave the nest, but I imagine it would be so much more painful to see them stay stagnant and wither on the vine, as they say.

I regret I cannot deliver this letter in person, but I trust my darling Drizella will get it to you on my behalf. I trust her, but not nearly as much as I love her.

With warmest regards and deepest respect,

Lady Tremaine

Drizella reads it through twice, surprised to find her eyes wet after the second read-through. What would her life be like if this were how Lady Tremaine really spoke, really felt? Would she and Anastasia fight less, do more, be happier? What would it have been like to have a mother who openly declared her love for you, who never made you scrabble for crumbs of affection like chickens pecking each other for food?

Drizella blinks twice to dry her eyes, then shakes her head a little. No point in worrying about that now. Her time with Madame Lambert has taught her that you can solve a problem only by looking at the truth of it, and to pretend or wonder about anything besides the facts is a waste of time.

Drizella's mother does not love her.

It's time to leave.

She waves the paper to dry the ink, then carefully rolls it up and slips it into her pocket next to the office key. It's strange to think that she'll probably never be in this room again, and she wonders if her father would have felt the same way had this been his home. Would he have stood here and looked at the big windows, the stacks upon stacks of books, committing it all to memory? Or would he have done what he did with his family, just walked out and never looked back?

Drizella gives the desk a quick goodbye pat, then turns to go. She's not sad to leave at all, and she tries to ignore the voice in her head, the one that has started to sound an awful lot like Lady Tremaine, as she locks the door behind her for the last time.

You're just like your father.

Better to be like my father than like my mother, Drizella thinks with a satisfied smirk, then goes down the hall, stopping only to grab her coat and bonnet before heading out the door.

⚜

It's not particularly hard to leave the house during the day. Even if her mother finally emerges from her bedroom and demands to know where Drizella is, she knows Anastasia will cover for her. Plus, with Ella locked away, it's easy to say that Drizella had to go into town to get some food: butter, salt, staples that they can't make on their run-down farm.

The farm. Drizella scoffs to herself. She hates the farm. Now that the possibility of Paris is on the horizon, their sagging barn and haggard-looking animals seem even more dreary and dilapidated than before. Paris will have lights and color and bridges and architecture, everything that Drizella cannot yet get, and she quickens her step as she walks, desperate to close the space between her and her brand-new adventure.

She knocks before opening up the door to Madame Lambert's studio. "Hello?" she calls. There are boxes everywhere, the walls and shelves now half bare, the plants already tucked away into their own separate carrier, and Drizella's heart leaps somewhere between her mouth and throat. "Hello?" she calls again, stepping into the room. Madame Lambert couldn't have left without her, right? She could never leave without even saying goodbye, especially not after promising Drizella the possibility of Paris, of a life—

"Hello, my dear!" Madame Lambert says, and Drizella's knees go weak with relief. "I had no idea you were coming by today. How lovely to see you." She smiles, her face as kind as it was two nights ago, and it takes all of Drizella's reserves not to run toward her for a hug, to feel that comforting warmth again, to feel cared for and safe.

Instead, she shuts the door behind her and digs into her pocket for "Lady Tremaine's" note. "I brought this," she says, thrusting it toward Madame Lambert like it's a hot potato and not a permission slip. "My mother, she's . . . ill right now—she can't leave the house—but she wanted me to give it to you."

Madame Lambert raises a concerned eyebrow. "Oh dear, your poor mother," she says. "Does she need medicine? I just made a new blend of tea. Perhaps I could—"

"No!" Drizella yelps, then clears her throat and tries to look as serene as she can. "No, thank you, she's just resting. She gets terrible headaches." She *gives* terrible headaches is a more accurate statement, but Drizella reassures herself that it's just one little white lie, that it will all be worth it soon enough.

"But I told her about your offer," she continues, and she once again extends the note to Madame Lambert. "And she wrote this and told me to give it to you."

"Well, let's see, then," Madame Lambert says, patting the desk. "I know my glasses are around here somewhere. I just had—oh!" She laughs to herself as she glances down and sees her reading glasses on a chain around her neck. "I swear, they would have bitten me if they had been any closer. Now, where were we?"

She puts the spectacles on the edge of her nose and frowns at the letter, reading it without even moving her lips the way Drizella does. Drizella stays still, trying to ignore her quick heartbeat and sweaty palms, acting like she hasn't forged a letter from her mother in order to secure her freedom.

Madame Lambert reads for a long, long time, then removes her glasses and carefully looks up at Drizella. "Your mother wrote this?" she asks.

Drizella nods without any hesitation whatsoever.

"Well, she seems to be quite loving toward you," Madame Lambert says. "Although I do recall that it sounded like you were having your difficulties the other night . . ." Her voice trails off, and she sits down at her worktable and pats the space across from her.

"Sit down, my girl."

"But the letter—" Drizella starts to say. She needs an answer, needs this panicky, desperate feeling to stop swelling inside her chest, needs to know.

"We'll discuss the letter in a moment," Madame Lambert says, gesturing toward a chair.

Drizella sits down, keeping her hands in her lap so that she doesn't leave sweaty palm prints on the table.

"How are you doing?" Madame Lambert asks her. "You were quite a sight when you left here last, I don't mind saying. I've been thinking about you, hoping you're feeling a little better."

"I'm fine," Drizella says, and then smiles.

Madame Lambert looks a bit doubtful. "You had quite a difficult time," she says. "Is your sister doing all right?"

"She's fine, too," Drizella says. "We're all fine now."

Madame Lambert laughs a little. "Drizella, if I didn't know better, I'd say your house was on fire and you were in a hurry to get back and put it out."

Drizella laughs, too, even though it comes out sounding garbled and weak. "I apologize," she says. "I'm just anxious to hear what you have to say."

Her face softens into the same expression Drizella saw on

Saturday evening, concerned but also reassuring. "Well, my dear, as touching as this note is, I'd feel much better speaking with your mother in person just to make sure that—"

"She doesn't leave the house," Drizella blurts out. "That often, anyway. And she doesn't like people coming over, either. She's very . . . private. And shy. After my father left, she became very reclusive."

When she started speaking, Drizella thought that what she was saying was a lie, but as she talks, she realizes that, for once, she's telling the truth. Her mother *is* reclusive. Even at the debut ball that evening, Drizella never saw her speaking to anyone else, just a few respectful nods here and there. And she doesn't leave the house that often, hardly ever now that the girls are old enough to go into town by themselves, preferring instead to huff around in their hallways, telling Ella what to do, letting her oppressive, suspicious personality set the mood in every single room that she enters.

"Well, I'm very sorry to hear that," Madame Lambert says. "I'm sure that your father leaving had quite a negative effect on all of you, including your mother. But if it's at all possible—"

"Madame Lambert," Drizella says. The shortest distance between two points is a straight line, after all. "I truly do understand why you'd like to speak to my mother, but what I just said is, unfortunately, very true. And I'm just afraid that if I stay any longer in that house with her, I'll end up that way, too." Drizella bites back the tears that she can feel rising up. She's already annoyed with herself for crying so much on Saturday night, and she'll be damned if she lets the waterworks start up again. She has no time for emotions right now.

"If you'll let me, I would love to accompany you to Paris and assist you in your laboratory. It would be an honor. But even if you say no, I *will* be leaving this village and my house, because I am not going to stay there for another minute when I know I could be somewhere else. If I don't go with you, I will *still* go, I promise you that. So please let me come with you. Please."

Drizella's lower lip is trembling, so she bites down hard on it, willing her face to stay still. Her mother used to say, when ranting about their father, that he was a terrible cardplayer, that he could never say no to just one more hand, one more prospect, and that was the reason they lived in such poverty. But after her speech, Drizella feels like she'd be pretty good at cards. She even believed herself for a minute.

"Well," Madame Lambert says slowly, glancing down at the table, then looking up at Drizella with a sly grin. "I have to say that I would also be honored to have you assist me."

"Is that a yes?" Drizella cries before she can help herself, and Madame Lambert barely manages to nod before Drizella lets out a joyful shriek and hops up to run around the desk and hug her.

"Oof, my dear, goodness!" she says, even though she's laughing. "I must say, I don't think I've seen you so happy!"

"That's because I've never been this happy!" Drizella says, squeezing the tiny woman with all her might. "Oh, thank you! Thank you! I promise, I'll be the best, most quiet, most studious assistant you've ever had!"

Madame Lambert chuckles as she pats Drizella's back, then lets go of her. "Well, if that is indeed true, then you can begin by helping me pack up my studio. We leave in three nights' time, and will you just look at this mess!" She throws her arms up in the air and lets her hands smack down at her sides. "Globes and plants and jars and paints and, goodness, everything else!"

Drizella's smiling so hard that her ears hurt. "It all sounds wonderful to me," she says. "Put me to work. I'm ready to assist."

The two women spend the next hour or so packing up the studio. Drizella takes great care as she carefully wraps up jars and specimens and test tubes in soft, worn paper, tucking them into boxes the way mothers might tuck their babies into bed at night. "I'll see you soon," she whispers to a row of old magnifying glasses, giving them a quick pat, and feels the warmth bubble up in her chest at the idea of unwrapping them all in Paris.

When she leaves, she stops at the door, one hand on the

doorknob, her bonnet tied around her neck. "Thank you again," she says to Madame Lambert, then lets go and gives her another hug. Drizella barely recognizes herself. She's just hugging all the time now! It's amazing for Drizella to feel how different she is when she's not around Lady Tremaine, not being suffocated by her oppressive darkness. She feels so much lighter, like she could float away from happiness, from the sheer *possibility* of happiness.

"Of course, my dear," Madame Lambert says softly. "I will see you here at seven o'clock in three nights' time. We'll take the overnight train so we don't have to travel in the heat of the day. Don't be late!"

The train! Drizella can barely contain herself.

"I will be here" is all she says, though, then shoots another grin at her brand-new mentor. She feels like she has to memorize everything, memorize this moment so she never forgets it, never once takes it for granted.

She imprints the feeling on her heart, then leaves the studio for the last time, making sure to shut the door softly behind her as she goes.

She's almost out of the village when she sees a royal carriage heading toward her, and she scurries out of the way before it nearly runs her over. She frowns at the rudeness, then sees a young man hanging off the back of the carriage as it rushes past her. He has dark hair and dark eyes, and even though she's never seen him before, Drizella is fairly certain that, based on Anastasia's description, she knows who he is.

She runs the rest of the way home.

The house is still dark, the draperies drawn against the heat of the afternoon, and Drizella rushes upstairs, looking everywhere for Anastasia. She finds her in her room, lying on her bed and carefully brushing out an old doll's hair for lack of anything else to do.

"Annie!" Drizella hisses, and Anastasia startles so hard that she falls off the bed.

"Oops," Drizella says.

"What was that for?" Anastasia cries. Her hair is in her face, and she tries blowing it back, without much success.

"I was just in town," Drizella says, clutching the doorway to support herself as she catches her breath. She might be getting good at hugging, but running is still tricky. "But there's a carriage there. A royal one. I think I spotted Dominic! I saw that little—" Her hands go to her hairline, twisting a small piece of hair up in the air to imitate his cowlick.

Anastasia is up and off the floor in a flash. "Oh, my goodness," she says.

"Go, go!" Drizella says to her. "You need to talk to him now! I'm going to Paris on Thursday night."

Anastasia freezes mid-frenzy. "You are?" she says, her voice suddenly small. "Really?"

"Go talk to him!" Drizella says in a fierce whisper, lest they disturb their mother and ruin all of their hastily laid plans. "You can come, you can follow us!"

Anastasia is back in action, quickly running her hands through her hair before dashing out of the room. But then she doubles back, going up to Drizella and putting her hands on her shoulders before giving her a kiss on the cheek.

"We're getting out," she whispers with a cheeky grin, then squeezes her shoulders before hurrying down the stairs. Drizella waves her away, her own smile wide and true, before slipping back into her own bedroom and shutting the door behind her, the house falling silent yet again.

The tower is especially quiet this afternoon. It seems that Ella has finally stopped crying.

14

ANASTASIA

A lifetime of bruised elbows, skinned knees, and bumped shins has made Anastasia realize that she'll never be considered athletic by any means.

But this afternoon, she runs like the wind.

Her bonnet bounces on her back as she dashes toward town, the dust kicking up and settling into the skirts of her dress. Just thinking about seeing Dominic again makes her pulse pound under her skin, and between that and the physical exertion, she's nearly breathless by the time she gets to the village, her eyes scanning wildly for the royal purple carriage that once nearly killed her and now feels like the only thing that could give her life.

When she doesn't see it upon first glance, she heads toward her music studio. It seems like years since she's been in there, practicing without any improvement whatsoever, but really, maybe it's only been several weeks? Anastasia feels like she's lost track of time entirely, that she can gauge the hours and days only by how long it's been since she last saw Dominic and how soon she'll lay eyes on him again. He's the sun in her sky, she thinks, and feels warm all over.

She hurries as fast as she can without attracting any extra attention to herself, searching down every empty street and dusty road. Maybe the carriage was just passing through? Maybe Drizella didn't see him at all? Maybe Anastasia got her hopes up for nothing and her disappointment will weigh her down for the rest of the day, pulling her back into her bed so she can hide there, dreaming instead of living.

No, she thinks. He's here. She's going to find him. And she will be damned if Drizella goes to Paris without her, Dominic right by her side. Anastasia isn't used to this sweet new air she's breathing, the kind that's full of light and hope and all good things, and she wants to have it for as long as possible, as long as they both shall live.

She's currently breathing a lot of that air, huffing and puffing as she hurries around corners, looking everywhere for the carriage. Just as she's about to give up in frustration, she spots a dash of purple behind a large building, and her feet seem to leap before her heart does, pushing her toward what seems to be a new millinery.

And then she gets closer and sees a shock of dark hair, hears a laugh, and feels the world settle around her.

"Monsieur?" she says tentatively, and Dominic turns around, his smile turning brighter before realizing his place.

"How can I assist you, Mademoiselle Tremaine?" he says, bowing as she gives him a wobbly curtsy. It feels so strange and silly to be formal with him after their evening spent on the palace grounds, and as they both come back up, they exchange small, secret grins.

"I was wondering if I may speak with you for a moment?" Anastasia says, trying to sound as grown-up as possible. It honestly feels more like she's playing dress-up in her mother's clothes (which, of course, she never did, because their mother was not *that* kind of mother), pretending to be an adult when she really feels like exactly what she is: a nervous, lovesick teenage girl.

"Of course, Mademoiselle," Dominic says, his eyes nearly dancing with glee. He's really liking this whole "mademoiselle" thing, she can tell, and she has to resist the urge to slap his arm when he offers it to her. Instead, she fits her hand into the crook of his elbow and follows him around the corner under the watchful gaze of two other courtiers, both of whom are snickering under their breath.

They're not fooling anyone, Anastasia thinks, and a bashful color blooms in her cheeks.

As soon as they're down an alley and hidden from view, Anastasia throws her arms around him, burying her face in the starched, stiff collar of his jacket. Dominic smells like hay and sunshine and that palace smell, so new and yet still so familiar that it makes her shiver. "Well, hello," he says, running his arms around her back and holding her tight. "What's all this about?"

"My sister saw the royal carriage and told me you might be here," Anastasia says, then looks up at him and lets him kiss her quickly. "If anyone sees us—"

"They won't," he replies. "You look much better than the last time we were together."

Anastasia rolls her eyes a little. "Let's forget about that night," she says. "Or at least the terrible parts of it."

"So . . . this part wasn't terrible?" he says, leaning in to kiss her again, still chaste but longer this time, and Anastasia has to put her hand on his shoulder to brace herself.

"Hmm, I can't quite remember," she teases as he kisses her one more time. "All right, we have to be serious now."

Dominic pulls a mock serious face, his brow so furrowed that deep wrinkles appear between his eyes, and Anastasia giggles at his expression. There's no silliness in her life, she thinks, nothing fun or amusing. It's just fear and walking on tiptoes, waiting for the next bad thing to happen, and in that moment, Anastasia realizes that if she ever loses Dominic, she'll lose the very best parts of herself, as well.

"I know a few weeks ago, we talked about how you'd travel to Paris if you could." She takes a deep breath before continuing. "Would you be willing to go there with me?"

He smiles. "Sure. Why not?"

"No, I mean, are you *serious*?" She stares at him, lowering her face so she can look up into his eyes. "Because I am if you are. My sister, she's going to Paris with her mentor on Thursday night. We could go with them."

Dominic blinks down at her. "Okay, now it's my turn to ask if you're serious. Do you realize what you're suggesting?"

"Of course I do! It's what we talked about. We could start our lives. We wouldn't have to answer to the palace, to my mother, to anyone. It could just be us, together."

Dominic's expression keeps going back and forth between amusement, confusion, and affection, even as he takes a step back to regard her. He blinks several times, runs a hand over his mouth, faces away, then turns back to her.

Anastasia has no idea if any of that is good or bad, so she holds her ground.

"You think it's just that easy to be on your own, Anastasia?" he asks. "I've been on my own before. It's not as easy as it sounds. It's not as romantic, either."

"But we wouldn't be on our own," Anastasia protests. "That's what I'm trying to tell you. We'll have each other. If I have you, I can do anything, I know it."

He still looks unsure, so Anastasia presses harder. "Dominic," she says. "This is the only thing that I've ever wished for in my entire life. And I don't know how to choose between my sister and freedom and staying here with you, so please don't make me do that."

Dominic looks down at her. "You really want this, don't you?"

"I really do." She looks up shyly at him, then gives his chin a sweet kiss. "I do," she whispers.

Dominic nods slowly as he picks up a lock of her hair and twirls it around in his fingers. "I have a little bit of money saved," he says. "It's not much, but it's something."

"It's more than I have," Anastasia says. She's so twitterpated at this point that she hasn't thought through any of the logistics, but love has a way of being better than everything else, including critical thinking skills and logical reasoning.

That's why it's so wonderful.

"I'm sure I could find work somewhere," Dominic says. "I've picked up more than a few skills at the palace."

"Plus it's Paris," Anastasia says. "There are jobs everywhere. I could work in a factory or mill, or maybe a fabric store or dress shop." She can see herself now, being so dressed up to go to work in the morning, coming home at night to the love of her life, sixteen years old and on top of a world that she's never even seen before.

"So are we going to Paris?" Dominic asks, tucking the lock of hair behind her ear, then pulling up her bonnet so the sun isn't on her face. "It sounds like a yes to me."

"Yes," Anastasia smiles, then leans forward to try to kiss him again, but the brim of her bonnet hits his forehead, jolting them apart. "Oops! Sorry, sorry."

He winces even as he laughs, rubbing at the sore spot. "Perhaps I was a bit hasty," he says, then lowers the bonnet, kisses her again, and then pulls it back up. "Thursday night?"

"Seven o'clock," Anastasia clarifies. "They're taking the night train."

"I'll get tickets," Dominic says. "If you're late, I'm still going without you." He winks and laughs, though, then picks her up and twirls her around, his arms tight around her waist, holding her close, and Anastasia's brain chants the word *safe* over and over again.

This is happening, Anastasia thinks. *This is actually happening. I'm making my* life *happen, life isn't happening to* me. She's taken matters into her own hands, changed her fate, and in just three nights' time, she'll be a whole new person—no matter what.

She'll burn the world down to get what she wants.

Just like her mother.

✤

Anastasia walks home in a happy daze, kicking at the dirt with the toe of her slipper as if she's doing a little dance. Will she dance in Paris? Probably. Will she eat rich food and drink wine and light candles and decorate her home so that Dominic is happy there? Of course she will. Anastasia wants light everywhere, all of the curtains open day and night, candles and oil lanterns illuminating every space so that there's never any darkness in her life ever again. Even if they don't have any money, even if they're poor for the rest of their lives together, it will still be okay, because they'll be together.

Anastasia is still young enough, of course, to believe this.

Drizella is thrilled at the news of Anastasia and Dominic's joining her and Madame Lambert, or at least as thrilled as Drizella can get. The two sisters talk and plan and talk some more, and at a quarter to seven on Thursday evening, Anastasia stands in her bedroom and lets her gaze fall on everything one last time. She grew up in this bedroom, after all, smiled and cried and dreamed and lost. She was a little girl in here, but now she is grown, going on to her own life, one that she can make for herself, and the feeling causes new and strange emotions to bubble up in her chest.

She's packed just the basics: a few dresses and under-things, her brush and comb, a tiny mirror that her father gave her back when she was a small child, a leaf she pressed that is the exact same size and color as a heart, and a pair of sleeping clothes for nighttime. Anastasia gives a fleeting thought to where, exactly, they will sleep, but she brushes it aside for now. If she's with Dominic, she can sleep anywhere, even on the streets of Paris if she must.

She takes a final look at her room, then closes the door on this chapter of her life and goes to meet her sister.

Anastasia finds Drizella inside her room checking her packed things, her hand smoothing over her perfectly made bed like it's a kitten. Not a kitten like Lucifer, of course. An actual cuddly, friendly kitten.

"I never thought I would say this," she says, "but I'm so happy."

"Me too," Anastasia says. "There's an entire world out there, Drizzy, and we're actually going to get to see it." It makes her eyes glisten, the sudden rush of tears a surprise to herself even as she quickly wipes them away.

"You big crybaby." Drizella giggles. "But yes."

Anastasia watches as Drizella pats her bed one last time, and then they leave the room together. Drizella doesn't glance back once, doesn't even flinch when her door clicks shut behind them. "Come on," she says. "We need to hurry. It's already getting late."

"Where are we—" Anastasia starts to say when they hear footsteps on the rickety back stairs, and both sisters freeze.

"Is that . . . ?" Anastasia whispers.

"Yes," Drizella replies.

They wait until the footsteps stop, and then there's the unmistakable sound of a door being unlocked and opened, the hinges creaking with rust and age.

The girls stay absolutely silent as they place their luggage inside Drizella's room and head down the staircase, tiptoeing toward the back of the house. Even though the sun is still up in the sky, this part of the house is always dark, and Anastasia hangs on to Drizella's skirts as they walk.

"Stop pulling at me," Drizella says, slapping at her hands, but there's no malice in her touch. Anastasia grabs her hand and hangs on to that instead, and this time, Drizella doesn't protest.

Their mother's voice is soft in a way that's neither reassuring nor comforting. "Do you think you've stayed here long enough?" she's asking, the words floating down the stairs. Anastasia presses her forehead against Drizella's shoulder blades and takes a deep breath. She knows that tone all too well. She knows how cruel it can be.

"Y-yes!" Ella sobs out her response, and both sisters can hear the desperation and exhaustion in her voice. She sounds wrecked, even more upset than she was the night her father died, and in the quiet hallway, Anastasia can hear Drizella swallow hard.

"I'll never do it again!" she adds. "I promise, I'll never sing again. I won't ever—"

"What have I said about not speaking unless spoken to?"

Drizella swears under her breath. Anastasia closes her eyes. "Stop talking, Ella," she whispers. "Just *stop*."

But the girl is too far gone. "I swear!" she continues. "I can't stay in here another night. The rats . . ."

Anastasia shivers, and Drizella squeezes her hand hard.

"Well, maybe you can sing for them the way you did for all of the lovely people at the ball." Their mother's voice is so sweet that it's poisonous. "Another day or two should be a good reminder of that. Or perhaps a few more. Maybe a week. Maybe even forever."

Ella bursts into tears again, pleading even as the sisters hear the door click shut and lock, even as her cries turn into moans. Anastasia and Drizella scurry fast, heading back toward the drawing room and picking up something, anything, that will make them look busy, like they haven't heard a word of what was just said, like Anastasia's hands aren't trembling violently.

"Girls," their mother says, and they both look up with innocent eyes. If she asks why Anastasia's so flushed, she thinks, she'll just say that she got a bit too much sun today.

"I have developed a severe headache and am going to retire to bed early tonight." Their mother smiles a bit, then pats her thinning hair. "I'll see you soon. Be my good girls while I'm asleep."

The way she says it makes it sound like a threat.

They wait a few minutes after the door shuts behind her, Anastasia's needlepoint project trembling right along with her, Drizella's book held upside down as Ella's moans turn back into racking sobs.

"Should we . . . ?" Anastasia finally says.

"No." Drizella is insistent. "Absolutely not. What if Mother comes back and finds us up there? What if she's just playing a trick to see if we'll disobey her? We have to get going, Annie."

Anastasia bites her lip, her eyes drifting toward the back of the house. "She just sounds . . . I know how she feels, Drizzy. It's so awful."

Drizella's shoulders slump a little bit. "Fine," she finally says. "But just for a minute, all right? Then we head out."

Anastasia's already running out of the room, though.

They both climb gingerly up the stairs, lest this be the day that the splintered steps finally give out and send them plummeting to the ground. Underneath the first step, a pair of green eyes squints at them, Lucifer's tail swishing before he pounces at their feet. "Quit it, you," Drizella says, giving him a nudge with her foot, and Lucifer hisses in sulky defeat.

Ella's sobs cut off abruptly once she hears them. "Hello?" she calls.

"It's just us," Anastasia says. "Me and Drizella."

"Please let me out!" Ella sobs, and there's a banging on the tower door, insistent and strong, Ella's fist seeming to almost break through the wood. "Please, I'm so sorry, I'm sorry! I'll never sing again. I never meant—"

"Stop," Drizella says, but not unkindly. "I mean it. Stop. You'll make yourself sick."

Anastasia sinks down to the floor, resting her head against the door. "Ella," she says. "We can't let you out. You know that. She'll lock all three of us in there, and then what?"

She and Drizella exchange silent glances. They both know what. If they get locked into that tower, they'll never be able to catch the train to Paris.

"Just breathe," Anastasia says, hearing Ella's gasps. "I know what it's like in there, trust me."

"Then you know I need to *get out of here!*" Ella cries.

Drizella drops to the floor beside her sister, then stretches her palm underneath the crack of the door. "Here," she says. "Look down. Take my hand."

There's a brief silence before Ella's shaking fingers slip into Drizella's hand. Her nails are raw, the cuticles and nail beds bitten down to nubs and scabs. "See?" Drizella says, and Anastasia is reminded of all the times that her sister has been there for her after a nightmare, straightforward and steady, never sentimental. "We're here."

Anastasia leans forward and puts her own hand over theirs, and for a minute or two, the only sound is of their three breaths rising and falling in tandem, Ella's shaking a little on every exhale. She coughs harshly, and Anastasia remembers that part, too, the dampness of the tower making her lungs feel swampy and heavy. The cough had plagued her for nearly two months afterward.

They sit together as Ella collects herself, Anastasia's head leaning against the door as Drizella rests her head in her free hand, her fingers covering her eyes. It's not comforting, but it's contact, a warmth that all three of them desperately need.

"We can only stay for a few more minutes," Drizella says.

"You have to kick the rats," Anastasia adds, ignoring the incredulous look that Drizella gives her. *"Hard."*

Ella just sniffles. It's hurting Anastasia's finger to hang on to her hand, but she does it anyway. She can remember the desperation, the complete terror of not knowing when she'd see sunlight again, when she'd be able to see Drizella. There's no hope in this tower, and having no hope is what can drive a person absolutely mad.

Anastasia can't let Ella suffer that way.

"Ella," she says, studiously looking away from Drizella, "we're getting out of here tonight and going to Paris."

Drizella jolts at Anastasia's words, her face both shocked

and infuriated. *What are you doing?* she mouths at her, waving her free hand in the air.

Anastasia ignores her while, behind the door, Ella starts to cry again.

"No, no, please, don't leave me here with her, please. . . ."

"We are going to get you out before we leave, I promise," Anastasia says. "Drizzy and I both swear on our lives."

Drizella's shaking her head, her jaw jutted forward, absolutely furious.

"Dr-Drizzy?" comes Ella's trembling voice, and Drizella closes her eyes and lets out a sigh.

"I'm here," she says, her voice flat. "And yes, on our lives."

Ella just shudders. Her fingers are so, so cold, even with Anastasia and Drizella covering them with their own warm palms. "All right," she says.

Drizella grabs Anastasia's hand and pulls her away from the door and back into her bedroom. Only when they are in Drizella's room does her sister speak.

"What were you thinking?!" Drizella asks. "Why would you tell her our plans, Annie? We don't have time for this!"

"You don't know what it's like in there, and I pray you never do, either!" Anastasia yells back. It's rare that she raises her voice to her sister, but she does now, her eyes flashing. "But it's so terrible, it's like a living nightmare, and if I can just tell her something that can—"

"You told her about Paris!" Drizella shouts. "All she has

to do is tell Mother and boom, she's out of there and then Mother is on her way to drag us back here!"

"You think Mother would actually believe her? And that's why we will just let her out now! Can you please just have a little faith, Drizella?"

"And what if we can't?" Drizella says, seething, "When you were in that tower, how desperate were you to get out?"

Anastasia pauses for a second. "I would have done anything," she admits, and Drizella huffs out a breath and raises her hands before letting them slap down against her thighs.

"Exactly my point!" she says. "You just gave her something better than a key! You gave her ammunition!"

In the reflection of the bedroom mirror, Anastasia can see her mouth set in a tight, thin line. "I did no such thing," she says. "I gave her hope. Maybe for just once in your life, you can try to be understanding, Drizzy, and not so judgmental all the time. Believe it or not, feeling something for someone else isn't such a bad thing. Maybe you could try it sometime."

There is a moment of silence while the sisters glare at each other. Finally, Anastasia speaks.

"We have to let her out," she says.

"I know," Drizella says.

"So how should we—" Anastasia starts to say, and Drizella turns to her, holding one hand up.

"I'll handle it," she says, and there's a set to her jawline that makes Anastasia back down. She's never not trusted Drizella before, but this time her sister looks different, older, almost like a woman rather than a girl. "Grab your things. Stay close behind me, and if you hear or see Mother, run."

Anastasia nods and does as she is told. She places her packed bag under her arm, which makes her sweat a little bit. No matter. The evening air is already cooling down, and a dense fog has rolled in, blotting out the sun and making Anastasia shiver.

If their house is cold, she thinks, the tower will be freezing.

"Where are we—" Anastasia starts to say, but Drizella just shoots her a sharp look and Anastasia closes her mouth, instead trailing behind her older sister as they head down the stairs and toward the drawing room. Drizella is walking with purpose, her brow furrowed, and she passes her bag to Anastasia before going over to a potted plant and shoving her hand into the dirt.

"Drizella!" Anastasia gasps. "What are you doing?"

Drizella just roots around for a few seconds, then pulls out the tower key. It's large and bulbous at one end, the iron knotted together in a way that would conveniently make it impossible to pass under a door. Anastasia recognizes it immediately, her hand going to her mouth.

"How did you know where it was hidden?" she whispers.

Drizella finally looks at her, and her eyes are both cold

and pained, determined to go toward her future even though she can't forget the past. "From when you were in there," she replies. "I saw her put it there after . . . you know."

She brushes the dirt off into the plant, then tucks the key into her hand and nods toward Anastasia. "Come on," she says. "We have to hurry."

They both go up the stairs as quickly and as silently as possible, Anastasia leading the way. One of the stairs lets out a squeak that causes them both to freeze, and Drizella's hand comes up to Anastasia's back as if to hold her in place. "Shh!" she says, even though it's already too late to be shushed.

"It's not like I did it on purpose!" Anastasia hisses back.

As soon as they're sure that they haven't woken their mother, the girls continue their climb, arriving at the top of the stairs just as Ella's hand pops out at the bottom of the door.

"Is that you?" she says, her voice thin and hoarse. Anastasia's heard her coughing at night. "Are you leaving?"

Drizella doesn't respond, but her face is grim as she inserts the key into the lock. "Don't worry," Anastasia murmurs. "We're letting you out. If she asks, you don't know who opened the door."

"Yes, because our mother will really believe that," Drizella mutters. Her brows are knit together as she starts to turn the key, then stops and jiggles it. "It's stuck."

"No, it's not," Anastasia says. "Just turn it harder."

Drizella takes it out, reinserts it, and tries again, but it won't turn at all, and Anastasia feels a cold prickle of sweat go down her spine. "It won't go," Drizella says again, and Ella's hand disappears from under the door as they hear her scurrying to stand.

"It has to fit!" Ella cries. "It has to! How else will I get out?"

Anastasia and Drizella exchange worried glances. "It's the fog," Drizella says. "It has to be. The humidity is making the key stick and not turn."

"Try again," Anastasia urges, patting her sister's arm. "Maybe it just needs a minute or two to warm up."

"It's a lock, Anastasia, not an oil lamp." But Drizella tries a third, then fourth, then fifth time, and all the while the clock creeps closer and closer to seven.

"Please, please," Ella is chanting, and Anastasia can hear the desperation in her voice, the way her hands are scrabbling at the wooden door. "Please, just let me out."

"She said she was going to lock her in here *forever*, Drizzy," Anastasia says. "You heard her yourself. There's nothing stopping her from doing that. We need to get her out of here!"

Drizella looks at Anastasia and shakes her head.

"No, Drizella, we have to!" she says quietly. "We have to. We promised. We *swore*."

"You try it, then," Drizella says, taking a step back, and after a few minutes of twisting and turning, Anastasia has to admit that her sister is right: the lock is stuck. Ella is trapped.

And from the village comes the faintest sound of clock tower bells chiming seven slow times.

Anastasia feels like she could throw up. "Drizzy," she whispers. "It's time. We were supposed to—"

"Ella," Drizella says. "We can't get it to open. I'm sorry, I'm so sorry." Drizella really does sound sorry, too, not like when she apologizes for *accidentally* digging her elbow into Anastasia's rib cage.

"You're not leaving, though, are you?" Ella pleads. "You said you'd let me out before you went to Paris!"

Drizella shoots a dark look at Anastasia, who studiously ignores it. "I told you we shouldn't have told her!" Drizella whisper-yells.

"I won't tell her!" Ella is starting to sound like she's on the edge of hysteria, babbling promise after promise as she gasps for air. "I won't tell a soul, just *let me out of here!*"

"Ella," Anastasia says. "I'm sorry. We can't get it to open. But we'll come back for you, I swear. Cross my heart and everything, we'll come back!"

Now Anastasia is crying, hot tears running down her cheeks as Drizella takes the key and tucks it back into the pocket of her dress. "Annie," she says quietly. "We have to go."

"Nonononono!" Ella is sobbing, and Anastasia can see the door shake as her fists pound against it. "You said you wouldn't leave without me! Please, Annie, Drizzy!"

I'm sorry, Anastasia tries to say again, but she can only mouth the words, her throat too tight to speak. Drizella's grabbing her by the arm, pulling her back toward the stairs, and Anastasia puts her hands against the door. "I'm sorry," she finally manages to say, and Ella bangs harder, cries louder as Drizella pulls Anastasia away before their mother can wake up and come to investigate.

They hurry down the stairs in silence, hearts racing along with the clock as Ella's sobs fade away, and then run through the sitting room toward the door. Drizella diverts just long enough to shove the key back into the potted plant, then takes Anastasia by the arm as they fling the front door open and run.

They both go as fast as their legs will let them, holding hands as they dash down the dirt road, away from their home and their lives, their mother and stepsister, away from all the pain and loss that the château holds. Anastasia gets a stitch in her side that leaves her gasping, but Drizella won't let her slow down.

"Hurry!" Drizella cries. "Madame Lambert said not to be late! She said to be there at seven sharp!"

"I'm going as fast as I can!" Anastasia yells back, but the

memory of Ella's tears is weighing her down, making her heart ache and her lungs burn, even as she does her best to match her strides to her sister's.

Once they get into the main village square, Anastasia lets go of Drizella's hand as they veer off in their separate directions. "I'll try to make her wait!" Drizella cries, but Anastasia can't hear her, is already bolting toward her meeting space with Dominic, suddenly and ravenously desperate to see him. The plan was for Anastasia and Dominic to meet near her music studio, then hurry over to Madame Lambert's atelier. Anastasia was eager to meet this woman Drizella has told her so much about. A female scientist! It seems nearly impossible for such a thing to exist, but what seems to have made an impression on Drizella is the woman's kind and gentle nature. Anastasia knows for a fact that Drizella is unimpressed by most people, so to see her sister's face light up as she talks about Madame Lambert and her studio has been a new experience.

But now all she wants is Dominic and a seat on the train and a ticket that takes her far, far away from the horrible mess that she's managed to create.

She rounds the corner and, with a relief that surprises even her, realizes that Dominic is late, too. He's not there, either, and Anastasia screeches to a stop and bends at the waist, clutching at her corset and trying to catch her breath. She sounds like one of their workhorses after a day toiling in the fields, huffing and heaving and panting, and she puts a hand on the side of the studio and tries to suck down air.

And she waits.

And waits.

And waits.

And waits.

Anastasia has no way to contact Dominic. She has no way to find him other than walking up to the palace doors and requesting to see him, which seems like an impossible thing to do. She pictures herself screaming into the sky, him hearing her from wherever he is and swooping down to save her, covering her in kisses and apologies for being late and worrying her, but even as her fantasy starts to shimmer like it's only a mirage, he's nowhere to be found.

If you're late, I'm still going without you.

Anastasia wonders if Madame Lambert and Drizella have already headed to the station. Surely their train is waiting at the platform, or perhaps it's already left, leaving Anastasia behind. She twists her hands in the skirt of her dress, feeling that terrible pull between her sister and her suitor, her love turning into a tug-of-war as she tries to quickly decide who she would miss more, Drizella or Dominic.

Anastasia is starting to realize that she's going to have to say goodbye to one of them tonight, and she doesn't know who it will be.

The sky turns dark blue, then purple, and with it, Anastasia's spirits grow darker and more tangled. She cranes her neck to check on anyone walking toward her, but the streets are mostly empty, and before long it's only her, a girl standing alone.

15

DRIZELLA

When Drizella breaks off from Anastasia, she's finally able to take a breath.

She's been trying to keep it together for her little sister, knowing that Anastasia is the sensitive, emotional one, the sister who will piggyback onto everyone else's feelings until they also become hers, and Drizella also knows that if she shows Anastasia just how nervous and anxious she really is, Anastasia will melt down with her own worries, and Drizella does not have the time for that right now.

But as soon as Anastasia is out of her sight, Drizella doubles over and takes two huge, gulping breaths, trying to calm her galloping heart even as she sees the clock tower's hands approaching 7:20. She is so very, very late, the one thing she wasn't supposed to be.

She's also nervous and anxious, with fear lacing around the edges, something nameless but familiar that she can't quite define. She's never done anything like this before in her life, so of course she's feeling this way, she tells herself, but that doesn't help ease any of her worries.

She puts one foot on the stairs leading to the atelier, takes another breath. "You're going to be fine," she whispers, and then begins her ascent.

The studio is dark, but the door is open just a bit, and Drizella runs forward and jerks it open, stumbling into the space. "Madame Lambert, I'm here!" she cries happily. "It's me, Drizella, I'm—"

The words die on her tongue as she realizes that the atelier is completely empty. There's not a single trace of Madame Lambert, not a leaf from a plant or even a small star still stuck to the ceiling. It's as if no one has ever been here at all, and that tiny curl of fear blooms into panic as Drizella begins to wander around. "Madame Lambert!" she cries. "Are you there? I'm ready to go with you!"

There's no response, of course, because not a single soul is in the room with her, and hot, angry tears spring to Drizella's eyes. Madame Lambert wouldn't have left her behind, even if

Drizella was a little late; not the woman who let her cry in her arms and helped her out of her terrible dress, and who taught her the phases of the moon and explained stardust and polar opposites and a thousand other things that are now all crashing together in Drizella's brain, their collision big enough to shatter her heart.

She'll just wait, Drizella finally decides. Madame Lambert probably went to check on the tickets or to make sure their train won't leave without them. Maybe she had so much luggage that she needed to check it earlier and got delayed on the way back. It's too far to walk to the train station, so maybe a wheel on her carriage broke and has made her late. One of the things Drizella learned in the atelier is that each problem has many possible solutions, so she will just sit and wait until the answer presents itself to her.

When she sees the first star appear in the night sky, Drizella feels a knot of dread twist up inside her. And when the moon starts to rise as the lamplighter makes his way down the quiet street, Drizella allows herself a single sob as she presses her hand against her mouth. "No," she whispers, and is surprised by how much she sounds like Ella, begging futilely behind the door for someone, anyone, to rescue her.

Madame Lambert did not wait for her. Despite all her kind words, her gentle touches, she left Drizella behind, the same way her father did, and Drizella, standing alone outside an empty atelier, can't help wondering if it's her. On one rainy afternoon, Madame Lambert taught her about common denominators in mathematics, and now Drizella thinks that maybe that's what she is in this equation: the reason everyone seems to leave.

Drizella wonders if Anastasia and Dominic have also left her, have gone off to start their new lives in a city that Drizella will probably never get to see. She didn't think that she wouldn't see Anastasia again tonight, and Drizella clutches her own hand as she remembers gripping onto her sister's as they dashed down the road. Was that the last time that she'll ever get to hold Anastasia's hand, see her sister's face? Will they be old women before they are reunited again?

Drizella allows herself another sob. She's lost a father and a stepfather, but nothing could have ever prepared her for losing Anastasia.

Once she feels like she can stand, Drizella gets up on wobbly legs and heads toward the door of the atelier. Her hand is heavy on the cold brass knob as she pulls it shut behind her. The night fog is thicker now, and Drizella reaches into her bag for her coat. She imagined wearing it in Paris, and the disappointment as she shrugs into it floods her eyes again. She wonders if everything will be sour from now, forever tinged with the broken promise of her future.

"Drizzy!"

Anastasia is there, flushed and tear-streaked and her hair flying in all directions as she runs down the road toward Drizella.

"Annie!" Drizella shouts, and then she's jogging down the stairs as quickly as she can go, like the speed of light even, which is much faster than the speed of sound, and she doesn't stop until she has her sister in her arms, clutching at her like she's the only good thing left in Drizella's life.

"I thought you would have left!" Annie cries, her arms so tight around Drizella that it feels like she's wearing a second corset. "Why didn't you leave? Where's Madame Lambert? What are you doing here?"

But Drizella has her own questions. "Where's Dominic? I thought he was going to buy tickets. Why didn't you go? Why are you still here?"

The words are spilling out of both their mouths so fast that it's just a rattle of words, and then Drizella pulls back and holds Anastasia at arm's length. "Annie," she says, and Anastasia looks up at her with puffy, bloodshot eyes. "Where is he?"

"I—I don't know," Anastasia admits, and she looks like a child as her lower lip begins to wobble. "I don't know where he is. He said he'd be there, Drizzy. He *promised* me."

"Where's Madame Lambert?" Anastasia adds, glancing up toward the atelier. "Is that her space? Can I see it? Where— Drizzy?"

Drizella, despite her stubborn, furious pride and her best efforts, is crying again. "Drizzy," Anastasia says. "Oh, no. Drizella, oh no."

"I don't know where she is, either," Drizella admits, cupping her hand over her face so Anastasia can't see her humiliation. All she wants is to be back in her own bed, tucked under the covers, and at the same time, that's the last place she ever wants to be again.

She's about to say more, that they should just keep waiting, but as she opens her mouth, a figure appears in the fog. Drizella takes a step forward, her heart pounding with anticipation, hoping for the round, soft figure of Madame Lambert to suddenly materialize in front of them, but as the person gets closer, Drizella can see that it's someone taller, narrower, her long, thin fingers wrapped around the top of a walking cane, one eyebrow arched and an all-too familiar smirk on her face.

Oh, no, Drizella thinks.

Oh no, oh no, oh no.

Lady Tremaine is standing there, looking at her two children with a gaze that is both disappointed and delighted. "Hello, my darlings," she says as soon as she's close enough, then sticks out her bottom lip in an exaggerated pout. "Why so sullen? Did Madame Lambert leave without you?"

Hearing her mother say her mentor's name makes Drizella

flinch hard, as if she's been slapped across the face. She has so many questions but doesn't want any answers, doesn't want to know how any of this is happening, because that will make it real and true, and Drizella doesn't know if her heart, brain, or body can handle this much crushing disappointment.

This was the fear, she realizes, that nameless, familiar thing that's now surrounding her like fog. The fear was of her mother, of this horrible woman finding and strangling the one precious thing that Drizella had, and when she bends at the waist again, she starts to chant the word *no* over and over again.

Anastasia is still standing there, dumbfounded and frightened, and their mother walks over to her and gives her cheek a not-so-gentle pat. "Anastasia," she says. "Were you waiting for someone, too? Someone tall, dark, handsome?"

Drizella drops to her knees and puts her head in her hands and feels every single good thing get sucked right out of her soul.

"Get up, Drizella," Lady Tremaine says, sounding annoyed and firm, and Drizella tries, but her legs are shaking too much, and then Anastasia has a hand on her arm, helping her to her feet. Her hands are icy, and when Drizella dares to take a look at her sister's face, she wishes she hadn't.

Anastasia doesn't look like herself at all. It's as if someone has taken the life out of her, turned her into an unblinking, expressionless doll. Even her eyes seem as if they're a different color, and if it weren't for Drizella recognizing her dress—a light blue dress that, if Drizella knows her sister well enough, was probably chosen because it's Dominic's favorite color— she wouldn't know her sister at all.

When her mother walks to stand next to her, Drizella grits her teeth and waits for a slap, a flick to the forehead, something physical to match her emotional pain, but all Lady Tremaine says is "Let's go home, girls. Back where you belong."

"We're not going anywhere with you," Drizella manages to spit out. Just the idea of being thrust back into that hell after seeing the potential of heaven makes her feel a fury toward her mother that feels all-consuming, like it could burn Drizella up into ash. "Just go back home without us."

"Darlings, I would gladly leave you here to fend for your-selves." Lady Tremaine shakes her head with pity, as if *they're* pitiful. "Let you see what it's like to be on the streets by your-self, no money, no food." She pauses before adding, "No love."

Anastasia shivers next to her. Drizella suspects that it has nothing to do with the rolling fog.

"But unfortunately, as your mother, I am still responsible for you. Responsible for your care even as you constantly bite the hand that feeds you." Her voice goes sharp and low. "Maybe it's time that I bite back."

Drizella is trembling, her spine feeling like the jelly that sometimes dances when its glass jar is set down too hard on their dining table.

"You truly thought you could just run away—run to Paris—and I wouldn't find out." Their mother chuckles, but it sounds more like a growl. "You little idiots. You silly, silly children."

Paris.

"But it seems that your saviors have made other plans, as well." Their mother makes a show of squinting into the fog as if waiting for someone, anyone, to appear. "No mad scientist, Drizella? No suitor, Anastasia?"

"You leave them alone," Drizella manages to spit out.

"Quite the opposite, my love. I'm afraid that *they're* the ones who have left you alone."

The words sting worse than a slap. Anastasia even flinches.

"I've known about your cute little plans for a while now, and yet I've let you two have your fun," their mother says as she examines one long fingernail. "It was almost amusing watching you scurry around like two little mice with a piece of cheese, I have to say." She smiles in a way that makes Drizella's heart pound. "I thought that I'd let this dream play out, see if my two silly girls could actually make their way to Paris. You've got none of my grit, of course, but still, I thought it could be possible."

"How did you—" Anastasia starts to ask, but Lady Tremaine waves the question away.

"I have my ways. In any case, I'm sure you can imagine my absolute *shock* to see you standing here, alone once again, no scientist or suitor to take you under their wing. A lot of people seem to leave you behind, don't they, my darlings? It appears to be a theme with you girls."

Anastasia's head is hanging down, fat tears falling on the ground as she cries silently, but Drizella feels only rage, the kind of anger that will consume her if it doesn't escape, taking every last piece of kindness and goodness along with it. Her hands clench, but she knows she'll never do anything with her fists. The fire inside her is too hot for her to move.

"I've tried to tell you both for so long that love and desire will never survive, and yet you always refuse to listen to your mother." Lady Tremaine taps her cane against the ground, and Drizella waits for a strike that never lands. "And yet, here I am, rescuing you from your own foolishness yet again. It seems as if I'm the only one who ever shows up for you, doesn't it?"

Drizella tries not to think of Madame Lambert's kind smile, the way her arms were both soft and strong, how she laughed in delight when Drizella correctly guessed the answer to a question. That warm studio, the golden light, all the stars fastened to the ceiling, all of it so close and then ripped away from her.

Maybe even *because* of her.

"I would urge you both to follow me home if you know what's good for you, but if you'd like to stay on these streets, please be my guest," Lady Tremaine continues, her voice sounding like she's reading the headlines in the morning paper, disconnected from all the horror happening around her. "But, my children, if a constable finds you out here tonight and takes you back home, it will be so, so much more painful for you." Her voice drops until it sounds feral, more animal than human. "I'll let you decide how you'd like this to end: badly, or even worse."

Anastasia looks over at Drizella, and Drizella feels like the worst sister in the galaxy. It was her idea to go to Paris, her idea to run away and follow a dream that now feels like the cotton candy at their yearly town festival, sticky and ephemeral, evaporated into nothing.

"Drizzy," Anastasia whispers, and then she reaches over to take her sister's hand. Lady Tremaine walks a few confident strides ahead of them, her posture reminding Drizella of her own determined walk. How was that less than an hour ago? Her bravado humiliates her now, and she watches the ground as she takes Anastasia's hand and walks back in the dark. The moon is just a sliver in the sky tonight, not offering any sort of light to guide them back. Waning, Drizella thinks, and the word suddenly has a new and terrible meaning for her.

❖

When they arrive home, both girls take off their coats and hang them up, but neither of them moves after that. If this were a chess game—and really, isn't *everything* just a game to Lady Tremaine?—then this would be checkmate, the two of them knocked down by the queen, lying motionless on the board.

Ella comes into the room then, her face so pale and drawn that Anastasia gasps and takes a step back. She's thinner, too, and her hands are trembling, and there's dirt gathered all around the edges of her worn dress. She smells like rot and mold and dirt. Drizella thought that Anastasia looked terrible once she was let out of the tower, but Ella appears ten times worse.

Ella, who opened her mouth and sang at the debut party, who made a stupid choice and suffered its consequences. Ella, who dared to beg for their help even after she never once tried to defend Anastasia and Drizella from Lady Tremaine's wrath. Ella, who made them late for their one chance at escape, who doesn't look even the least bit regretful or sorry.

It's as if the ink Drizella found in her stepfather's office is pouring over her, soaking her in darkness, coating her fresh wounds with numbing fury.

"You," Drizella whispers. "We were late because of *you*."

Next to her, Anastasia's eyes widen and then narrow. It's as if her sister's accusation is contagious, the cause of their late arrival in the village taking root in Anastasia's brain, her mouth opening and closing like a gasping fish's.

In the back of her mind, Drizella knows that she's not being fair, but she's way past fairness now. Nothing is fair, after all. It's a dumb concept for small children, ones who still have enough hope to think that the world might forever spin in their favor. Drizella may be the only one yet to be locked up in the tower, but now she knows that hopeless feeling of entrapment, of never escaping, of the absence of hope. Only instead of damp walls and a rusty lock, it's her stepsister, Ella, who held her back, who kept her from leaving, and Drizella bites back the animalistic urge to claw at her, to feel her skin under her hands, to tear her apart.

Lady Tremaine reaches down to their settee, and Drizella turns to see her pick up what she now realizes is Madame Lambert's cloak. Her voice is strangled as she instinctively reaches for it, the way a child might clutch for a beloved blanket, but Lady Tremaine pulls it back, a smug gleam in her eye.

"Ah, ah, no touching what's not yours," she says as she heads toward the hearth. "Besides, I doubt you'll be needing this again."

"No!" Drizella says, her words stuck in a sob, and before

the word has even left her lips, the cloak is thrown on the fire, turned into flames, and Drizella watches as the last connection to her most beloved person is quickly burned into ash.

It turns out that when a world comes crashing down, it barely makes a sound at all.

And when she looks back up at Ella, Drizella's eyes are ablaze.

❧

16

ANASTASIA

Anastasia watches as Drizella's cloak burns.

Next to her, Drizella makes a tiny sound in the back of her throat, more of a growl than a whimper, and Anastasia thinks suddenly of Lucifer, of his need to approach everything with teeth bared and claws out.

Ella lets out a soft sniffle, and Anastasia's eyes snap over to her, a fresh wave of anger consuming her. How dare Ella be the one who's crying right now? How dare she stand there and seem anything other than absolutely despondent over ruining their futures, their *lives*?

A tiny thought pings the back of Anastasia's mind, a quiet

reminder that her mother is standing there, smirking at her own daughters' anguish, reveling in the triumph of seeing them defeated. But when Anastasia looks up, she knows she's no match for her mother, that any angry outburst would be quickly—and painfully—extinguished. Her frustration and fury are so intense, though, that she can't hold it all inside of her; it has to go somewhere. She needs to get it out of her body before it eats her alive, and there's Ella standing right there, so weak and pale, with no strength to fight back.

It's all her fault, Anastasia thinks, and feels better.

It's not fair. Anastasia knows that.

But she no longer cares.

"Both of you girls," her mother snaps. "Look at me."

It takes a few extra seconds for Anastasia to obey, but when she does, she can tell that her mother has gone serious, her amused grin now gone.

"You two will never fail me again," she says, her voice low and firm. "But after tonight, you will always be a disappointment to me. Is that clear?"

"Yes, Mother," the girls chorus. A fresh tear falls down Anastasia's face and onto her dress, the one she picked especially for Dominic because she knew it was his favorite color. How foolish, she now realizes. Here she was, picking out the color of a dress for a man who couldn't even wait twenty minutes for her.

"Now," their mother says, brushing her hands down the front of her dress like she's ridding herself of specks of dirt. "As your mother, I should punish you for such insolence, for such treachery. Trying to leave, to abandon your own family to fend for themselves. That tower should hold both of you for at least two weeks—"

Both Anastasia and Drizella gasp despite themselves.

"But I believe that what you're going to endure over the next few weeks will be suffering enough. A broken heart, after all, is much worse than anything I could conjure up.

"And of course, there's always a chance that your little heroes can come back for you. What's stopping them? Maybe Paris will be boring. Maybe they'll just miss you." Lady Tremaine pauses before adding, with a sharp-toothed smile, "One can always hope."

Then she presses her palms together as she heads for the stairs. "Make sure to get to bed soon, my dears. You have lessons tomorrow, and you'll need to look well-rested."

All three girls stand frozen in the room as she walks upstairs and shuts her bedroom door quietly behind her.

"What," Anastasia says quietly, her eyes shooting into Ella, "did you *do*?"

"Nothing!" Ella cries. "I promise! I swear!"

"We promised and swore, too!" Drizella shouts, taking a step forward, Anastasia right behind her, until both girls are just centimeters away from her. "Is this your revenge on us for leaving you here? Even though we tried to save you, you just decided to betray us?"

"I didn't tell her—" Ella starts to say, but she's weak from the tower, and she dissolves into a wet-sounding coughing fit. Anastasia and Drizella just watch, neither of them offering any help or assistance.

"I didn't tell her!" Ella says as soon as she can speak again.

"She said she had her ways of finding out!" Anastasia yells. "What do you think that's supposed to mean?"

"Why would I do that? And besides, she hates me, she absolutely loathes me! Maybe she has her ways, but we all know that I'm not one of them!"

The silence hangs heavy among the three of them.

"Fine," Anastasia finally says. "But that doesn't change the fact that we were late because of *you*."

"That's right," Drizella adds. "Madame Lambert and Dominic left without us because we were trying to help you. We missed our train, we missed everything, all because of you."

"Help me?" Ella finally says. "You let her leave me in there for nearly a week, and you call that help? You try to open the door for five minutes and then just give up? You have no idea what—"

"No, I do!" Anastasia screams. "I *do* know what it's like up there! And I also know how awful the rest of your life in this house is going to be!"

"It already is awful!" Ella yells back. "You made me a servant! My father died and you and your mother just swanned in and treated me like I was worse than trash, worse than—" She falls into a coughing spell, this one sounding worse than the last.

"Then why did you get up there and start singing in front of everyone?" Anastasia shrieks. "Why didn't you just stay back instead of getting yourself locked up there? Was seeing me go through it not enough for you?" The evening's events are starting to compound in her brain, narrowing her vision to nothing but pain and loss and Ella. "I was in that tower all by myself, and I managed to deal with it! Why couldn't you? Why couldn't you think of someone besides yourself for once?"

Drizella waits until Ella's next coughing fit passes before speaking. "You had to go get yourself locked up in that tower and then expect *us* to help you," Drizella says. "If we're stuck here with her for the rest of our lives, then so are you."

"You will never know love," Anastasia adds, and her voice is trembling, because, it seems, neither will she, not again. "No one will ever love you, do you understand? Not *ever*."

Ella's eyes are dripping tears, but her chin is high.

"Enjoy your stupid mice," Drizella says, then grabs Anastasia's arm. But as they walk past the fireplace, Anastasia jerks away and grabs a handful of cold cinders that are lying on the hearth. She turns and hurls them at Ella, staining her old cotton dress with black soot. Ella gasps and steps back, but Anastasia holds her ground, glaring at her.

"That's all you are now," she says. "I'll make sure of it."

"Come on, Annie," Drizella says, her own voice tired and worn, and Anastasia follows her up the stairs. She waits for her sister to say something, to fix it, to come up with a solution that will save them, but instead Drizella just walks slowly into her bedroom, and Anastasia follows her because she doesn't know what else to do, then shuts the door behind them.

They both stand there for nearly a minute in complete silence. Outside the window, Anastasia can just see one of the palace's turrets, its purple flag waving jauntily in the evening breeze, and the image makes her want to throw up.

"Do you remember what they said?" Drizella says, and Anastasia jumps at her sudden words.

"Who?"

"At the party." Drizella turns to look at her as the moon begins to rise in the window behind her. "Do you remember what they said?"

Of course Anastasia remembers. Even if she had gone to Paris with Dominic, even if she had begun a brand-new life with him, made a home and had babies and raised a family and been surrounded by love every single day, she would always have remembered those words. They were the kind of words that no girl will ever forget, no matter how hard she fights against them.

"Ugly stepsisters," Anastasia replies. "They called us ugly."

Drizella nods, then smiles. There's something in the look on her face that would have scared Anastasia before tonight, but now there's a familiarity to it, the darkness in Anastasia rising up to meet her sister's.

"There's all kinds of ugly," Drizella continues. "If people thought we were ugly then, just wait." She turns back and looks at the moon, waiting a few beats before speaking again. "We will be absolutely wicked."

"Wicked," Anastasia repeats, and there's a small relief in saying the word, in finally owning it. She's so tired of chasing what she can't have, after all; of not meeting expectations, of always being kind to people who only turn around and hurt her in ways she could never have imagined hurting them. She thinks of Ella, of Dominic, of the ballroom of people laughing at her, of her mother's hands dragging her up to the tower, of her father tiptoeing out of their home and lives forever, paving the way for a lifetime of betrayals.

"Let's just stop fighting it," Drizella says, then reaches under her bed and pulls out what Anastasia realizes is a small calendar. She lights a candle and holds the paper bundle over it, waits for it to be halfway consumed, and drops it into the water basin, where it continues to burn. Anastasia thinks of heat, of hell, of fighting fire with fire until her whole world is ash. The warm glow of the fire illuminates the planes of Drizella's face, shedding light on who she is—who *they* are—now.

When Drizella looks up at her, Anastasia nods.

"All right," she says, and when Drizella smiles, her teeth are sharp in the flames.

When Anastasia finally goes back to her bedroom, it's the same as it was when she left earlier that evening, everything just as she tried to remember it, and yet it's wholly unfamiliar to her. It's the room of someone who was naive, who's had every last bit of goodness burned out of her, and before she can even realize what she's doing, she picks up an old book and hurls it into the mirror in front of her.

And as it breaks, Anastasia watches her old self shatter and fall to pieces on the ground.

Epilogue

LADY TREMAINE

Never have daughters.

That's what Lady Tremaine would say if anyone ever asked her about becoming a mother. But if you do have to have daughters, she would add, make sure they're not as stupid as the three currently living under her roof.

Honestly, sometimes Lady Tremaine is embarrassed by just how naive her own flesh and blood can be. Running off to Paris with no money, no plan, no permission? It's so childish that it almost makes her laugh to think about it now, sitting in front of her dressing table and carefully removing each piece of jewelry.

Ella has always been a lost cause, of course, drifting around the house in her own little world; no matter how much Lady Tremaine piles on top of her, she still seems untouched by everything. But Anastasia and Drizella? She expected so much more from them, but apparently they take after their father.

Just thinking about Monsieur Tremaine still makes her blood boil, even after all these years. Leaving her nothing except two dependent children. She thought she loved him, of course, followed him to this dust-trap village when she was just sixteen years old, the same age Anastasia is now. Of course, her mother warned her against it, told her that he would break her heart and leave her cold, but did Lady Tremaine listen?

She did not, and she has regretted it every day of her life ever since.

One day, she knows Anastasia will be grateful to her. Yes, the girl has a broken heart now, but broken things often become stronger when they heal. Just look at Lady Tremaine, after all. She was broken, but now nothing can touch her. No weakness will ever be allowed to burrow under her skin again, and she will make sure her daughters are the same way. She has to protect them, after all.

The world is such a harsh, harsh place for a woman.

It was Lady Tremaine who discovered that boy's— Dominic, what an absolutely ridiculous name—missing jacket button, plucked it off the ground one morning, and immediately recognized the engraved royal symbol on it. She didn't think much of it at the time, assumed that a magpie had swooped it up and then dropped it, but when she went looking for Anastasia after that mortifying debut evening, she glanced out an open palace window and saw Anastasia and that boy far out in the royal garden, her own daughter sobbing like a child in his arms after behaving so egregiously.

It didn't take much to put the pieces together after that. Lady Tremaine watched the two of them from that window for a long time, the boy drying her daughter's tears like they even mattered to him, then waltzing with her across the dew-covered grass before kissing her. The childish romantic act made Lady Tremaine roll her eyes. Anastasia looked so dopey, so in love, even though she could never know what that truly meant, not at her tender age.

"You," Lady Tremaine said to a passing servant, jabbing a finger in the direction of her daughter and the velvet-clad boy. "What's his name?"

"Dominic, madame," he replied with a quick bow before scurrying off.

Marrying for love, Lady Tremaine knew all too well, would always be the worst thing a woman could do.

So she took care of it.

She visited the castle a few days later, asking for Dominic by name, and she explained quietly and softly that he was going to leave that evening, that he was going to leave their village, or she would tell everyone what he had *really* done to her daughter, how she had caught him nearly defiling her, how frightened Anastasia was of him after such brutish overtures. "By the time I'm done with your good name, it will be in tatters and you will be an outcast in this village and in every village in a twenty-kilometer radius from here."

"Those are all lies!" the dumb boy tried to protest, but Lady Tremaine just shrugged a slim shoulder.

"In these small spaces, gossip is just as good as the truth," she replied, then held up his missing brass button. "Maybe even better."

"Anastasia and I really love each other!" he continued to shout, and oh, it was like watching a small child have a tantrum, both adorable and annoying. "We do! We're going to *Paris*, and—" Dominic suddenly went pale, realizing his slip of the tongue.

Just as Lady Tremaine suspected: absolutely useless. Her daughter would have ended up in a brothel if she had gone to Paris with this boy, both of them too stupid to make any money on their own. But that's Anastasia, always like her father, always thinking that every shiny trinket is actual gold.

"I will give you until this evening to take your leave of this town," she said after a few seconds of cold silence. "Anastasia will not marry some stall mucker. She will not marry for romance or any sort of foolish reason. And if I see you again, or if you try to take her with you, I will set the wolves on you, and we'll see just how far your love will get you then."

Drizella's schemes were easier to uncover, which disappointed Lady Tremaine tremendously. Between her two daughters, she always thought that Drizella had more grit, more *fire* in her, but it turned out that she was as naive as her sister. Coming home from the debut ball wearing nothing but her underthings and a cloak—did she *truly* think that Lady Tremaine wouldn't go looking for the garment?

She dug in the laundry for all of thirty seconds before finding it and seeing *Madame Lambert* stitched into the back collar with a kind of embroidery that was way too adorable for her liking. Back into town she went, this time asking a few people if they recognized the name and soon finding herself outside the most run-down, decrepit, silly rooms she had ever seen. A grown woman with stars painted on the ceiling? A bunch of useless globes used as decoration? Frankly, Lady Tremaine was embarrassed for Drizella for falling into such an absurd thing.

Madame Lambert was delighted to see Lady Tremaine, even showing her a permission letter that was clearly written in Drizella's loopy handwriting. (Apparently, calligraphy lessons hadn't paid off, either.) Lady Tremaine took it in her gloved hand, read it twice, and then carefully tore it into four neat pieces in front of Madame Lambert's shocked face.

"My daughter forged this letter," she said coldly. "I would think that a *scientist* of all people would recognize that."

Madame Lambert tried to argue at first, then cajole, then bargain, saying that Drizella had a brilliant mind, was a hard worker, could focus on her studies as well as any of Madame Lambert's students at university. As if any of that matters to Lady Tremaine. Drizella is her eldest and therefore her strongest hope. Once she is married, she can read whatever books she wants, study whatever she desires, but Lady Tremaine will be dead in the ground before she lets her daughter become an unwed scholar.

Finally, she had enough of the woman's babble, and she leaned in close. "If you do not take your leave of this town by Thursday, I will let everyone in this small, narrow-minded, old-fashioned village know that a female scientist has not only set her sights on my lovely daughter Drizella, but has actually planned to abscond with her to Paris without my knowledge, leaving her own family behind." Lady Tremaine paused before adding, "I wonder how that kind of news would be received in this little rural enclave. Don't you wonder, too, Madame Lambert?"

The woman looked flushed and furious. "You can't just decide that for Drizella—" she started to say, but Lady Tremaine cut her off.

"Of course I can. I'm her mother. Not you. I'll make the

decisions about what's right for my daughter, and if you try to interfere with that, I'll make sure that you're never able to settle in a town in France again." She paused before adding, "Just go to Paris, Madame Lambert, and leave Drizella where she belongs. With me."

Lady Tremaine has to pat herself on the back, though. Not only did she effortlessly get rid of the two biggest obstacles in her life, but both of her daughters think that it was Ella's fault. *Ella*, who had the gall to open her mouth and sing at the debut ball. Ella, who was favored by her own father, the man who left his every last cent to her. She has no idea, of course, and Lady Tremaine will make sure she never does. That money is rightfully Lady Tremaine's, after she spent years feeding and clothing the child.

No, there is a lot coming to Lady Tremaine, and if there's one thing she knows, it is how to take it.

As she continues to remove her jewelry, she can hear her two daughters yelling at Ella, followed by Ella's hoarse cough and her own muted shouts. Normally, Lady Tremaine would insist on silence after such a long evening, but she's rather enjoying hearing the three of them fight. Much better than the alternative, where they become friends, share secrets, work together.

She smiles to herself, so pleased with how everything has worked out. She will not have those three girls allying against her. If there's going to be any mutiny in this house, it will be from Lady Tremaine and not those stupid, simpering children.

The brass button with the royal insignia glistens in her jewelry box as she carefully closes the lid and stands up from her chair. Lucifer, the darling, is waiting for her on her bed, his fat tail swishing back and forth like the pendulum on a grandfather clock. Probably the only thing the girls have ever done right in their lives was bring this cat home with them. Lucifer appreciates her efforts, she can tell, and she runs a bony, ring-free hand down his soft head, stroking his fur.

Lady Tremaine sighs as she dons her nightgown for bed. If she hears anyone but Ella shed a single tear in her house this evening, she'll drag both her daughters back into the tower, so help her. When their father left, she didn't have a single minute to mourn his loss, to rage and cry and stay in bed with the covers pulled up over her head. Anastasia and Drizella have no idea how good they have it, she thinks, untangling her hair from its knot and brushing it out, not looking in the mirror at her bald spots, the ones that have never seemed to fill back in even after all these years.

She glances out to their yard as she reaches to shut the window against the cool night, feeling satisfied after a job well done, ready for a good night of sleep and the promise of a better tomorrow. She drifts off easily, her daughters' distress not disturbing her once.

Outside, the pumpkin patch is still overgrown, the dead vines going wild, rising up over the new shoots of green and pushing them back down, down, down into the ground, swallowing them whole, burying them alive.

Acknowledgments

My biggest gratitude to Elana Cohen, who brought this project to me over breakfast one morning and shepherded it through its initial stages with all of the joy and excitement that it deserved. An equally great amount of gratitude goes to Holly Rice, who picked up the reins and provided great conversations, beautiful notes, and thoughtful edits throughout the entire process. To work with not one but two excellent editors was a dream, and I am so thankful to both of them. Additional thanks to the rest of the team at Disney: Nathanna Érica, Jean-Paul Orpinas, Scott Piehl, Soyoung Kim, and Tim Retzlaff.

As always, thank you to my agent Lisa Grubka for her endless support, enthusiasm, and professionalism.

Thank you to Maret Orliss and Katie Cotugno for reading early outlines and drafts and listening to me ramble on about mice wearing clothes for days on end.

I had the best time working on this project, but it was because of my family that it was such a fun process. Thanks to them for providing inspiration, ideas, and many, many, *many* viewings of *Cinderella*. When I think of this book, I think of you. All my love forever.